ISBN: 978-1-7324984-6-4

**Cover Design**
Amalia Chitulescu
**Editor**
Krystal Dehaba from Blaze Edits, KDehaba@blazeedits.com
**Interior Formatting**
Melissa Stevens, The Illustrated Author Design Services

"But it is one thing to read about dragons and another to meet them."

*-Ursula K. LeGuin*

JACOB DEVLIN

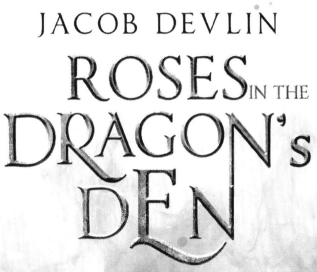

ROSES IN THE
DRAGON'S
DEN

A NOVEL

# DEDICATION

For Karina. For Uncle Ed. And for all whose hearts lie
off the beaten path.

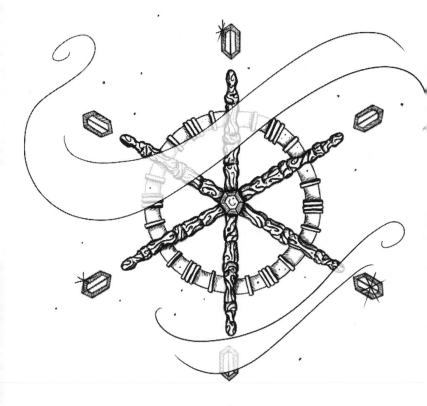

# PART ONE

---

OFF
THE BEATEN
PATH

# KARINA

## OUR FAMOUS
## ESTRANGED UNCLE

·:◆━━━◆:·

"Here, there be dragons," Uncle Diego declared in a forced pirate voice. These were the first words any of us had spoken since we'd gotten on the Fernweh Express a few hours ago.

My twin brother, Charlie, raised an eyebrow, not looking up from the Spider-Man portrait he was sketching in a notebook. "Doesn't that mean you don't know where we are?"

Uncle Diego frowned, his lips a perfect crescent moon under his aviator shades. "How'd you know what that means?"

"I learned it in school. People used to put it on maps to mark areas where they didn't know what was actually there. Duh."

*Duh* was Charlie's new thing. A step up from his last thing, which was *so?*

"Smart guy." Uncle Diego turned back to the train's window.

Even though it was our summer, we had a view of snowcapped mountains that reminded me of a scene on the front of a Christmas card.

"This is my first time traveling this route. I haven't hiked these mountains yet. But I'm excited to spend a few easy days, eating some authentic Swiss chocolate and doing a little stargazing with my favorite niece and nephew."

"Aren't we your only niece and nephew?" I asked.

Nobody could look at our family and miss the blood between us, and people glanced all the time. Only nobody stared because of our resemblance. They stared because my uncle was famous, and he was unmistakable. When people saw the golden-brown skin, shiny raven hair, and tall, lean figure, they at least did a double-take to see if it was really him. Then they'd zoom in on the full eyebrows and the dimples, and they'd remember exactly where they saw him, be it a TV show or a fitness magazine cover.

"So you are." Uncle Diego tinkered with the necklace at his throat, a thin silver chain with a spherical pendant he kept twirling between his fingers.

There was a time when I would've been proud to call him my uncle.

That time passed when Charlie and I were in kindergarten. Our mom brought us to our uncle's house for a mini-camping trip, despite the iron-gray clouds brewing in the desert sky that night. When it came to camping, Uncle Diego went all out: s'mores, a striped bedsheet tent, and *horchata*.

We spent a few hours in the tent, playing with some toys Uncle Diego helped us win at a pizza place. The man was a Skee-Ball demigod, and as we learned from the photos he showed us from his travels, Skee-Ball wasn't his only area of strength. One day he pushed back against the Leaning Tower with one finger, and a few nights later he held the Pyramids of Giza on his shoulders. I'd heard stories of him surviving bear encounters, of the day he crossed the Sahara with only an empty water bottle and half a credit card, and I imagined he was the kind of invincible hero who could star in our bedtime stories—the kind who sweeps kids and princesses out of dragon-guarded towers.

When the sun went away, Charlie confessed to a fear of the dark and Uncle Diego brought out a hulking flashlight he probably used to do arm curls. "That better?" he asked. "Now you can see all the little crickets and those big, strong muscles of yours."

And then this epic roar gurgled in the distance, probably no more than a couple football fields away, and I swear my heart was going to explode.

"And it helps us see dragons, too," Uncle Diego said.

"Dragons?" Charlie repeated.

Somewhere over Uncle Diego's fence, a fiery light burned on the horizon and raced in our direction. The shrieks and moans repeated, growing louder.

I screamed and clung to my brother with the fierce grip of a *luchador*.

But Uncle Diego stood tall and lean and marched to the fence, cool as Superman.

"Don't let it eat you." I gripped Charlie tighter. But after only seconds, Uncle Diego turned around, grimacing as his bare feet padded along the gravel between the blanket and the fence. Clearly he didn't understand the danger we were in, because he laughed.

"Aren't you going to fight it?" Charlie asked.

"C'mere." Uncle Diego wrapped his arms around our shoulders. His warmth stopped my tears in their tracks. "Rina, Charlie, that's just the train. It won't hurt you. Watch—let's go look at it. I'll be right behind you."

There's a famous drawing that circles the internet sometimes, where they ask whether it looks more like an ancient witch or a youthful princess. Well, for the longest time, I looked at that train and only saw the dragon spewing fire, sparks, and smoke. But after a minute, the wings collapsed into tight metal boxes on squeaky wheels, the fire crystallizing into warmly lit windows, and I couldn't unsee the train blazing its path into the mysterious desert night.

"See?" Uncle Diego pumped his arms twice. "*Choo choo.* That's all it is. We're okay."

"It's not a dragon?" Charlie asked.

"Not that one, no." Uncle Diego winked. "But you know, even if it was a dragon, you guys still wouldn't need to be scared. Sometimes dragons are nice. And the mean ones?" He stretched his arms over his head, grasping at stars. "Your *tío*'s bigger than all of them, and so are you. If one of them ever took you away, I would find it and would punch it in its stupid face."

Charlie smiled, showing off his baby teeth. "Really? You would punch a dragon in the face?"

"Always. I would punch all the dragons for you two." He cleaved a fist through the air. "And if a dragon ever took me away, you can punch that one, too. But you know, maybe try to give it a cookie first. Remember, nature's kind if you're kind." I'd heard him say that on TV before.

"Dragons like cookies?" I scrunched my nose.

"Well, doesn't everybody?" Uncle Diego tousled my hair and beckoned us inside.

We shuffled into the kitchen behind him, where he pulled a new pack of Oreos out of the cupboard. I immediately decided I liked him more.

"And if you meet a dragon that doesn't like cookies, that means we get all the snacks, right? More for us."

We nodded, fascinated by Uncle Diego's logic. Our mom would never have agreed, and he knew it. He showed off his bare palms, rubbed his hands together, and reached behind my ear. When he pulled his hand away, he held an Oreo. My jaw dropped.

"Does your mom know you hide cookies in your ears?" he asked.

I rubbed my earlobes, feeling for crumbs. "I don't. I swear!"

Charlie looked astonished and then appalled. "Gross, Rina."

"And Charlie! Look at you." Uncle Diego replicated his magic trick with my brother, to his embarrassment. "You two have some explaining to do. Don't tell your mom we're about to eat all these cookies at midnight. Deal?"

We nodded again. I wasn't going to argue.

Uncle Diego poured some cold and frothy milk in the glasses he pulled from his freezer. "Look. There are some scary things out there," he said. "I wish we could protect you from them all. But there are many more beautiful things out there, like bees and—"

"Bees are scary, though," I argued.

"Even the scary things can be beautiful. Did you know bees make honey to put on your waffles? And spiders eat mosquitoes so you don't get sick from them."

I twisted a cookie open. No one would ever convince me spiders were good. "What about chupacabras? Werewolves? Or giant squids? What do they do?"

Uncle Diego took a few gulps of milk, made an *ahhh* sound, and wiped his upper lip. "I don't think I'd ever want to mess with a werewolf." He winked. "But one day, I'll get another break from my show and we'll have a real adventure together, just the three of us. Then I'll show you what I mean about all the beautiful things out there." He paused, and crickets and cicadas chirped their symphony outside. The train had passed, carrying away the ghostly echoes of the dragon. Uncle Diego must've read my mind because he slid me another cookie. "Don't be afraid of dragons, either of you. We won't be seeing those around."

Well, we wouldn't be seeing him around either. At least, not for about seven years.

A tap on the window compartment door startled me out of my memory, rocketing me seven years ahead to the present. I turned my head, and a tall guy who looked about nineteen years old with bright-red hair, a

black flannel, and suede hiking boots tapped his finger against the door. I pushed it open.

"Hey, sorry, our compartment's full," I said.

"Excuse me." The guy turned a light shade of pink and swept his hand over the back of his neck. "I'm sorry to bother you all, but are you . . . are you Diego Rosas?"

*Oh brother. Here we go again.*

Uncle Diego flashed his million-dollar smile, one I liked to think Charlie and I inherited. Our uncle tipped his cap, and I understood why he wore it so low with those big aviators. He was trying to avoid conversations like this one. Still, he extended his hand. "Sure am. What's your name, man?"

"Oh man, I knew it was you." The traveler took a deep breath, wiped his sweaty palm on his jeans, and shook Uncle Diego's hand. "I'm Evan. Dude, I want you to know I've seen every single episode of your show and have all your travel guides. I'm a huge fan. Do you think I could get a selfie with you?"

Uncle Diego took off his sunglasses. "Evan, good to meet you. Would you settle for a high five?"

Charlie and I had already heard this spiel a couple times in the airport, the train station, and everywhere. Uncle Diego didn't like to do photos with fans anymore because he said it diluted the magic of actually meeting somebody. Plus, it took away his privacy. One simple photo sometimes led to a hundred retweets, and suddenly Uncle Diego had stalkers in Rome.

Evan nodded. "Heck yeah, man, I'll take a high five." Their palms connected with a smack like thunder. "Can I have your autograph, too?"

"Sure thing." Uncle Diego fished into his leather backpack for a pen. "Anything you'd like me to sign for you?"

"Oh. No." Evan turned his pockets inside out, producing a wad of Euros, a rail pass, and a gum wrapper. "Uh, maybe you can sign my arm?" His eyes lit up. "Yeah. I'll go home and tattoo your signature to my arm." He rolled up his flannel sleeve.

The half-hearted, casual smile on Uncle Diego's face suggested he'd heard this way too often. I, on the other hand, swept my phone out of my pocket and texted my brother: *Ugh*. Purple demon emoji. Uncle Diego uncapped a black marker with his teeth and made a flashy scribble across Evan's freckled forearm.

Everything about these interactions boiled my blood. We hadn't seen Uncle Diego in years, and still he let all these actual strangers hijack our time with him and give him hugs and express their undying adoration just because they saw him on TV. None of them knew him like Charlie and I, and after all the time we'd spent apart, we hardly knew him at all.

"Wow, this is so cool." Evan beamed from ear to ear. "You inspired me to travel the world, Mr. Rosas."

"Is that right?" Uncle Diego swept the finishing stroke on his autograph, the harsh Sharpie smell stinging the air. "Where are you from, Evan?"

Evan marveled at the fresh ink on his arm. "Uh, D.C., sir."

"Just call me Diego."

"Sorry, sir."

"D.C." Uncle Diego capped his marker, waved his hand over the signature, and dried the ink with a quick blow. "Home of the Lincoln Memorial, one of my favorite places in the US. Reminds me just how small I am and how big I can become."

Even I had to admit that was deep.

"I've never actually been to it," Evan confessed.

"Well, may you see everything you want to see, Evan. Including your own back yard." Uncle Diego gave Evan another handshake.

"I will, sir."

"Diego."

"Well, uh . . . thanks, Diego. It's cool to finally meet you. Sweet necklace you're wearing, by the way."

"Likewise, and thanks. Safe travels."

Evan walked away with a spring in his step, bouncing toward the back of the Fernweh Express.

When my phone buzzed, three puking emojis from Charlie lit up my screen. I smirked at Uncle Diego. "So, how often does that happen?"

Uncle Diego popped his shades on and pulled his hat over his eyes again. "Every. Day."

"Do you ever wish for something different?" Charlie asked.

Our uncle shrugged. "I have my grumbles sometimes. But I'd never trade it away. Somewhere down the line, I inspired that kid. That's a good feeling."

Seriously, people were crazy about my uncle, and not for the dragon-fighting, Oreo-munching Skee-Ball warrior I used to know. They loved the man he disappeared to become. Around the world, he was known for his travel show, *Off the Beaten Path*. His program appealed to people who wanted to know things like where to have the craziest rafting adventure and where to safely snap an amazing photo of an active volcano. Often, he would tackle a new place with minimal resources and show his viewers how to survive. *Now here's how to fight off a grizzly bear. Here's how to stay warm on Everest. Here's how to purify your own pee.* Things the average twelve-year-old really needs to know, right?

Practical or not, people watched, and that meant I had to put up with my fellow seventh graders squealing over him, along with all the school posters my gym teacher hung up with the speech bubble coming out of my uncle's mouth: *"Eat right, exercise, and climb your mountain."* Which he's never said in real life, by the way.

I would always be proud of him, but the cost to his fame was that we hardly ever heard from him. We gave him a lot of grief for this at the airport, right until he revealed that June 2nd—the day after we'd arrive in Switzerland—was his birthday and that we were the only ones he invited to spend it with him.

After Evan left, Uncle Diego picked up one of his boots and flipped it upside-down. Gripping it by the ankle, he swatted the rubber heel a few times. He always checked his boots before he put them on. One of his habits was to check his footwear—and his bedsheets—for scorpions, spiders, and creepy-crawlies that like to sneak into warm, dark places. I knew this about my uncle, but until recently, I had no idea when his birthday was. "I'm going to find the coffee car. Want anything?"

Charlie wrinkled his nose. "Coffee? Gross."

A metallic bang sounded beneath us.

The Fernweh Express literally shook and lurched as if it had gone over a nasty bump in the tracks, and my forehead hit the window with a hard *thunk*. The impact sounded worse than it felt, but it was still enough to rip my phone out of my hands, webbing the screen with deep cracks. Charlie lost control of his pencil and cleaved a jagged, messy line through his Spider-Man sketch. Uncle Diego had a white-knuckled death grip on his armrest.

His eyes went wide, and my heart responded with a leap against my ribs.

"Um," Charlie said. "Are trains supposed to go *whumph* like that?"

As if in answer, the train bumped again. This time, I swear it teetered on its wheels a bit, shaking my view of the mountains. Instinctively, I reached for Charlie's hand, my heart drumming on my bones. "Uncle Diego?"

Uncle Diego aimed a palm at us. "Just stay seated, all right? We're okay."

But when I looked outside our compartment door, passengers were doing anything but staying seated. They pushed from the back to the front in panicked globs. Women herded their children through narrow halls and doors. A man in a suit ran with a baby clutched firmly to his chest while a teenage girl pushed a man in a wheelchair.

"Do you think we should follow them?" Charlie asked. "Are there bombs or something?"

The intercom blared to life, and the air crackled with static. "This is your conductor speaking. We have an emergency situation on board. All passengers please—"

Another boom rocked the train.

This time, an orange glow painted the walls, seats, and windows. The Fernweh Express whistled, and I flashed back to when I was five years old, panicking in Uncle Diego's yard.

*It's just the train, Rina. It won't hurt you.*

But this dragon of a train swept me up with my family, ready to zoom us all away on wings of fire. There was nowhere to brace. Uncle Diego stood and shoved the door open.

*He'll protect us. We'll be okay.*

The crowd had packed forward as far as it would go, banging on doors and windows and trampling over each other in panic. Smoke, thin and wispy, curled through the air, and my throat rejected the fumes. I ducked down and covered my nose with my shirt, coughing until I thought my lungs would burst.

There was one more boom, and it was the loudest and most haunting of all. Uncle Diego turned and wrapped his arms around me and Charlie in a sort of cocoon, throwing his chest against my back with such immense force that all three of us hit the ground.

"Karina," Uncle Diego coughed. "Charlie—"

Then the Fernweh Express rolled over, tipping me like a log against the wall. The windows flashed from milk-white to pea-green, and suitcases hammered together over my head. A hard, blunt force struck my temple, and the world faded to black.

# CHARLIE

## HAPPY
## LITTLE TRAIN WRECKS

I woke up with bees in my stomach and a fire in my skull. Ma always told me to be grateful I didn't inherit the migraines that ran in the family—Karina had them real bad—and here was my first one, like a train wreck in my head.

*Train wreck.*

I blinked until my vision swam into focus. I remembered the accident. Somehow, the Fernweh Express to Switzerland flew off its rail. My mind replayed our tio throwing his body over us like a shield and that burst of crisp-orange light, like flames.

Only now, the world was green.

*Too* green. Like emeralds.

Instead of snowcapped mountains and frosted ground, everything around me was covered in grass and leaves. The view couldn't have been more different from the sky-spearing, snowcapped fangs we saw from the train.

With concrete in my arms, I pushed off with my left elbow and made myself sit. The world flipped right-side-up again, revealing rolling hills all around me. I coughed into my fist, and my stomach lurched. Warm blood trickled down my arm. A scrape marred my skin from elbow to wrist. My jeans were ripped at the knees.

"Karina?" I called. My throat stung like I'd swallowed a thumbtack. "Tio?"

A bit stiff in the neck, I turned my head and studied the hill behind me, studded with smooth gray stones and lumps of earth that looked like they might burst open at any minute and release some kind of shaggy green monster. A crimson bird cawed overhead and tore across the sky. I rubbed my shoulders and then my throbbing temples. How had I been thrown so far from the train that I couldn't even see it anymore? That I couldn't see the mountains? In fact, there was no evidence I had even been through snowy land. The air was warm, about seventy-five with a breeze that smelled of pine, and there wasn't a single cloud in the sky. Switzerland was nothing like how I pictured it.

"Karina," I yelled, my heart leaping into my throat. "Tio, where are you?"

*Where is anyone?*

Fear drenched my palms in sweat. What if Karina and Uncle Diego hadn't woken up? Or what if the

Fernweh Express spat me out and rolled on without me? If it crashed, tons of people should have been all around me. Luggage, torn leather, shredded metal, train tracks—anything.

I peeled myself off the ground, dusted my knees, and fished my phone out of my pocket, surprised to find it unbroken. *Whew*. Thirty-nine percent battery. No notifications. No service bars. And even though the sun blazed high above, the clock on my phone read ten at night.

I started for the hill, my calves protesting with every step. *Maybe I'm dreaming. This is some twisted nightmare, and I'm still asleep in a burning train. Or maybe I died.* All this greenery and too-perfect temperature did kinda look like Heaven, at least the way I pictured it. Hell wouldn't have been this green, or so I'd been taught.

When I approached the top of the hill, a thin, barely detectable plume of smoke appeared from the other side, charmed from an unseen source like a snake out of a basket. My heart rose in my throat, and I ran.

*The train.*

I expected to see my fellow passengers cleaning each other's wounds, dialing home, and helping each other out of the wreckage, sharing hugs and a round of *Kumbaya*. I wished this nightmare would end with a fist in the air and a freeze frame, Captain Underpants style.

But no. An empty, deserted train wreck stared back at me.

No passengers, dead or alive. Just the steaming metal husk of the Fernweh Express planted in the grass.

And that meant I was alone. No Tio. No Karina. Just a single, lonely Charlie.

*Check the wreckage*, my brain said. *Comb through every train car, and look for signs of your family.* Maybe I'd find them sleeping or see the conductor calling home. But my heart was a bloody mess, and in the epic war between my heart and brain, my heart won. *Cry*, it urged me like the devil on my shoulder. Obediently, I fell to my knees and bawled out a waterfall.

By the time I was a red-eyed, goobery mess and convinced my entire life was over, I saw my sister trudging up the hill with her pink-streaked hair in a tangle. And Mom always said I wouldn't get my way by crying.

"Rina." I wiped the tears from my face. "You're okay."

Karina and I met in the middle and hugged like we'd never hugged before. She smelled a little smoky, and she was almost as scraped up as I was.

Words poured from her like water from a bottle. "Oh my god, Carlos, I've been freaking out. Are you okay?" She grabbed my arm. "You're bleeding."

Most days I might've told her not to use my full name, but she got a pass this time. I wasn't alone, and that was enough to make me laugh off my crying fit. "I thought we died."

"What happened to us?" Karina asked. "Where's Uncle Diego? What do you remember? The last thing I remember is hitting my head in the train car. Ay, Mom's gonna freak out. We must have made national news by now. Does your phone work?"

I skipped to the last question, unable to keep up with Karina's pace for asking them. "No service."

Karina bit her thumbnail. "Mine didn't survive." She paused. "But we did. We're lucky."

"Lucky." I rolled my eyes. "Sure."

"I'm just saying—"

"I'm glad you're looking on the bright side, Rina, but I don't feel lucky at all right now," I said.

"Then let's change that," Karina said. "Let's search the train."

I considered the metal monster in the field. Now that I wasn't completely on my own, I was ready to face the wreck. Seven charred, broken train cars lay scattered in ruins along a seemingly infinite plain. Everything about it looked wrong. The landscape would have been fit for a Bob Ross painting if it weren't scarred by a steaming skeleton of aluminum and leather. Happy grass. Happy hills. Happy train wrecks.

We were probably stupid to crawl back into the train that exploded and spat us out. We had no idea what had really happened. For all we knew, a bomb could've gone off and there could be more. Maybe there were terrorists in Europe blowing up railways. But we knew two things for sure: We needed help, and the wreckage was the best place to start.

My arms prickled when we ducked back into the train. The first car we explored was upside down, and some of the seats dangled from what used to be the floor. Suitcases and backpacks lay torn and open, but the weirdest thing was what we didn't find: anyone else.

The Fernweh Express brimmed to the max with people when it departed, and yet every bit of evidence told us we were the only ones wandering the wreckage.

I wouldn't have been able to handle seeing any bodies, but I would've felt a lot better if someone else was in our situation. I doubted the passengers had all got up and left. So where were they?

We also didn't find any clues about where we were or any way to communicate with the world beyond the train. I looked for a radio but couldn't even find the conductor's cabin. The café car wasn't around either, which would've been nice because I was starving. From what I could tell, the back seven cars seemed like they were scattered around the field. And that was it. Karina and I checked the only other phone we could find lying on a seat. No signal. Even the Map app put our little blue dot on an empty grid.

"We're in the middle of nowhere," Karina said. I think we'd both known it for a while, but neither of us wanted to name it. *Nowhere.* "Do you think someone's coming to rescue us?"

"Don't they monitor the railways for obstacles and stuff? I feel like somebody would've been here already," I said. "According to my phone, it's almost eleven. We should've been in Switzerland by five. So if we crashed somewhere in the middle, that would've left at least six hours for them to send a rescue team to come look for us. It can't take that long, can it?"

Karina didn't say anything. She bit her lip and dug her knuckles into her hips. She could have started crying and I wouldn't have made fun of her, but she didn't. She was a lot like our mom, tough and strong. Karina gathered her hair in a ponytail, sighed, and then knelt next to a random suitcase and unzipped every pocket.

"Whoa, hey, what are you doing?" I asked. "That's not yours."

"Looking for bandages and snacks. Help me."

"You can't just dig through other people's stuff."

Karina gave me the look she learned from our mom, only it made me laugh when my sister did it. "Where's our stuff then?"

Good point. I didn't know.

I opened a random duffel bag, where I found ankle socks, boxers, jeans, crisp button-downs, a pair of boots about my size, earbuds, and all the men's extras from deodorant to hair gel. Bandages weren't on this guy's packing list, but I did find some nutty granola bars. I tossed one to Karina and tore another open right away, feeling a little guilty at first. I promised myself if I ever met the owner, I'd share some Oreos with him or something.

Karina found bandages in another bag and managed to scavenge some snacks, but nothing our mom would be super proud of: chips, crackers, candy. I wasn't complaining.

The last car we checked turned out to be our own, and that's where we found what we really needed.

"Uncle Diego." Karina waved her arms, her eyes wide with fear. "Charlie, he's here."

He lay unconscious over one of the train seats, which flipped upside down and carried him in a lopsided L, his arms dangling under him and his knees bent side by side.

"Tio." I ran to his side, my heart in my throat.

Karina grabbed one of his hands, calling his name with heavy breaths. "Wake up. We're here."

When Tio didn't move, my blood ran cold. I pressed the back of my hand to his forehead, relieved to feel some warmth radiating from his skin. His lips were slightly parted, but his eyes were shut tight. I put my ear by his mouth, listening for breaths and hearing nothing.

Karina squeezed his hand. "Uncle Diego?" Her voice cracked. "Please wake up."

When he didn't answer, I gripped Tio's shoulder and gave it a rocky shake, the way Mom did when I missed my alarm. "Hey." I thumped his forehead. "Quit fooling around."

"Charlie." Tears burst from Karina's eyes and carved smooth paths down her cheeks.

"What?" I bit back. "If this is his idea of some sick joke, it's not funny. It's stupid. This whole idea to come to Europe with him was stupid."

"Stop," Karina hissed. "You're going to regret talking like that if he doesn't wake up. Stop it right now or—"

"Or what? Huh?" I was on a slippery slope now, and I couldn't calm myself down. "You're gonna tell Mom? Good. I hope you do. Because in case you haven't noticed, there's a good chance we might not ever see our parents again. So you keep threatening to rat me out, and I'll keep jabbing and poking our stupid—"

Tio lurched and his eyes snapped open.

I leapt back against the wall, startled by the sudden movement. But the relief after that was like a warm hug.

Tio took in sips of air, rolling his shoulders and tilting his head back and forth. His eyes grew wider and wider as he soaked in the wreckage. "What the—"

I knew exactly how he felt.

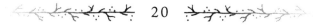

Karina swatted Tio's shoulder, fury in her eyes. "Don't scare me like that." She punched him again for good measure and slumped down against the wall, pulling her knees to her chest as the tears spilled freely. "I thought you . . ."

I couldn't help but roll my eyes. She *Mom'd* me for barely tapping him, but suddenly he wakes up and she gets to jab him like Muhammad Ali? Okay. "How you feeling, Tio? Here, let me help you up. Are you hurt?"

Tio braced his weight on me. "We crashed." It was more of a statement than a question. Luckily, he didn't scream or reveal evidence of injuries besides a drop of blood crusted onto his forehead. He looked somewhere past my shoulders, and a faint light sparked in his eyes. "My hat."

"Awesome," I grumbled. I didn't mention that I might have accidentally crushed his aviators a few minutes ago. "We crashed, but at least your hat's okay."

Tio let out something between a cough and a laugh. "That's your ma's sarcasm."

"Nice of you to know that after all this time."

He leaned on me until he could support his own weight. "Thank you." He clapped me on the shoulder and turned to help Karina up, wiping her tears. "Hey, chin up, Rina."

Karina buried her face in Tio's shoulder. "I'm so glad you're okay."

"Okay seems . . . generous, but look. We survived a train crash. Can you believe the luck? Both the good and the bad. Of all the things that could've happened in this world. We can be grateful." He knelt, caught his breath, and picked up his hat. "Maybe your mom won't kill me after all. Did you call her yet?"

Karina shook her head. "No signal."

After he beat the dust off his hat, Tio put it on his head. He patted his pockets and fumbled around for his phone. "Maybe somebody has a hotspot or something. So we can send a message and let her know you're okay."

"That's the thing, Tio," I said. "We're alone. Karina and I looked all around, and . . . there's nobody."

He narrowed his eyes. "Nobody? As in—"

"As in no bodies. There's only us."

"But that's impossible."

"Look out the window."

Tio obeyed, and I watched him cycle through all the same realizations I'd struggled with on the hill. "What? Where's the . . ." *Snow? Mountains? People? Cell signal?* He buried his fingers in his hair, pushing his hat back to the ground. "Never mind. Your mom is definitely going to kill me."

# KARINA

IT'S A BAT! IT'S A CICADA!
IT'S . . .

◈—◆—◈

We had two good things going for us: We had our uncle back, and we found our backpacks. Together, we retraced our steps through the train cars one more time, sifting through wreckage and stuffing our packs with random goods from protein bars to compact mirrors. At one point, I unzipped a leopard-print suitcase and discovered a blue dress, a teddy bear covered in faded marker scribbles, and a passport belonging to a woman from Tennessee. My heart broke when I saw the passport. I didn't remove a thing—not even the half-eaten bag of M&Ms or the fully charged tablet. Matching its contents to an actual woman's identity made it feel wrong. Well, more wrong than I'd felt collecting items from faceless, nameless individuals.

I patted the teddy bear, zipped up the suitcase, and then pushed it into a corner. When I turned around, I found Charlie fishing a phone charger out of a bright-red bag. "A charger? Really, Charlie?"

"I'm at thirty-five percent, though." He wrapped the cord around his wrist.

Uncle Diego applied a fresh bandage to his temple and tightened his backpack. He processed everything with minimal hysterics, rationalizing our situation as well as he could. Like me and Charlie, Uncle Diego didn't know how to explain the complete change of scene and lack of bodies, but he stood tall and put on his adventure face, the same way I had a writing face, Charlie had a soccer or drawing face, and our mom had a cooking face. We all had this really intense stare when we were focused on something. I could only imagine how Mom would've reacted over everything that happened. Jorge, our stepdad, probably would've lost his mind and started doing the rosary. But Uncle Diego stood tall. All things considered, we couldn't have picked a better person to get into a train wreck with.

"Here's what we know. We have no cell signal, no data, no remote communication." Uncle Diego's first idea was to try the conductor's cabin. I was proud Charlie and I had already thought of that. "We wrecked somewhere between Florence and Switzerland, a roughly three hundred and fifty-mile gap. And we haven't broken any major bones. So now? We're going for help. Staying put won't do us any good."

"Are you sure?" I asked. "What if we miss the helicopters and rescuers and everything?"

"Someone should have been here a long time ago, Rina," Uncle Diego said, confirming Charlie's theory. "We gotta go to them."

I slung my backpack over one shoulder. "Then I'm down to leave. Going through all this luggage is depressing." I took another look at the Tennessee teddy bear, and my heart burst all over again. "How far are we going?"

"As far as we need to," Uncle Diego said. "I'd maybe bring all your stuff, just in case."

"In case what?" I asked.

"Exactly." Uncle Diego nodded. "In case what. Always assume there will be a what. Make sure you have enough snacks, water, bandages, whatever you need. Shut your phones off. You'll wanna save battery life in case we find good reception again. All we need is one call."

"You don't want a selfie with the train wreck first?" Charlie joked. "Sign my arm, please?"

I rolled my eyes, hoping Evan and the other passengers were okay.

"It's just like hiking," Uncle Diego said. "Hiking on uncharted lands, looking for lost civilization. That makes this sound like a lot more fun, right?"

I managed a weak smile. "Here, there be dragons?"

"Here, there be dragons." Uncle Diego put on that pirate accent again and swung his fist in front of him. "We're gonna be okay. Think of it as an adventure. If you see me freak out, then you have permission to freak out. But I'm Diego Rosas, and I promised your mom I'd take care of you. I don't freak out."

"Never?" I asked.

"Never ever." Uncle Diego stepped out of the train car, and we followed him into the rolling greens. "And when you get home, you can tell your friends and brag about how cool you are, and your ma will never let me back into your life again. You'll go back to the safety of the city, and I'll slip quietly into the night."

"So another seven years will go by before we see you again?" I asked. "Great."

I didn't mean to throw so much shade, but the last he knew, I was still into *Dora the Explorer* and Charlie's career goal was "the red Power Ranger." There was too much history in that gap. Charlie and I had a combined total of fourteen years of life between us since we'd last seen Uncle Diego. Fourteen birthdays, first days of school, and summer vacations. Did none of that matter?

Uncle Diego averted his gaze, taking a second before he responded. "That hurts, guys."

Charlie shrugged. "Sure does."

"Look. I know I haven't been an active figure in your lives. But I do care, and I always did." Uncle Diego put a thumb to the horizon, which was something I'd seen him do on his show to figure out when the sun would go down. "Let me get us out of here, and I promise we'll make up for all that lost time. Every minute of it."

"Then how do we get out of here?" Charlie asked. "We don't even know where we are. What kinds of things could we run into? Scary animals and stuff?"

"You don't have to be afraid of anything in nature if you know what you're dealing with," Uncle Diego said. "You just have to respect it, treat it right, and know how to respond. You see a wolf in the wild, and you earn its respect by making yourself bigger. You see a bear, and . . . well, you have to know what kind it is before you do anything."

I tried to remember what he meant. Was brown bear *play dead* and black bear *try to scare it away?* How did Uncle Diego manage to fit so many random tidbits of nature information in his head? "What if we're wandering around for days?" I asked. "How do we survive?"

"This kind of setting, we should be okay in. It wouldn't be too different from camping on Mt. Lemmon, for example. A rolling green like this doesn't hold a candle to a place like Everest."

I thought about the posters up at school. The cheesy *Climb Your Mountain* ones. Everest was Uncle Diego's personal mountain—his biggest challenge. He was one of the youngest people to attempt the climb, and he almost didn't survive. But not only did he reach the top, he went back a second time and filmed it all, teaching his viewers about the dangers of the cold and the funny ways elevation can mess with the mind.

We walked for what felt like hours, until I couldn't ignore the burn spreading up my legs and the sweat beading down our faces. I started to get the sense that we'd been walking through the plains for days. Uncle Diego made us stop, drink, and eat protein bars a couple times, and we'd sit on the ground where he'd stretch his legs and touch his toes.

"I'm sure we're getting close to something," he said. "Any minute now."

Charlie was the one to finally say what I'd been thinking for a while. "Tio, I'm exhausted." He curled his hands behind his head and caught his breath. "Can we just rest our eyes?"

The sun had finally met the horizon, throwing the plains and hills into a pinkish glow.

Uncle Diego shielded his eyes with a palm and squinted into the distance. "Are you sure you don't want to keep going a little more? We could be five minutes away from a town or something."

"My legs are on fire," Charlie said. "This is the most I've ever walked in my life."

"Karina? Do you want to stop?"

I brushed the back of my hand over my forehead. "Please."

After a brief moment doing that famous Rosas concentration stare, Uncle Diego agreed. "Real quick then, okay?" He pointed to one of the hills beside us. "Let's get on the other side of this hill and see if it'll give us some shade."

We moved around the giant hill, and as Uncle Diego predicted, it threw a patch of land into shadow. It had also been concealing something strange: a squat cylindrical monument resting just beyond the base of the hill. The object might've been polished stone, a shimmering gray obelisk adorned with a huge carving of a wheel, the kind I imagined a pirate would use to steer a ship. Jagged and narrow, the stone leaned toward the hill on a steep angle. Had it been standing straight, it might have been about as tall as Uncle Diego.

"What is that?" I asked.

"I've never seen that in my life." Uncle Diego dropped his backpack at his feet and approached the stone, wild curiosity in his eyes. He used a finger to trace the wheel, which was chiseled with smaller symbols on the spokes. "Let's see . . . we've got a rose and a tree and a teardrop and a crescent moon . . . This looks like maybe the sun . . . How have I never heard of this?"

"Never? In all your travels?" I asked.

"I have no idea where we are. Maybe I hit my head too hard. I have no knowledge of anything like this in Europe, or anywhere."

"Do you think it means we're close to help?" Charlie asked. "Maybe it's a historic landmark by some sketchy little town off the maps?"

"Could be," Uncle Diego said. "Maybe you two can rest in the shade for a bit and I'll go see if we can get any closer to help."

"I don't think we should split up," Charlie said, pulling the words right out of my mouth.

Uncle Diego crossed his arms, squinting like he was running through a hundred scenarios in his mind. "All right. We'll rest here together. But not for long, okay? I didn't sign you guys up for a camping trip. We need to get ourselves to Switzerland or get you two back home."

Charlie and I exchanged shrugs. "We don't mind camping," I said, though every syllable hurt my soul. "For a little bit, I mean."

So we sprawled out in the shadow, took off our shoes, and enjoyed a meal of granola bars, water, and chewing gum.

"Dinner of champs," Charlie said.

Uncle Diego laughed. "Right? I'd really prefer some *carne asada* right now, but all we need are a few candles and we'd have a five-star meal."

The thought of beef wrapped in warm tortillas made my stomach rumble. That was one thing Charlie and I loved about our stepdad. Jorge rocked the *carne asada*.

I stretched out on the ground, letting my hair fan out on the grass. The sun had almost completed its descent below the horizon, throwing the sky into a light tinge of purple. "It's so nice outside," I said. "So quiet and peaceful. I sort of understand why you do this."

"I love everything about it," Uncle Diego said. "The things it can teach you about the world around you and about yourself. You don't get the depth of that experience in front of a screen." He crossed his legs and brushed his palm over the grass. "Just look at that stone. That sunset. These plains. Doesn't it all make you feel like you're a part of something bigger?"

I smiled, but Charlie looked disinterested. "Speaking of phones." He pulled out his smart phone and powered it up. "Still no service. But apparently it's two forty-three in the morning."

"And the sun's barely going down," Uncle Diego marveled. "This doesn't fit the time zone." He dug through his own backpack, brushing aside a rope and a pair of jeans before producing a cracked leather book.

Uncle Diego unwound the strap that held it together and coiled it in his hand. "I need to make some notes here."

The first time I saw him take out that journal in Florence, my heart leapt. I loved paper and notebooks and filled many diaries of my own. Uncle Diego kept different kinds of notebooks, some for tickets and photographs, some for rubbings and drawings of interesting things he found, and some he purely enjoyed to write in.

He flipped the diary open and scribbled a few notes. When he finished, the sunset cast a melancholic gleam in his eyes. "Guys, I'm sorry about all of this. I wish we were doing this under better circumstances. But this moment? This here is perfect. If you really listen, I think I can hear the wind."

I shut my eyes and concentrated, letting the breeze sift through my hair. For a second, I almost forgot how the Fernweh Express derailed my life only hours before— and the strange place I'd woken up in. For this second, Uncle Diego was right, and everything was perfect.

But then I heard the wind whispering.

And it wasn't a gentle whisper, the kind friends used to share secrets. The wind was cold, the kind used to whisper a curse. The harder I concentrated, the louder it grew and the more I hated it. My eyelids flew open. "Uncle Diego?"

He held up a finger and shushed me. Even Charlie looked creeped out, his lips in a perfect circle as the breath of the wind intensified to a cold, voiceless shriek, penetrating the air in every direction.

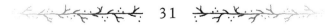

"Cicadas?" Charlie guessed.

"Shh," Uncle Diego hissed.

Charlie swallowed, his Adam's apple bobbing up and down. He fidgeted with a blade of grass. "Bats?"

"Be quiet," Uncle Diego ordered. "I'm trying to figure out what that is."

Then came the harsh sound of a *whoosh* beating metronomically from the sunset . . . the sound of something cleaving the air, the way a parachute snaps open.

After hours of being alone, the unexplained *whoosh* and the shrieking wind raised the hair on the back of my neck. I'd never heard anything like this back home.

"Wings," Uncle Diego said.

I crinkled my brows. "Wings?"

Uncle Diego pointed into the sunset, and the last thread of hope I had for the Fernweh Express and our way home came unspooled. Maybe that thread was my sanity. Uncle Diego hadn't been kidding. The source of the *whoosh*, *whoosh*, *whoosh* had leathery green wings that spanned as big as five train cars laid end-to-end. The creature rose over the horizon, flapped upward, and made a deliberate beeline in our direction. In fact, I was certain the glowing emerald eyes were drilling straight into my soul as it moved, a gold serpentine tail whipping back and forth behind it like a pendulum.

Charlie gulped. "Not a bat."

"Not the wind," I whispered.

There was no mistaking what it was, even though I'd never seen one before. Any other day, I could identify one in a book or a movie with a thousand percent certainty that I would never encounter one in the real world.

But wherever I was now, it couldn't be farther from Europe.

Not even Switzerland was home to dragons.

"Rina? Charlie?" Uncle Diego threw on his boots— without checking them—and scrambled to his feet as an orb of fire hurtled from the dragon's mouth to the crest of the hill. "Run."

# CHARLIE

## THE
## OREO THEORY

•:—•—:•

Yep. *Here, there be dragons.*

Here, on the horizon. Tio had to jinx us, didn't he? He'd probably done some weird *brujeria* and brought that dragon to life just by saying the words earlier.

I changed my mind. We obviously did die in that wreck, and this wasn't the nice place at all.

"Whoa," I breathed.

For two seconds I became everyone I've ever hated in a monster movie—not the villain, but the people who stand and marvel at the dinosaur while I scream, *Run, you fool!* I was paralyzed, my legs like stone.

A harsh tug on my collar sprang me out of my paralysis, more like hypnosis from the dragon's eyes.

Those green orbs seemed to find a direct pathway into my brain. I couldn't stop staring.

"I told you to run." Tio waved his arms in front of him like he was shooing the world's biggest fly.

As if Tio had hexed me, my legs sprang to life, carrying me after my family. "What in the world is that thing?"

"What does it look like, Charlie?" Karina threw her arms up.

"Like a . . . a flying death lizard!"

The creature shrieked, reminding me of rusty metal gears grinding together.

"It's a dragon!" Karina shook her head, and her hair became a wild, frizzy mess. "Uncle Diego, what do we do?"

Tio's face was red and drenched with sweat. "Less talking, more running."

"Permission to freak out now?"

"Granted."

I gritted my teeth. "You're supposed to be the survival expert."

"Yeah? Well, that guy behind us is just a little out of my expertise."

"You're useless." I imagined a huge vein protruding out of my forehead and wished I had a mirror.

With every step I took, the earth itself trembled beneath me like it wanted to run too. The individual blades of grass shivered, trees rustled in the distance, and even the hair on my head rattled as the dragon loomed closer. Each beat of the beast's leathery wings was louder than the last.

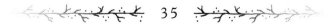

The dragon roared—a deep, gravelly sound like a moving mountain—and its shadow spread over me like a cold blanket in the purple sunset.

Against my best judgment, I looked up. The beast covered half the sky, an emerald monster drenched in flecks of gold. It must have been a hundred feet wide, and suddenly I felt like an ant.

*We are so dead.* I peeled my sweaty collar from my skin. *So entirely dead.*

Tio aimed a finger ahead of him, indicating a thick, dark crack in the earth where tangled red roots the size of human legs curled into the air. "We're gonna jump into that ravine together. Get ready."

I would never be ready.

"Uncle Diego, *eres loco.*" Karina dug her hands into her hair. "That could be a hundred feet deep."

"We jump in or we let Smaug here barbecue our bones."

"Who?" I asked. "Is there an option C?" *Like go back in time and refuse to come on this trip?*

With that, the dragon propelled ahead of us, spiraled downward, and planted itself between us and the ravine, stopping us in our tracks. The beast stood on legs like tree trunks, and its steamy breath made little waves in the air. It snorted a few times and clawed at the grass, swiveling its neck to look upon me, Karina, and our uncle in turn.

Tio stood stone still, arms locked at his sides. Sweat streaked his face, no longer a sunny golden tan but pale with fatigue. His backpack hung from his elbows, exposing his journal, some jeans, and a rope. The lazy way the bag unfurled made it look like a wide open mouth, just as beat and tired as the rest of us.

Out of the corner of Tio's lips, he mumbled, "Charlie. Karina. Don't. Move. A muscle. Just remain. Calm."

It would've been easier to plant roots in the ground and become a cactus. My calves and knees rattled beneath me, and my lungs were in flames. It took every ounce of energy to stop myself from screaming, collapsing to the ground, or straight-up bawling. Karina squeezed her eyes shut, curling her hands into fists.

With slow, careful movements, Tio slid his backpack off and reached inside. "Nature will respect you if you respect it first." He took a deep breath and made eye contact with the dragon. "Hey, big guy. My, you're a beautiful beast, aren't you? Yes, you are. Such a fascinating, handsome thing."

*Beautiful?* Karina and I exchanged a quick glance. *Tio is a lunatic.* How could he smile or keep his voice lullaby-sweet with the beast?

The dragon responded with a grunt, almost a whimper, and tilted its head—a reaction that built Tio's confidence.

Tio pulled an Oreo from his pack and twisted it into halves. "You hungry, buddy? I bet you like the taste of chocolate, don't you? Chocolate and *crema*? Oh, you haven't tried it? It's phenomenal." He nibbled off the good half and held the creamy one over his head. "See? Mmm."

I watched all of this happen with one eye open, but to Tio's credit, he never blinked once. He looked every bit as strong, brave, and cool as I remembered him as a kid. Like Thor.

The dragon bowed and sniffed the cookie, first hesitantly, and then more boldly. I couldn't stand to see its mouth so close to Tio's bare hand. At least Thor had a hammer. "You like that? Go ahead, buddy. Take it."

The dragon tilted its head, appearing to consider the food.

*Whoa*, I thought. *It's actually working.* At long last, I knew we were gonna be okay.

Until the dragon straightened its neck, spit fire into the air, and swatted the cookie from Tio's hand, showering the grass with creamy Oreo crumbs.

"Oh, he's mad." Karina clapped her hands over her mouth.

"Whoa." Tio spread his arms, reminding me of a lion-tamer. "What'd you have to go and do that for, huh? I was trying to share with you."

The dragon spread its leathery gold wings and took a menacing step forward.

"No." I took a jerky step back.

"It's okay, guys," Tio said, reaching for his pack. "We'll just have to make a better offer. He needs respect. That's all anything in the wild ever wants is—"

Before Tio could finish, the dragon leapt up and snatched him off the ground with a flick of its tail. The tail curled around Tio's torso twice, squeezing his pack against him and leaving only his panicked face, messy hair, and dangling feet exposed as the dragon hovered higher.

I buried my fingers in my hair, immobilized by shock. "Oh, man . . . Tio, try not to panic, okay?"

But Karina lost it. "Uncle Diego!" Then she did probably the dumbest thing I could think of off the top of my head: She picked up a rock and chucked it at the dragon's belly. "Put him down."

The rock bounced off the dragon like a Ping-Pong ball, and the beast didn't react. By the size of its scales, I don't even think he felt it. Beating its wings with increasing speed, the dragon rose a bit higher.

"Hey." I jammed my finger in the air, talking through my teeth. "We're talking to you."

"Guys?" Tio's voice trembled. "Don't be afraid, all right?"

Karina hurled another rock, and this time she didn't even hit the monster. We couldn't reach anymore. She burst into tears and screamed until it sounded like her throat might tear. The dragon swooped in a circle, locked its gaze on me, and threw its head back.

The fire came a second later, a broiling tower of embers raining from its mouth. The wings fanned the flames, ushering them into a cocoon that rocketed toward me like a solar flare. The world became an oven, and I was going to roast in this unfamiliar land. Rooted to the ground, I threw my arms over my face, knowing they weren't going to protect me, and—

My sister tackled me from the side and knocked me off balance. My shoulder and hip exploded with pain, and when I took my arms away from my face, Karina was rolling through the grass like a log down a hill, putting out bright flashes of orange on her pants and shirt.

The dragon let out another roar, reared higher into the air until its shadow barely covered me, and then sped into the purple horizon.

Uncle Diego was gone.

"Karina," I called, cupping my hands around my mouth to project my voice.

"I'm down here."

I looked to the enormous crack in the ground and tumbled into the ravine after my sister, bracing myself for a long, hard fall. Mercifully, it was shallower than I'd expected, and I landed on a patch of rocks and damp, fragile twigs. There I lay face-up, dizzy, starved for breath, and heartbroken.

Tears in her eyes, Karina knelt over me, her hair matted with sweat. She plucked a dry leaf out of my hair and looked me up and down.

"You okay?" she wheezed.

I managed a nod, but the slightest movement nearly gave me vertigo. I planted my hands beneath me and reminded myself that I was on stable ground. "I'm okay. You?" Okay. We were never going to think of that word the same way again. My sight drifted to Karina's reddened skin, rough and charred on her arms. "You're burned."

"No, no. I'll be fine." Karina wiped her eyes and stared up at the stars. "If that's what you call this. Lucky is probably a better word."

"No." I grabbed Karina's wrist and pointed at the burns on her forearms. "You need to treat that. And you call this lucky? A train crash and a dragon assault in the same day?"

"And living to tell the tale," Karina added. "We are the luckiest siblings on the planet right now."

"But that thing took Tio. The dragon swiped him off the ground and carried him away." I picked up a stick and snapped it in two. "And in case you haven't thought about this, dragons shouldn't exist. I don't even think we're in Europe."

Karina buried her head in her hands. "Charlie . . ."

"You know it's true. That train blasted us into some weirdo freak land, and we don't know how we're gonna get home. Tio was our best chance, and that death lizard carried him away. And gave you burns."

"Then we'll get him back. We're *familia*, Carlos." There she went using my real name again. "We're going to get our uncle back." Her mind was only in one place. She didn't care about her burns.

"How? You wanna go crawl into a giant nest in some thousand-foot tree and ask nicely?"

*Excuse me, Mr. Dragon, can we please have our uncle back?*

*Oh, what in tarnation, this is yours? My bad, y'all. Happy trails!*

Karina must not have known how to respond, because she started crying. Maybe I was being too harsh. I was right, but I also didn't need to yell at my sister, even if she was being completely naive. We were going through the same pain right now. I had to be her rock, and she had to be mine. We had no one else.

Nobody.

Through a film of tears, I stared up at the darkening sky, where even the stars seemed too afraid to come out yet.

For the first time in our lives, we were truly alone.

# KARINA

## WANTED DEAD OR ALIVE (BUT PREFERABLY DEAD)

—◆———◆—

Charlie and I spent the night in the ravine, agreeing to sleep in shifts in case the dragon came back. Except Charlie passed out for the whole night. It worked out because my mind was too full to sleep. Instead, I lay awake and argued with myself.

*I need rest; I'm no good to Charlie and Uncle Diego if I can't see straight.*

*I need to go find my uncle now; in a matter of minutes the dragon could eat him, maul him, burn him, or whatever a dragon actually does.*

*We need to stay down here until somebody finds us.*

*We need to get out of here before something finds us.*

I tossed these thoughts around like a hacky sack, wishing sleep would come. My body was like a limp marionette, but my mind raced on hyperdrive. It didn't help that tight spaces made me want to crawl out of my skin, and that every other thought in my head was *ow, ow, ow.* I studied my burns, throbbing as if someone had run a piping hot iron over my arms. Charlie and I were blessed with our mom's golden-brown skin and never even got sunburns. Dragon burns? How was I supposed to deal with these? I blew on them, wishing that would have the same effect as blowing on hot soup did.

A couple times I climbed out of the ravine—slow and quiet in case there were more monsters—wondering what we should do next. I looked to the skies, then up ahead, and finally to the ground, and the second time I found my uncle's journal.

It lay spread open with the leather strap undone, all the ink pointing up at the stars. When had he dropped it? I picked it up and pressed it to my chest, careful not to move my arms too much, and I breathed in the pleasant aroma of leather and Uncle Diego's cologne. Like his hugs.

Something fell from the journal and thumped my foot, taking me by surprise, and I found my uncle's necklace on my shoe—the little pendant he always twisted around. I hadn't even seen him take it off, but he must have tucked it into his journal. When I picked up the necklace, it was a little heavier than expected. I rolled it in my palm and then slipped it into my pocket.

My gaze wandered to the diary's open page. While I'd never want to violate my uncle's privacy, I couldn't pull my attention away from the smooth, dark ink:

*The Greatest Adventures:*
+ Everest
+ Snorkeling in the Caribbean
+ Crossing the Sahara with Danny and Jake
+ Couch-surfing in New Zealand
+ Meeting Karina and Charlie

Below the number five, which was underlined three times, a weathered piece of tape clung to the corner of a photo I'd never seen before, but I definitely remembered when my mom took it. It was when she picked us up from his house after the night of our back yard camping trip when Charlie and I were five. A tiny, gap-toothed version of myself smiled back at me, along with a little Charlie and his Power Ranger pajamas. Uncle Diego stood between us, tall, young, and happy.

I smiled through my tears and ran my finger across the ink, feeling the little grooves in the creamy-white paper. "We'll save you, Uncle Diego."

The air stung my eyes from all the crying, and the world weighed a thousand pounds on my shoulders. I closed Uncle Diego's journal and carried it back into the ravine with me. With this small comfort, sleep hit me like, well . . . like a train. The night passed quickly, with no dreams.

I awoke to sunlight and the swish of turning pages.

For a fleeting moment, I thought I woke up back home and heard my stepdad reading the newspaper. But the biting sensation of rocks in my elbows and the searing scream of the burns on my arms killed that hope fast. I sat up, flexed the kinks out of my neck and shoulders, and found Charlie sitting cross-legged against the ravine with Uncle Diego's diary in his hands.

"*Buenos dias*," my brother said. "So much for sleeping in shifts, huh?"

"That's Uncle Diego's journal." I rubbed the crud from my eyes and shook dirt out of my hair.

"I know. It's fascinating."

"Don't read it," I said, reaching to snatch it from his hands. "It's rude to go through people's private writing. It's like if someone went through your undies."

Charlie turned the page. "Tio's a celebrity who's been in *Men's Fitness* like five times. Half the country's seen his undies. He doesn't have a private life."

"I can't even with you right now. Put it down," I said. "And I hope you got good sleep, because we're leaving. We never should've slept. Uncle Diego would've spent days and nights looking for us without even thinking about shutting his eyes. We're going to give him that same priority from now on. No excuses."

"Are you sure?" Charlie slammed the book shut and tossed it back to me. "He'd give us priority? Because the past five or six years suggest otherwise."

I stuffed the book into my backpack and slung it over my shoulders, wincing when the strap sizzled against the raw skin on my arm. I hated to admit it, but Charlie's words burned with truth as well. Uncle Diego hadn't made us a priority for years. But if we were in his shoes right now, *he'd give up everything, wouldn't he?*

"What would Mom say? No matter what, we're still familia. If we think positive, we can make it up to him. We can get him back."

I climbed out of the ravine, and my brother followed. We stretched, turned in a circle, and greeted our strange, new world.

"It's gonna be hard to be positive," Charlie said. "When a beast like that snatches a six-foot-tall man off the ground ..."

"Then we need to hurry," I said. "We don't know anything about dragons. But if there's any chance our uncle is okay, we owe him everything. It's his birthday."

All he wanted to do was spend time with us, and we spent the whole trip quizzing him and burying our noses in our phones.

After a few minutes of walking in silence, I caught sight of something else I'd never seen here before—the sort of thing I wouldn't pay attention to if I saw it at home, but here ...

Two wooden poles rose from the ground, and between them, a wide plank displayed a sign painted in flowing, white letters. I never thought I would be happier to see a sign, both physical and symbolic.

"Charlie," I said, "we're not alone."

Relief filled my lungs. Whatever this country ... world ... land was, people lived here, and they were close by. An arrow pointed to a path of smooth, red stone winding deep into the hills and into a faraway forest where paper lanterns hung from the trees. I couldn't believe I'd missed it from the ravine. Charlie and I were going to get help.

## FLORINDALE SQUARE: STRAIGHT AHEAD

"Yesss." Charlie pumped a fist in the air and closed the gap between us. We met in a bone-crushing hug and jumped in a few circles. The last time I jumped in circles was . . . hmm, probably never. "We're gonna get help."

"I know." My heart fluttered at the thought. "Florindale Square. Somebody there has to know something about the dragon. Maybe they saw it fly over them last night. Do you think they're getting ready to fight it?"

"Do you think it belongs to them?"

I clutched my pack tight against my back, dusted my knees, and stepped toward Florindale Square, repeating the name of the town in my head. *Florindale.* Like chicken soup, the name warmed me from within. I couldn't wait to find out what kind of people lived here. I just hoped Charlie was wrong about the dragon belonging to them. What if they were barbarians?

Charlie jammed his hands in his pockets. "What a weird name for a town."

"But it's pretty," I said. "I wonder if it'll be anything like my story. I wrote a novella about a town called Floral Falls once. It was cute and quaint and colorful, and there were little fairies everywhere." And elves and robots, but Charlie didn't need to know any more.

"Yeah?" Charlie asked. "Well, I watched a movie on Netflix about these creepy townspeople who make sacrifices to the moon, and I didn't sleep for weeks. That's what the name Florindale makes me think of."

I sneered at my brother. "Maybe you shouldn't watch those low-budget D-list movies. Mom said we were gonna get nightmares."

"But sometimes they're funny, though. And they make me feel like it's not hard to make a movie."

I smiled. He had a point. "Isn't the Florin the coin they used to use in Florence? Back in old *Italia*? It can't be that scary."

Charlie pinched all his fingers together and made a kissing motion. "*Parmigiano*? Mario? Hey, maybe we'll find lasagna."

I gave him the side-eye. "You can be done now."

But then I smiled. We would need his goofy sense of humor. I tried to imagine how I would feel—how I would live—if I had to face this situation without Charlie by my side. The idea alone was too painful.

As we walked into the grove, I understood that the paper lanterns weren't hanging from the trees at all, but rather they were floating in midair high above our heads.

"That's a cool trick," I said.

Charlie shrugged. "Drones, probably."

Meanwhile, the road flickered with tiny specks of life. I stopped to kneel and stare at a gold circular bug with tiny legs that reminded me of a perfect coat button. I had almost touched it when it lifted a waxy pair of wings, exposing its shimmering shell. When the bug lifted off and left a thin stream of vapor trailing behind it, I squealed and burst into joyful laughter.

Charlie wrinkled his nose. "Don't go touching stuff, Rina. What if these bugs bite or sting or something?"

I immediately thought of Uncle Diego always checking his boots for bugs and what he would do if something actually stung him. "Put ice on it?" Which reminded me, I really needed to do something about the screaming burns on my arms soon. "I could use some for my arms."

"A: No, Rina. You're not supposed to put ice on burns. B: Where do we get ice, wandering the open road like this? Don't touch things."

Not even a minute later, Charlie plucked a rose from a bush and twirled the stem in his fingers, forgetting his own advice. "Check this out. It's so perfect. The symmetry and everything."

Before I could scold my brother, the petals darkened on their stem, first becoming a deep, bloody shade of red, then withering to black. As if they'd been burned, the petals turned to ash and spilled onto the ground, leaving only the stem intact.

Charlie tossed the stem away and clenched his fist. "What the . . ."

As soon as the stem hit the grass, a fresh new rosebud sprouted on the end and unfurled into a brand new flower.

"What did you do?" I asked.

"I didn't do anything."

We watched as the rose repeated the cycle in loops, crumbling to dust and blooming again, leaving the breeze to sweep up the ashes and carry them away.

"Do you think it's magic?" Charlie whispered.

"No." The answer came as a reflex, my ears rejecting the word Charlie produced so casually. But it was a fun idea. "Okay, maybe. If there are dragons and floating lanterns, then who knows what else there is?"

Charlie bent down next to the rose and studied it from a couple angles. "Would that make this thing cursed?"

"How would I know?" I asked. "Just leave it alone, Charlie. Let's just get to the town. Okay? Keep your hands in your pockets."

We walked the road until our legs screamed and our feet swelled inside our shoes, and when we didn't think we could take another step, a wooden sign and a leafy archway announced the entrance to Florindale Square.

"Have we died?" Charlie asked. "Are we about to go to Heaven now?"

I sank to the ground and massaged my legs again. "It's so close, yet so far. I can barely take another step."

"Come on," Charlie said.

He tried to pull me up, but I yanked my arms out of his reach. "Ow, don't touch, Charlie. Every little tap is like a billion hot needles. It hurts."

"Then we need to treat your burns. We need water and a place to sit. We need help."

When we stepped through the archway, we had to catch our breath again, and this time it was awe rather than exhaustion that took the wind out of our lungs.

Beautiful red bricks lined the path below, though vibrant grass and plant life speckled the town in carefully curated patches. A merchant popped out of a crimson tent, the curtain making a crisp fluttering sound behind her, and walked over to a stand where a man arranged boots and leather vests on iron racks. The two greeted each other like lifelong friends.

In the center of the action, a tower of polished stone stood proudly over the people of the town. I admired the gargoyles and the intricate statues of men and women standing together in harmony. A set of shimmering bronze bells hung from stone arches at the top. Signs near the tower pointed to hidden destinations such as *The Woodlands*, *Grimm's Hollow*, and *Dickory Dock*.

"Wow," I breathed. "This place is breathtaking."

"Tio would flip out." Charlie turned in a circle, sticking his nose in the air and sniffing. "Karina, I have to know where that smell is coming from right now. You don't understand—I must know what god or goddess of food magic hath blessed this Florindale Square and how we can get them to smile upon Tucson."

A warm, sweet, zesty scent greeted my nose and tickled my stomach. With all the running we'd done, a handful of protein bars wasn't going to last us much longer. I fixed my gaze on a shop near the bell tower. In gold letters, somebody had painted the words *Hansel and Gretel*, and a thin veil of steam drifted from the open windows.

"It's that little bakery," I said. "Should we go get a bite and start asking questions?"

A *Closed* sign went up in the window. A middle-aged man and a girl about our age stepped out of the bakery, turned a large copper key in the doorknob, and then sauntered on their way.

"Never mind, then." I slumped down at a picnic table and dropped my backpack at my feet. Charlie and I didn't have any money, and even if we did, I was pretty sure dollars and cents weren't a thing in a place like this. "I. Am. So hungry. I can't even, Charlie. Are we doomed to become beggars and shake a tin cup at all the happy . . . Florindalians?"

Charlie sat next to me and rubbed his face. "We'll figure this out, one way or another. Things always happen for a reason."

"You don't believe that."

Charlie threw his hands up. "Come on. I'm trying to be positive."

"I've known you my whole entire life, and you don't believe everything happens for a reason."

"We're still young, Rina," Charlie said. "Maybe I changed my mind. That's why everyone respects Tio so much. He's all about that self-discovery business. Journaling and stuff. I think it's a little cheesy sometimes, but hey, it works for him."

I retrieved the journal from my backpack, leafed through a few pages, and then hugged it against my chest. "Do you think we're here for a reason right now? Or do you think it was all just bad luck?"

Charlie stretched out and rested one foot on top of the other. "I don't know. Maybe everything that happens to us is like a game of Uno. Half of what happens to us is luck, and then we do what we can with it. Blowing up and landing here? Those are the cards we got. We couldn't have controlled that."

"But maybe we can control what we do with them. Now we have to be like our uncle to save him and get out of here. We have to play our cards right." I nudged Charlie with my elbow. "We're so deep, huh?"

Charlie grinned, and for the first time since the train wreck, the smile was wide enough to show off all his teeth. "Super deep."

"All right," I said. "Let's play our cards. Let's get help."

"*Harrrumph.*" A deep grumble sounded behind me, where a burly man of a little less than four feet smeared a poster across a brick wall. The poster was wider than his arm span, and he shifted back and forth with increasing frustration, trying to smooth it against the wall. Every time he moved to one side, the other corner would curl as if to pester him, and the man grumbled and made a fist.

"A thousand curses." The man finally tore the poster off the wall, chucked it at his feet, and then kicked it into a crumpled mess. "This world has always had it in for us dwarves. Gah!" He kicked again for good measure.

Charlie sprang to his feet. "Here, man. Let me help."

The dwarf didn't acknowledge us at first, immersed in his flurry of kicks and grunts. When Charlie took a knee and picked up the battered poster, the dwarf froze mid-kick, stroked his iron-gray beard, and narrowed his eyes.

"And who the ivory queen are you?"

"Charlie Rosas." Charlie smoothed the wrinkles out of the poor broken poster, tattered and upside-down on the ground, and then he reached out to shake the dwarf's hand. "And this is my sister, Karina."

I raised my hand in an awkward wave as the man flicked his gaze between me and Charlie. "Hi."

"Stars." He looked us up and down, probably studying our jeans, sneakers, and the pink in my hair. "You're not from around here, are you? No, don't answer that. Whatever's happening in that other world this time, I'll not be having a part in it. No, I tell you. I've done my service! Hmph."

*Okaaay?* I shrugged, vowing to make sure Charlie and I started on the right foot with these people. "What's your name?"

"Zid," the dwarf said. "Yes, you heard me correctly."

I helped Charlie finish smoothing out the poster. "Zid. I like it. It's unique."

"Well shucks." Zid reddened and knitted his fingers together at his waist. "My gratitude for your help. 'Twas an insult for the town council to ask a dwarf to put up these hulking posters meant for giants."

"It's no trouble, man," Charlie said. "We were raised to help people whenever we can."

I flipped the poster over, and my breath halted in my throat. I tugged on my brother's sleeve.

Charlie's eyes widened. "No."

An inky reptilian monster glared up from the center of the poster, the beast's veiny wings and bulbous eyes rendered in terrifying detail, along with a tail that could coil around a grown man at least three times. Even in 2D, the dragon was the mayor of Nightmare Town.

"What?" Zid ground his knuckles into his hips.

"*Wanted, Dead or Alive, but Preferably Dead,*" Charlie read aloud. "*Verdoro, the Dark Dragon of the Old World.*"

I swallowed a knot in my throat. The monster had a name. A reputation. A history.

"*What?*" Zid parroted, a stark staccato. "You never seen a dragon before? Good. This one's the grandfather of them all. Even I can't knock any sense into that heathen, and I'm the best at what I do. You thank Lady Fortune that Verdoro's not your problem."

What an encouraging, wonderful man.

"Umm, Zid?" Charlie said. "We have seen this dragon before."

"Just last night, actually." I rolled up my sleeves to show Zid the burns on my arms and watched the color spill from his face. "We need your help. This monster took our uncle away."

# CHARLIE

## THE DRAGON TAMER'S TALE

---

Zid sat me and Karina down in the back of an old cottage, where he applied thick burgundy leaves drenched in oil to Karina's burns to repair her skin while she flipped through Tio's diary. "It took a human . . . a New World human. Stars, this is so much worse than I knew."

The dwarf paced back and forth, tugging his beard in alternating motions like cow udders. While he got over his fit, I checked out his home. This guy seemed like the least likely person to put wanted posters around the city for a dragon's death. Reptilian figurines lined his shelves, golden eggs the size of my head sat in silver bowls, and paintings of winged beasts clung to every inch of the wall. And yet, here stood a man who was blubbering like he had a phobia. When he finally stopped pacing, he poured three goblets of wine without asking. I wondered if it was juice at first, but the smell stung my nostrils, and I vowed not to touch it.

Zid gulped his wine, wiped his lips, and then slammed his goblet down in front of him. "I'll have you know that I used to be a dragon trainer. I've bred and raised a few. I fed them and exercised them and advocated for their rights. See that one on the wall right there?" He pointed to a painting of a dragon that oddly seemed to be smiling. "My Draco. I loved him dearly, so much that I had to move him into Grimm's Hollow with a friend. He was too big and too free for my little yard."

A tear sparkled like a marble in Zid's eye.

Karina offered a smile. "I can imagine you're very passionate about dragons."

"Was," Zid said. "Until Verdoro."

I gripped the sides of my chair, ready for some kind of story. We needed a thunderclap and a theater spotlight to properly set the mood.

Zid cleared his throat dramatically, rising on his toes to make himself look taller. "Verdoro first plagued Florindale Square some time ago. You can imagine my excitement when I first saw those scales. He was a dream. Most people ran in fear, but I wanted to talk to him. They can understand us, you know. They know our tones, our intentions, and our body language. But when he burned down Midas's Pub without provocation, I knew there was something . . . off about him. Dragons do not descend on civilization to burn or consume unprovoked. They're actually quite gentle. Leave them be—respect them—and they shall never hurt a soul."

Based on that statement alone, I knew Zid would've become fast friends with Tio. Coffee shop buddies. I tried to picture them broing out, and I almost laughed. The trouble was I didn't agree with Zid's statement at all, and Karina clearly didn't either.

"My uncle did nothing to the dragon," she said. "It came out of nowhere and took him away with no good reason."

"That's because this one's different," Zid said. "As if Hades itself spat him out. He cannot be reasoned with or tamed. Believe me, I was the only one foolish enough to keep trying. I considered that he might be a shifter—a human who's dabbled in dark arts to assume another form at will."

Karina and I exchanged wide-eyed glances. Real life shifters? Like Dracula and his bat form? Or the blue lady from the *X-Men* comics? Neither of them was very nice.

Zid must've sensed my discomfort because he waved a hand and said, "But I have doubts. Humans have different auras that don't go away when they turn. You can sense it. Go figure, we finally settle into a period of peace, free of curses and evil queens, and now we have Verdoro returning at random intervals to terrorize Florindale. Sometimes he engulfs buildings. The Woodlands are dying. Sometimes he batters a living being and leaves them there to suffer, as if he enjoys the sport of torturing people."

My stomach churned. What was the monster doing to my tio?

"I should say there are few who have ventured out to hunt him. None have returned, and not a soul wishes to attempt the journey anymore, even with the rather generous reward on Verdoro's head. It feels as though we are destined to settle into our fear, to keep one eye fixed on the clouds until the monster finally plummets from them. Unfortunately, the life of such a beast spans ages we do not care to wait for."

Rina and I grew up with some messed up legends. Mom liked to scare us with *La Llorona*, the crying ghost woman that took bad kids away. But never an actual dragon.

Karina put on that famous Rosas concentration stare, like she was taking an X-ray of Zid. "What do you think is the lifespan of somebody who's been taken by the dragon?"

Zid frowned, deep lines appearing on his forehead. "I'm sorry, younglings." He refilled his goblet and then drained it again. "Nobody's ever come back."

Tears sprung to Karina's eyes, and I covered my mouth with a fist.

"This is a nightmare," I said. "We're supposed to be in Switzerland with our tio right now. I knew I had a bad feeling about all of this, and now you're basically telling us we're never going to see him again."

"I only advise maintaining realistic expectations," Zid said. "We can say a few words for him tonight. I can prepare a feast. We can—"

"That's not what we want." Karina pounded the table, spilling a drop of her untouched drink. "It won't make us feel better. We want him back. We want to go home."

I knew we were speaking to Zid like five-year-olds throwing a tantrum, but I didn't care. I wanted answers, and so far, I'd been too afraid to ask one of the most important questions of all. "Zid. Where are we?"

"Ahh. I wondered when you'd ask." Zid sighed. "As far as we know, there are three worlds: the New, where you came from, the Old, where you stand before me, and the World Between, which is . . . trickier to explain. As hard as we work to keep them divided, someone always slips between the cracks. But never by train. Your presence here is a puzzle indeed."

A bitter taste climbed up my throat, and I buried my head in my hands. There we had it. This wasn't Switzerland or Europe or even the Earth we knew. This was another world entirely.

"We shouldn't be here," I said.

Zid folded his hands on his lap and stared at his fingers. "Then I should tell you I know a generous, wonderful young man who can send you home. He's a rather gifted Carver, a sort of mage who can slip between the worlds and bend matter to his will, and he also happens to be our king. If you so desire, younglings, say the word, and I shall take you to this man with no further question. 'Tis the best I can offer."

I lifted my head. An iron promise of home. It sounded too good to be true.

How much were Mom and Jorge missing us right now? How much did they know? I pictured Mom sitting in the living room, peering over a magazine to catch glimpses of the news and turning up the volume when they announced some breaking story about the Fernweh Express crashing—or even vanishing—en route to Switzerland. She'd probably call everyone she knew, trying to learn more information, and what could anybody give her? Who would know to say that her kids were in a fairytale land, and her little brother had been fed to a dragon?

The idea tore my heart into ribbons.

I turned to my sister. "We've gotta get back to Mom and Jorge. They're probably freaked, and I am too. If somebody knows how to get us home, we need to go."

Zid tapped his thumbs together, and we waited for Karina to agree with my flawless logic. But for some reason, she wasn't nodding.

I put a hand on her shoulder. "Right, though? Say yes."

Karina bit her lip. "I . . ."

"I sense you're considering an alternative plan given your uncle's situation," Zid said. "I cannot recommend you entertain it any further."

My sister dried her cheeks and cleared her throat. "That's our uncle. It's wrong to leave him here. It's the opposite of what he would do for us."

Zid looked like Karina had backhanded him. "You mean to go after him."

"Yes. I do."

"No, we don't," I said. "Karina, seriously, it's suicidal. It's really not a good—"

The dwarf held up a palm and shushed us. "Have you understood nothing? People—knights, warriors, sorcerers—are not coming back from their quests to kill Verdoro, and you are far less prepared than any of them. Beyond Florindale Square and in the isle of Kesterfall, our world is rife with dangers, especially for New World urban folk like you two. Dragons are but one such danger. Miss Karina, I urge you to reconsider. You can be home with your brother before the sun goes down. I can guarantee it."

*Warm bedding,* I thought. *Hot showers. Familia . . . Guilt.*

"No," Karina said.

I stood, nearly toppling my untouched goblet. "Rina, can we talk about this for another minute, you and me? Outside?"

Zid picked up his goblet, realized it was empty, then tossed it over his shoulder. He reached for my wine and sipped. "Take all the time you need. Talk sense into her, youngling. I'll be right here."

Karina followed me outside, the light of Florindale cutting into my eyes after being submerged in Zid's dim home. She shut the door behind her with a soft click and spoke before I could begin. "Look. I know this is a nightmare, but if I don't go after Uncle Diego, I'll never forgive myself for leaving him behind. Uno, remember? We have a choice about—"

"What do we owe him?" I asked. "He's been a shadow, too busy with his money and his fame to care about us. Even Mom feels the same way."

"Yes, but he's familia," Karina countered. "Nothing about this is easy, Carlos. Especially this decision. I know it's hurtful that he hasn't made much effort in the last seven years. But is that really a good reason to leave him behind for the rest of his life?"

I shrugged. "I dunno. Maybe."

"Look, if you want to go home, then I think you should. Tell Mom and Jorge what happened, and I'll go find our uncle. Then I can bring him back, and we can forget about this whole crazy trip." She paused. "I want you to go home. I'll be fine."

"You will not be fine." I threw my arms up and waved them with each syllable. "No offense. I wouldn't be fine. We wouldn't be fine. Tío's the most qualified person in the world to be 'fine' out there, and I don't even like his chances. I'm making the call as the older sibling, and we're both going home. Now."

Karina rolled her eyes. "You're literally only five minutes older."

"Seven."

This is what our mom would have called *causing a scene*, and it's one of the behaviors that made her threaten us with *La Llorona*—the crazy crying ghost woman—or a sandal until we were too old to care. *Take a picture, it'll last longer*, I wanted to tell them. But did this place even have cameras?

"Excuse me? You there, younglings," a woman interrupted.

She was beautiful and dark-skinned, about Tío's height, and strutting down the cobblestone path. Her hair fell down her shoulders in rich-black waves that matched every square inch of her leather coat and the high-heeled boots she wore. Under one arm, she carried a wide-brimmed hat with a crimson feather. On the other, she carried a burlap sack. She wore a smirk that made me feel about two feet tall, and she wiggled her eyebrows before she spoke again, pointing to Zid's home with a chewed-up fingernail. "You two see a little man go in there recently?"

Karina wrinkled her eyebrows. "A little man?"

"Oh, you'd know him if you saw him. Hard to miss. I just wanna parlay with dear Zid. You two carry on about your little . . . scuffle." The woman approached Zid's door, her heels clipping at the cobblestone. She beat a short rhythm into the door then entered uninvited. As she moved, I caught a whiff of ocean spray and sun-kissed leather.

I blinked a few times, dumbfounded. "Was that a pirate?"

This place was getting stranger by the minute, like a twisted joke. *So this pirate walks into a dwarf's home, right? And he's a dragon tamer, so then . . .*

"Don't change the subject." Karina scoffed, but her attention stayed on the door. "Probably. Anyway, it's cute how you think you can boss me around. Now I'm doubly staying behind."

"You are on another level, Karina." I tried out Mom's death gaze. "I will straight-up drag you back home by your annoying pink highlights if I have to."

"You're being super immature," Karina said. "Here I am trying to give you a choice, and here you are trying to take mine away. Way to be a good brother, Carlos.

Also, the death glare doesn't work when you do it. You just look hilarious."

Ouch.

She'd done it. My pride wilted. I was out of comebacks.

Karina sighed and took my shoulder. "Remember when we were little and Uncle Diego set up that campout for us? Even though a monsoon was coming, and we kept thinking there were dragons in his back yard? He was gonna punch them in the face or share Oreos with them?"

The memory replayed in my head like one of Jorge's old vinyl records, dust drifting from the surface and restoring in rich, vibrant detail. "Yeah. I remember."

"Look. I want to give this a real chance. I know the odds are against us. But think about how awful we'd feel if we left him here. Are we supposed to go back to school wondering if he's still here? If he's chained up in some dungeon or trying to punch his way out of a dragon's belly? Do what you want, but I won't leave him. The guilt would eat at my brain for the rest of my life."

"As opposed to a hundred-foot death lizard eating it instead?" I kicked a rock and didn't say anything for a while, wiping a stupid, embarrassing tear from my eye. Karina had won. If I kept up these emotional outbursts, my eyes would be red forever. "Well, if you're staying, then I guess I am, too."

Karina shook her head. "I told you, you don't have—"

"And all those things you said about guilt? It's the same if I go home and leave you here. You drive me crazy sometimes, but we're familia, and I'm pretty sure that means we're supposed to protect each other. And I can't believe I'm saying this, but . . ." I massaged my temples. "We should probably do whatever we can to protect our tio, too."

Karina threw her arms around me and squeezed like I was a teddy bear. "Thank you, Charlie. I love you."

"Yeah," I said. "You, too."

"Should we go tell Zid?"

"He's not gonna like it."

"It's not his decision."

We went back inside and found the dwarf sitting with the pirate woman as he traced a crinkled yellow map with a thick finger. Both of them looked up, their expressions flat and hard as though we'd interrupted an important business meeting.

"And so?" Zid asked.

I crossed my arms. "Thank you for offering to send us home, but we can't go. Not yet."

Zid wrinkled his bulbous nose. "So I see."

The pirate woman put her hands on her hips. "Making more friends from the New World, Zid?"

"It's complicated," he muttered. "Younglings, may I present Captain Niraya Storm of the *Red Hood*. It seems the three of you share a common goal."

*Captain of the Red Hood?* I thought.

"So you are a pirate," Karina said.

"Shh." I nudged my sister with my elbow.

Niraya huffed and crossed the room, looking Karina up and down. "Perceptive. Good. What's your name, wildling?"

"Karina. Karina Rosas."

"Charmed, Karina." The woman went for a handshake. Then she turned to me. "And this handsome boy?"

I swear I probably turned as red as licorice, and I didn't know whether to laugh or hide.

"Carlos. But call me Charlie." I went for a handshake of my own.

"Charlie. What a lovely name." After Niraya shook my hand, she cupped my chin in her fingers and tilted my head back and forth, nodding as she studied my face. "So the two of you fancy yourselves dragon hunters? Zid tells me your uncle was taken by Verdoro not so long ago?"

Karina straightened her back, like she was trying to make herself feel as tall as possible. "Yes. Just last night. We're going to get him back."

Niraya let go of my face, took a step back, and then drummed her fingers on her arms, the sound like rain against her leather coat. "You know it's dangerous to tango with dragons."

"Well, yeah, I think I have a general understanding of how dangerous this is. It's not like I'm expecting it to be easy." Karina stuck her nose in the air.

Niraya smirked, evidently more impressed than annoyed by Rina's snark. "Good. Because that same dragon took my love away from me several weeks ago . . . plucked him and his ship from the middle of the Joringel Sea"—she reached out and made a plucking motion at nothing in particular—"and didn't look back."

Just how much damage had the dragon caused in Florindale? How many lives had it ruined?

"To be fair," Zid said, "you did suggest that the scoundrel provoked him. Classic J—"

"There's nothing fair or classic about it." Niraya pounded the table with a fist, sending ripples through Zid's drink. "Verdoro set my blood on fire, and I want my vengeance. I want the beast's head on a silver platter."

Zid cleared his throat. "Captain Storm means to set sail for the island of Kesterfall tonight, where the dragon is thought to reside. She's the first in weeks to announce her intention to make the journey. If you plan to do the same, then I suggest you go together. There is, as they say, safety in numbers."

Karina tugged on my sleeve. "Let's go with her."

In response, Niraya raised a thin eyebrow at Zid, and I raised one at Karina, who would never trust a stranger this easily.

"They're serious?" Niraya asked Zid. "Kesterfall isn't a playground, wildlings. And I can't afford to waste time looking after cubs. You'll slow me down."

"We can help you," Karina said. "Our odds increase if we travel together. We can save our uncle, your love, and look out for each other."

"Split three ways, the reward will still be enough for you to live like a royal when you return." Zid's voice went gravelly and low. Karina and I must've really worn him out.

*When you return*, he'd said. Not *if you return*. Apparently Zid had much more faith in Niraya Storm than he did in me and Rina. Heck, so did I.

My sister shook her head. "We don't want the reward."

I almost argued that yes, we did want the reward, but I doubted Florindale currency would work back home. If I couldn't buy video games or some sweet new Nikes, I wasn't interested. In the end, all that really mattered was Tio anyway.

I considered the situation. I never would have been comfortable traveling with an actual pirate. It seemed like something Mom would tell us not to do, if she could even imagine such a possibility coming to life in present-day Tucson. I'd seen enough movies, read enough books, and even written a five-page social studies paper to know pirates couldn't be trusted. They always had selfish motives, and they could be violent and deceptive to get what they wanted. And yet, I had to admit I would've liked our chances better with Niraya on our side.

Maybe a cold, hard pirate with a thirst for vengeance was what we needed to survive the trip and bring the dragon down. If only she felt the same about two city kids.

"Captain Storm," Zid said, "they're making the journey either way. You'd put my mind at ease if you team up."

Niraya brushed some dust off her sleeve, fixing her dark-eyed stare on me. "What can you offer? How do I know you can hold your own?"

I shrugged. "Well, we already outran Verdoro once. I'm a soccer player. Karina's got an awesome imagination. And our tio's an adventurist. We might've picked up a thing or two from him. It's in our blood."

Niraya took another minute to think, pacing like a wolf. I was positive she was going to say no, but finally, she placed her hat on her head and tipped it in my direction. "I suppose we have a deal. I could use the deckhands sailing to Kesterfall. If you're willing to join me, I only ask that you keep up."

"We'll hold our own. Promise." Karina snuck a glance at me. "What do you think?"

"I'm in." I half wished I could cram the words back into my throat, but the damage was done. "So you know where we're going?"

"You'll take my map." Zid passed me the parchment. "I should caution that it is largely rooted in theory, but I've a pretty good idea about what you're in for. Kesterfall is mostly abandoned now. Leave from Dickory Dock tonight. Sail to Jericho Harbor. Should only take you about a day. Of course, I expect you'll have a very long and difficult hike. But somewhere in Mount Blackburn, Verdoro is thought to have made his home. At the very least, you should be able to track him from there."

I took the map, and the words *Here, there be dragons* hovering over Mount Blackburn twisted my stomach into knots. I had a feeling, this time, it wasn't just a phrase to mark uncharted territory.

"I will prepare you some food and mer leaves and moon oil for burns. And before I forget . . ." Zid produced a handful of thick, shimmering coins that reminded me of the fake gold chocolates I sometimes got in my Christmas stocking. "Just in case you need it. Come back safe, and I'm sure the king will give you much more. Then you and your family can do whatever you want. Live happily ever after, I presume."

*Happily ever after.* I rolled up the map. *Yeah, right.*

"So, wildlings." Niraya extended a gloved hand. "Partners?"

We clasped hands and shook. "Partners."

# DIEGO

## EPISODE
## I

·◆——◆·

Sometime during the flight, I blacked out. Fear, fatigue, and the grip of a dragon's tail will do that to a person.

I woke up in the cold, fully convinced I had died and become a ghost. However, I seriously doubted the afterlife starts in a cave. I'd been sleeping in a sitting position, my back resting against a jagged wall of ice and rock. My breaths came out in short little puffs of vapor.

I looked down and inspected my body and clothes. Rips tattered my shirt, and tiny scrapes streaked my body, but otherwise I was whole. I rubbed my face, peppered with stubble that felt like sandpaper. I'd probably been here a few days already. My backpack lay tossed open beside me, a bit charred with the remaining contents spread around it: two remaining cookies and plenty of crumbs, a rope, an extra pair of jeans, and a notebook. I'd lost a few things. My travel diary. My hat. My pendant.

Darkness smattered my vision, but everything above me looked like a starry sky. Thin columns of light cut through and showered the murky terrain, damp and musty from the snowflakes that drifted in from the outside world. They settled on the rocks, the uneven cave floor, and the tip of my nose. Ahead of me, the walls narrowed into a sort of hallway. From where I sat, it seemed the only way out was that hallway, just wide enough for a grown man to push through.

But not wide enough for a massive dragon.

How in the world did I wake up here? Did the fire drake drop me through one of the holes in the ceiling? Could the beast change size? A crazy idea, I admit, but until recently, the existence of dragons was completely loco.

Was this what death felt like: cold, dark, eternal hunger, dread? Could the winged demon hear me? Was he coming back for me? Flying above me right now? I could only imagine the fear Charlie and Karina must've been feeling. Adrenaline is good for stressful situations, but the monster that took me was the stuff of pure, unadulterated terror that binds a person's feet to the ground and does nothing productive for the body.

I had to escape before I became part of a dragon family cookout.

I took my first step through the dark cave, searching for an exit, a lantern, and a living creature that wanted to eat me. I've been in countless caves, but the panic I felt in this one reminded me of those haunted house walkthroughs, which I despised. My sister used to tease me over my fear of strobe lights and clown makeup when we were Charlie and Rina's age. But Rina and Charlie handled themselves pretty well when the big guy appeared. We all put on a good run. They kept their cool while I tried to feed the beast Oreos. So maybe they were still alive. And maybe that meant they'd have a shot at getting home.

Unless they did something stupid, like come look for me.

I walked with only tiny slices of moonlight from cracks above to guide me, keeping my hands buried in my armpits and away from the icy condensation melting down the walls—since the outer limbs go first. The temperature and the frost-crusted walls reminded me a bit of a walk-in freezer, with all the cool mist obscuring the limited vision I had. I only hoped I wouldn't miss something beneath me and plummet deeper into the earth.

My legs already throbbed from the train wreck, from the hike, from running, and from what I could only guess was a very rocky landing after I blacked out. I had to remember I'm stronger than pain and bigger than fears. I walked through a simple meditation, focusing on my breath. *In. Out.*

But I could only keep it up for so long before my mind wandered, and I wished I had anything to listen to besides air through the nose and boots on the ground. An iPod. The wind in the trees. Even a storm.

Miraculously, I got my wish.

Somebody coughed, and the sound stopped me in my tracks.

The cough was human, distinctly male, and if it were any more aggressive, I would've mistaken it for a sneeze.

The cave's acoustics bounced and played with my mind, making identifying where the sound came from nearly impossible. I turned in a circle, fully alert and ready for anything. This was the kind of surprise I didn't like about haunted houses.

People can be so much scarier—so much more dangerous—than the wild.

I rubbed my knuckles and curled my hands into fists, determined to strike first if somebody—or something—snuck up on me . . . like the sudden tickle in my throat. Maybe the cold was getting to me. Maybe the coughing man was contagious.

Finally, I couldn't hold it anymore, and a cough burst from my lungs. I covered my mouth with my sleeve, but even against my arm, one cough sounded like a thousand.

The other cough stopped, and I knew I'd been heard. I shut my eyes and leaned back against the cavern wall. I'd given myself away.

"Ah, so I do have company. Reckoned I heard the beast drop a body through one of those crevasses the other day. Who goes there?" A gruff voice cut through the dark, and the echoes swam in my ears. *Who goes there? Oo goes there? Goes there?*

*Turn around*, I thought. *Walk away.*

"Show yourself." *Show yourself. O yourself.* "I command you in the name of the king."

King? I was in a regular Camelot here.

"Fine," I said. "I'll come out. You gonna be peaceful?"

"Such a fool," the voice said. "Taking one's word before you know what it's worth. I'm not looking to hurt anybody, lad. I'm unarmed, I'm alone, and if you mean well, I'm no threat to your existence. On my honor."

I broke an icicle off the wall and turned the corner, the make-shift weapon tucked behind my back.

A thin man lay slumped against the wall, his hair short but unruly, and his beard a grizzly brown nest flecked with gray. The man probably hadn't shaved in close to a month. Even behind the beard, it looked like somebody took his skin and stretched it tight over his cheekbones. When was his last meal?

He wore a dark leather coat, dusty boots that had seen better days, and black clothes that couldn't have done much to fight the cold. He kept his hands tucked under his coat.

Water gathered at the tip of my icicle and coated my palms.

"So, the beastie got you, too." The stranger stretched his arms over his head, and the icicle slipped from my fingers and shattered when I realized the man was missing a hand. Instead, a rusty metal hook protruded from his tattered sleeve.

A pirate, of course.

"Welcome to purgatory, lad. Make yourself comfortable."

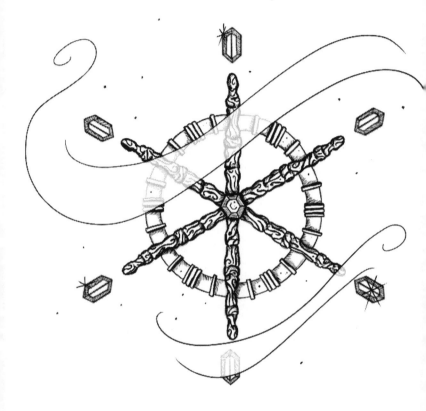

# PART
# TWO

ON THESE
DARK
WATERS

# CHARLIE

## THE LEGEND OF LADY FORTUNE

*·———·*

*I am so uncomfortable*, I thought.

I gawked at the *Red Hood*, the ship that was supposed to deliver me, Karina, and Captain Niraya Storm to Kesterfall. True to its name, most of the vessel was the color of blood, and it didn't help that there were cracked planks like scars all over. Barnacles clung to the underside like pimples. A rickety bathtub might've looked more comforting, especially because I'd never been on water before. I wished I'd brought some Dramamine with me. I didn't think to ask Zid for any, if it even existed here. Karina didn't have a problem with motion sickness. She sometimes read books in the car. I tried that once and threw up.

"Niraya," I said. "There's only three of us."

The captain raised a brow. "Your point?"

"Well, don't you need a whole crew to sail a ship like this?"

Zid burst into laughter. "Niraya Storm, needing a crew . . . ha! Captain Storm could sail a vessel blindfolded with her hands bound behind her back. She's done it before."

Niraya shrugged. "I won't contest that rumor."

"Consider this moment your greatest honor." Zid grinned. "You're about to sail with the greatest captain in all the worlds."

With a smug smile, Niraya started walking. "You coming, wildlings? The ocean calls."

Karina sauntered onto the boat behind Niraya, and I shuffled a few feet behind them. My stomach churned just stepping on the platform.

"Charlie," Niraya said, "would you help me hoist the anchor? There's the windlass over there."

I dropped my backpack, steadied my balance, and followed Niraya to a simple-looking contraption with a pulley and some handles connected to a thick metal chain.

"Clockwise." Niraya made a circle with her finger.

"Oh, that's all? I can do it on my own then." I gripped the handle and turned the wheel. First it came easily, but after a few spins, the machine resisted. Was I using this thing to move a bus? My fingers turned red, and I put all my weight on the balls of my feet. That's the thing about Rosas pride. Sometimes we don't know when to give up.

Niraya stood next to me with her hands on her hips, and I could feel her smirk zeroing in on me like a shrink ray. "You can do it on your own, hmm?"

Karina leaned over the side of the vessel and waved. "Bye, Zid. Thank you for your help."

I couldn't see the dwarf from where I stood, but when Niraya turned and saluted the ground, I heard Zid call back, "Come back with that dragon's hide. May the light be with you."

"Oh, you know it, handsome." Niraya spun on her heel and instantly put me to shame. The windlass turned effortlessly for her, like a doorknob. She winked and patted my shoulder. "We'll work on those muscles. Don't you worry."

I flushed, flexed, and checked my biceps. "They're not that bad, are they?"

Karina and Niraya pretty much ignored me and lowered the sails while I huffed through my nose. Despite little rips in the fabric, they caught the wind instantly. All it took was one gust to blow the ship out of Dickory Dock and into the unknown.

There was no turning back.

"Anchors away," Niraya called, "and to Kesterfall we go. Welcome to the *Red Hood*, wildlings. Welcome to the wild."

The wild.

After I adjusted to the waves swelling under my feet, I welcomed a calming sense of freedom. Karina and I stood at the rail and stared at the end of the world together. The wind whipped through my hair, and tiny droplets of ocean spray kissed my fingers when the water lapped at the side of the ship. I loved the *whoosh* of the wind against the waves, air and water in constant conversation. Call and response. This was how Tio must have felt every day. Young. Free. Infinite.

"It is quite beautiful, isn't it?" Niraya squeezed between me and Karina, interrupting my thoughts like a strange dream. I couldn't believe I'd agreed to sail away with this woman, a total stranger shrouded in secrets. I might as well have agreed to ride a roller coaster without strapping in.

"Who's at the helm?" I asked. I glanced back at the wheel, bewildered to see it turning and correcting course all on its own.

"Don't you worry, wildlings. It knows where we're going." Niraya smirked. "You know, my James gave up everything for the chance to experience this view every day."

The lower half of Niraya's face was smiling, but her eyes were sad. Distant. "The sea. It drew him in like a beautiful spell, the kind you only find in bedtime storybooks. And he did the very same to me. It was Cupid's arrow. He swept me up in a rogue wave, and I vowed never to return to shore."

Oh, brother. That was probably the corniest thing I'd ever heard.

Karina, of course, drank up every word, resting her chin on her hands. "What was he like?"

"What is he like?" Niraya corrected. "He's . . . wily. A little moody. Thinks he's intimidating, but deep down he's a hopeless romantic. A teddy bear, really. When I met him, he had just resigned from the Order of the

Bell, Florindale's elite guardians. He's a hero. One who saved the world then quietly sailed away to start anew."

"And how did you two meet?"

"Our ships crossed paths, and I tried to take his vessel," Niraya said. "But he took my heart instead, and we sailed to world's end together, side by side."

"Wow." Karina dragged the word out, a glassy look in her eyes. She was a living heart-eyed emoji.

Was this gonna be my life now?

Niraya leaned on the rail. "More on your uncle. What was he like?"

"What is he like?" I said. "He's an adventurer. The best known in the world, probably. He climbed the highest, coldest mountain you could imagine. People try all the time, but not everybody gets to the top. Tio was one of the youngest people to do it at the time. He's a legend."

Karina reached into her pocket and took out Tio's necklace, her eyes getting a faraway look as she rubbed the stone between her fingers. I remember glancing at the sphere a few times when Tio was wearing it, wondering where he got it, but I never got around to asking him.

I put my hand out. "Can I see, Rina?"

Like I'd brought her out of a memory, she blinked a few times, shook her head as if to clear it, and then nodded.

Niraya's gaze followed the pendant all the way to my hand, her eyes growing wider and wider as if Karina and I were passing a bar of gold around. "That pendant," Niraya said. "Where did you find it?"

I closed my fingers around it, instinctively protective. "It's Tio's. He must have dropped it or taken it off before the dragon came."

"And where exactly did it come from?"

Her tone freaked me out because it didn't match the question. It wasn't a hey, where'd you get those shoestone. It was more of a where'd you get that giant bazooka-kind of tone. Or maybe it was pirate greed I'd heard.

Karina must've heard it too, because she raised an eyebrow. "Why? It's a rock."

Niraya chuckled and looked back to the horizon. "Be that as it may, there are people who would be quite taken by that little artifact. Where you come from, your people know the legend of Lady Fortune, right?"

"Lady Fortune?" I asked.

The captain waved one arm in a grand circle. "Lady Fortune and her magnificent wheel. Because Fortune, as they say, is a beautiful woman not unlike young Karina or myself."

"Like Lady Luck?" I asked. "I've heard people say that before, but she's not real."

"I've watched *Wheel of Fortune* before," Karina said. "I'd be awesome on that show."

Niraya pointed back at Karina and gave her a nod. "So her influence is known in your world. My grandfather used to tell me this legend many nights before I closed my eyes."

I passed the pendant to Karina. "What does Tio's necklace have to do with her?"

Niraya straightened her back and pressed her fingertips together. "As I said, it's only legend, and so there are variations, but this is the story as I know it. Lady Fortune had the greatest task ever granted to one human: She was responsible for apportioning luck—and the lack thereof—to the people of the world. We have her to thank when we win a game of cards, when we dock the ship minutes before the storm, or when we first encounter our true love while reaching for the same loaf of bread at the bazaar.

"But luck is finite and limited, yet everybody always wants more. Imagine the burden our lady must have faced as the sole decider of who was worthy . . . the responsibility she feels when a decent human loses his estate to a royal flush, perishes in the storm, or arrives at the marketplace just half a moment after that dashing fellow acquires someone else's arm?"

Or like when a train explodes, sends a guy and his sister to another world, and a dragon sweeps their uncle away?

Karina pursed her lips, and I knew we were thinking the same thing: *Stupid Lady Fortune.*

"So, Lady Fortune commissioned a wheel from the fey." Niraya took a tiny blade from her belt and scratched a perfect circle into a weathered barrel. "This way, she could distribute luck in a fair, random manner. She couldn't blame herself for others' misfortunes, and she couldn't bask in others' strokes of good fate. All she had to do was spin, thus weaving a harmonious balance for Florindale. Fortune is cyclical. Some days your luck blossoms"—Niraya divided the wheel into six wedges and carved a rose into the top slice—"and some days it withers to dust." In the opposite wedge, Niraya scratched a dead tree.

In the remaining pieces, she drew a drop of water, explaining that fortune could run strong like a river; a flame, for the days when it could all burn to the ground; the sun, for bright, clear paths; and the moon, for paths of shadow, transition, and wonder.

"The fey forged seven orbs to place on Fortune's wheel: one for each spoke, and one for the center."

I was starting to think of that huge gray slab of rock we ran into in the middle of the fields with Tio, and the big wheel that had been chiseled into the stone. Niraya had just drawn us the same thing. A shiver passed down my spine.

"What were the stones for?" Karina asked.

"Each was thought to possess a unique power when it stood on its own, somehow tied to the being who created it . . . shape-shifting capabilities, or the power to fold its bearer through worlds, as examples. But somehow, the sum of these stones was the wheel's driving force."

"Well, that's a cool fairy tale," Charlie said. "Did Lady Fortune live happily ever after?"

"No," Niraya said simply. "She had a lover, you know. She could have lived happily. But luck wasn't so kind to them."

I frowned. "This is gonna get weird, isn't it?"

"It is a fairy tale," Niraya said. "And so it goes that somebody opposed true love and meant to drive Lady Fortune and her court jester apart. That's one way to tell the story. Others say the villain was jealous of Fortune's power and meant to claim the wheel for himself. Is either so hard to believe?"

I believed it. Every other story on the ten o'clock news was about people who got hurt wrestling for power, or doing stupid things for love.

"They speak of a small army that stormed Lady Fortune's castle. Most legends call the villain Lord Falk, a brutish man who charged into her home. In some variations, he wrestles Lady Fortune for the wheel, and it breaks. In others, he murders the court jester and Fortune destroys her own wheel in the ashes of her grief."

I cringed. This was one dark fairy tale.

"Either way, the destruction was so great that the seven orbs were scattered between this world and the next, presumably never to be seen again. And in his own fury, Lord Falk chained the fair lady to a house on a cloud, where she's forced to look down and watch him hunt down the pieces of her wheel to claim it for himself. 'For whoever wields the Wheel of Fortune controls destiny.'" Niraya took a deep breath, pocketed her knife, and took off her hat, spinning it on her finger. "But it's only a legend."

A fairy tale for people who lived in a world we considered a fairy tale. No wonder I had a headache.

"Do you believe it?" I asked.

"Not entirely," Niraya said. "A healthy dose of skepticism is good, you know. But so is a little belief in stranger things. I've never had a reason to care about the wheel. However, there are people who live by the story of Lady Fortune, obsessively hunting the orbs in honor of Falk or to find the wheel for themselves. Such people give treasure hunters a bad name. And you're hearing this from a pirate."

Karina studied the pendant for a while before putting it around her neck. "Wait, so let's say it's all true. Do you think this is one of the orbs that belongs on the wheel?"

"Just be careful who you show it to. Some people would poison your goblet to steal it from you."

*Great.* And I was actually convinced we'd only be fighting dragons. As Tio once said, other people could be a lot scarier than the wilderness. At least Niraya was scary, too, and she was on our side.

Karina dropped the pendant into the neckline of her shirt. "This couldn't be one of them. If Uncle Diego found it somewhere, he wouldn't have picked it up. He never picks random stuff up off the ground."

"Take only pictures. Leave only footprints," I said, half mockingly.

"A wise policy." Niraya consulted a compass in her pocket and dusted off her knees. "We'll say nothing more about it today. Let's eat, wildlings. I'm famished."

Food. Now it was my turn to be a heart-eyed emoji. Even though Karina and I hadn't been in the wild for too long, it seemed like I'd been on a steady diet of granola bars for weeks. What I wouldn't have given for one french fry dipped in ranch? The thought alone made my mouth water.

"Oh, sweet." Karina rubbed her tummy. "What do we eat?"

Niraya picked up a group of fishing poles near the helm. "Seeing as how we're on the water, we eat whatever we find." She tossed a pole in my direction. "Catch."

"Fish," I said.

Niraya raised an eyebrow. "And you were expecting . . . ?"

"Oh, I'm not being picky. Rina and I don't know how to fish, though."

"You don't know how to fish?" Niraya's jaw dropped, and then she clutched her belly and burst into uncontrollable laughter. "What? You travel around with your famous uncle who probably eats worms for dinner, and you don't know how to catch a fish?"

"Hey, stop laughing!" I clenched my fists. "It isn't funny. We didn't get to spend a lot of time with our tio before the other day. And you'd be surprised how many people my age, and way older, never learned how to fish. Nobody needs to know how to fish where I come from. We can buy it at the store." Sometimes we could even get it at a drive-thru window.

Niraya only laughed harder, turning around to wipe her eyes. I had this overwhelming urge to snap my fishing pole and chuck it overboard. Then she'd stop laughing.

"What a sad place you come from." Niraya steadied her breath. "What would you do if the markets shut down? If you had to fend for yourself?"

"Pick up gardening or something," Karina said. "I'm allergic to fish."

Niraya shook her head. "It's our only option today. There's no garden on the *Red Hood*." She opened her box, exposing a tangle of pink, writhing worms. "Is fish going to kill you?"

"She gets hives if she eats it," I said. "I don't want her to get sick. We have Zid's snacks, right?"

Karina nodded. "Crackers and grapes. Dinner of champs."

I leaned back against the mast, hands in my pockets. I didn't believe in Lady Fortune or her wheel, but after everything that had happened the past two days, I would have given up anything for our luck to spin back the other way.

# DIEGO

## EPISODE
## II

·❖——❖·

The pirate's name was James. He didn't have both oars in the water.

For a few minutes, I was sure I'd somehow hallucinated the hook-handed man in the dragon's den. If only I were crazy, it would explain a lot of the past few days' events, but my imagination wasn't quite this powerful. Rina got her brilliant creative mind from my older sister, and Charlie was pretty grounded in reality, I think. I had to assume all my gears were functioning and that James was real.

I took a seat next to the pirate. He had this hollow, faraway look in his eyes, like he'd already resigned himself to death.

"So," I said slowly, "a dragon carried you here, too?"

James scoffed. "Aye. Ripped me right out of the ocean, ship and all. The thing's a demon. It's a wonder we're alive to talk about it. At least, I'm alive. I'm not half convinced you're a real man sitting here next to me, Diego Rosas. I'm not half convinced I care, either."

"Is there anyone else around here?" Maybe this monster was just scooping people off the ground and rounding them up to roast later.

"Dunno." James gave me a lazy shrug, barely able to lift his shoulders. "Thought I might've seen a boy wandering around my first day. I wager he's probably in the dragon's belly now. Far more likely I hallucinated him. Feels like my sails are cast but no one's at the helm these days. Are you real, lad?"

*A boy wandering.* Charlie? Or maybe someone native to the land?

"I promise I'm as real as they come," I assured. "What else do you know about the dragon? Do you know where he is now?"

James tilted his chin up and studied the cracks in the ceiling. I wished I could see more of the stars from where I sat. As an experiment, I wanted to look for Polaris, but I had a feeling I wasn't even under my own sky anymore. In my own world.

"I wager it's on the hunt," James said. "It's far too quiet out there right now, but don't get comfortable. The dragon doesn't sleep. He leaves for long periods at a time, but he returns at the drop of a hat. I've been hiding here for weeks."

My ears perked up. "Hiding? In here? You mean it doesn't live in here?"

"Well, don't call me the expert. I only know he's never come in here before, though stranger things can happen. As it stands, he's far too big. You ought to have known that, mate, seeing him up close and all."

I rubbed my forehead. Maybe I was safe from dragons in this cavern, but I couldn't survive in here forever. I needed food, water, sunlight . . . Being a hermit in a dark cave simply wasn't sustainable. Plus, I was pretty certain Charlie and Karina weren't in here.

I had to get out and find them.

"If the monster's out hunting," I said, "then we have a shot at escaping, don't we?"

James forced a laugh and slapped his thigh with the blunt end of his hook.

I gave him the evil eye. "I don't understand what's funny."

"Mate." James cleared his throat. "You don't know where we are, do you?"

"No." I was probably a little more snappy and harsh than I wanted to be. "I'm supposed to be eating Swiss chocolate with my family and walking the Old Town Chur and taking selfies at the Matterhorn, but instead, my train blew up and blasted me into . . . wherever, and a dragon dropped me into a cave to die. I'm in the dark here, so please enlighten me, you hook-handed—"

In a second, James was on his feet, his hand around my throat, and our noses an inch apart. If a look could burn, my face would've burst into flames. "You'll want to watch your tongue from here on out, mate. I won't warn you twice. Comments about either of my hands are off limits, unless you mean to compliment me." He brushed the tip of his hook against my temple, inches away from my eyeball. "I think my hands are rather pretty, don't you?"

I refused to blink or look away, idiotic as it was to smart off to a pirate. "Take your hand off me," I choked, "or—"

James brought his knee up to my stomach with surprising power for a man who hadn't eaten in days. I swear, he probably had just as much metal in his legs as he did where his hand used to be.

I cried out in pain.

"Wanna try again?" James asked.

Letting go of that Rosas pride was always hard for me, especially when I felt like it made me weak. It took a lot for me to come to the conclusion that James wasn't my top concern and that getting off to a bad start with him wouldn't be worth the potential trouble it could put us in later on. So I let it go.

"You have very nice hands," I muttered.

James ripped his fingers away from my throat and took a sweeping step backward, a vein throbbing in his forehead. This man would be keeping one eye on me for the rest of our time together. And I'd certainly be doing the same. He sat down again and curled his knees against his chest. "Didn't wanna hurt you. For that, I apologize. But you never insult a pirate's pride. Let that be your first lesson, mate."

I held my stomach, my own pride fractured and splintered.

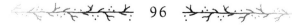

"Second lesson." James held up two fingers. "That beast didn't carry you here from Old Town Chur. You're clearly from the other place—the New World— just like our king. And unless he's coming for us, banish your hopes of going home."

I moved my hand from my stomach to my head. So the train blew me into another world entirely. Fun. I couldn't wait to explain this to my sister. I'd be better off just checking myself into a mental health facility. This couldn't be real. Maybe James wasn't even real. But until I could wake up from this new fantasy, I'd have to play along. "What else is out there?"

James tilted his head back against the wall. "I went out there once, you know. One time was all it took for me to abandon hope. It's not only the dragon we have to worry about. It's the terrain . . . the creatures the monster preys on. Out there, we're the bottom of the food chain. Out there, we die in pieces. But in here, we may die in peace."

That was probably one of the most cowardly things I'd ever heard. Withering in the dark was hardly any way to live at all. But I didn't want to risk the madman's anger again, so I only said this: "I need to see this for myself. Listen. Where I'm from, you can drop me anywhere on the planet and I'll find a way to brave the elements. I do it for a living. Deserts, tundras, rainforests—I've seen it all."

"No, you haven't." James kneaded his forehead as if to silence a headache. "Have you seen a cursed land? Specifically curated to keep humankind out and kill everything that gets inside, like a disease? I don't question your ability to brave the natural elements, mate. But sorcery . . . You aren't bred for that. I fought alongside some of the greatest warriors in this world to dethrone an evil queen, and I'm not bred to survive. Magic is poison."

My shoulders tightened. I was never overly superstitious, but I did grow up with a fear of the *what if*. My parents didn't care what time we came home or what R-rated movies we snuck into with our friends. Our dad even gave us candy to smuggle in. They didn't scold me when I started "running wild" and getting into adventuring. As long as I knew what I was doing and understood the consequences, my life was my own. Until one of my sister's friends brought a Ouija board to a sleepover. That earned us all a long, passionate lecture about how we shouldn't mess with things we don't understand. They never had to tell me twice.

"All I need to do is try to get out of here," I said. "You know how many people told me I wouldn't last a day in the Sahara? That I wouldn't make it halfway up Everest? Sometimes I told myself those things. But I'm telling you I'm not living out the rest of my days in a cave. My niece and nephew need me. My sister needs me. Do you have anyone out there, James? Kids? Family?"

That did it. His posture relaxed when he shut his eyes. He hummed a little melody under his breath, like a lullaby. "Aye."

"Think about it," I said. "Picture them."

A slight smile spread across James's lips. He barely looked like the same guy who threatened me a couple minutes ago. Once upon a time, this was a happy man.

"Tell me their names," I said.

James took a deep, savoring breath. "Her name is Niraya Storm."

Now I was getting somewhere. I chuckled. "Niraya. That's a pretty name. I'm sure she'd love to know you've been doing everything you can to get back to her. Am I right? She's probably looking for you, too."

James opened his eyes, and where I first saw anger, peace dripped from the cracks now. He smiled at the stars for a long time, and I didn't disturb him.

"I'm going out there," I said. "I'll leave it up to you if you want to come too, but whatever's outside this cave, the two of us stand a better chance together than we do apart." I couldn't believe I was reasoning with an unpredictable pirate, but times were desperate, and there was safety in numbers. "I imagine you're getting pretty hungry. I can show you how to dig for water, purify the snow, and find nutrients in the wild. And with the two of us side-by-side, if that dragon comes back, we have double the chances at taking him down. Am I wrong?"

"Double the chances." James's smile deflated. "I was never good with numbers, but I think that's still zero."

Well. I'd done my best.

"But you make a compelling case, mate." James pulled himself to his feet, matching my height. "I'll go out there with you. If nothing else, I'll show you exactly why we aren't getting out of here. Maybe then you'll make an educated choice to come back in here."

Far more likely, we'd agree to disagree and part ways. We shook hands.

And so we made our way through the cave. The terrain brought its share of challenges, mostly from the snow that trickled in through the cracks and coated the ground in layers of ice. According to James, it had been snowing the whole time he'd been here.

When the mouth of the cave appeared, he stepped aside and bowed, a sly grin on his face. He gestured for me to go ahead of him. "Well, do you still wish to play outside?"

I took in the landscape. The clouds overhead swirled in a dark circle, exposing the stars between the cracks. The sky looked like a vortex that might rip me off the ground and throw me in a black hole at any minute. As for the land itself, a dark jungle lay ahead of me, its canopy covered in frost. I turned around. The cave had only been the bottom of a massive mountain that stretched as far up as I could see.

But everything around me bothered me most. Far beyond the jungle, and in every degree of my vision, a thick wall of ice and rock protruded into the sky. The wall was a massive, unclimbable barrier between me and my family. The taller the ice rose, the more it sloped inward, like a cupped hand with the fingertips pointing back at me. I faced the facts: I was trapped in a massive, frosty bowl of jungle with a madman who had all but given up hope.

In a few weeks, this would probably be me too, if I haven't been eaten yet.

"Now you see why we aren't getting out, lad?" James stood by me and crossed his arms. "We're fenced in. There's nowhere for us to go."

I crouched down low, chest to knees, thinking I would be sick. *He's right. There's nowhere to go. There's no way up that wall. I'm actually going to die here.* But every time I thought I was going to die, the survival instinct kicked in with a vengeance, and I vowed to find a way. Always.

I stared at the frost-coated jungle, willing the gears of my brain to spin again and wondering what I could find under the canopy. "What's in the jungle?"

"Ogres," James said. "Among other monstrosities."

I scratched my jaw, swearing I'd misheard. "I'm sorry, did you say ogres?"

"I did."

"In the jungle?"

"Aye."

I shook my head, hoping the force might wake me from this nightmare. "Fun. What else should I know about?"

"Well, if my intuition is right, my ship should've landed in there."

A pirate ship in the jungle. What else?

"I tried to get to the wreck earlier, hoping to set off the flares I kept below deck. Never made it. Everything out there chased me back"—he pointed to the mouth of the cave—"in here."

"Flares." I leaned in, catching James's musky leather-and-sweat-and-too-much-cologne scent. "Which means potential rescue."

"Aye. But they're in my vessel. In the jungle."

"In your vessel. In the jungle," I echoed, my mouth going dry. There was hope out there. "But you couldn't get to the wreckage on your own. Only now that there are two of us together . . . maybe you'd care to try again?"

James's lip curled. He plucked at his coat sleeve, his gaze colder than the snow around us. "You really mean to do this. You're one sail short of a full mast, mate."

I shrugged. If he was calling me crazy, I'd heard it before.

"But I suppose I'll go with you on one condition." The captain stared up at the sky as if to say a silent prayer. With a bow, he stepped aside and pointed toward the jungle. "You lead."

# KARINA

## SOMETHING
## IN THE WATER

·•———•·

With so much on my mind, so little in my belly, and rolling waves churning beneath me, it was difficult to stay asleep on the *Red Hood*. Motion sickness wasn't really a thing for me, but I had fears. Oceans are ginormous, murky, and still vastly unexplored. Unknown.

I lay on the deck most of the night, staring at the sky and wondering if I'd find the North Star in another world. Under the celestial frontier, I was tiny. The ocean was massive, but the heavens were infinite.

I pretended that somewhere, somehow, Uncle Diego had made it out of the dragon's clutches and found a nice place to sit and marvel at the stars. Maybe that brought him peace. Or at least the sense of wonder and adventure he was always looking for. For him, peace, adventure, and wonder were the same things, and he found them all in nature.

Oddly, I felt that same calm by fishing with Niraya. Charlie was bored out of his mind, but I found something meditative and soothing about waiting for the fish to bite, which gave me a ton of writing ideas. I was glad I had a real excuse not to eat any of our catches, though. It all smelled bad. The crackers didn't really fill me up, but at least they didn't smell or make me want to scratch my skin off.

I dozed off a few times and always woke up to something different. The stars would be in a new arrangement, sometimes concealed by stringy clouds. When Niraya wasn't at the wheel, she paced around in her coat while consulting her compass, and I didn't think she'd slept at all. As for Charlie, sometimes I'd find him flipping through our uncle's journal, drawing in a notebook, or napping.

When I awoke for good, the clouds had fully veiled the stars. There was some chop to the water, making the ride bumpy. I sat up and gripped a barrel for support, inhaling its musky scent and the salt of the air around me.

"It's getting a little crazy out here," Charlie said. "I hope we're getting to the island soon. I'm so bored. Water for days. Where's Niraya?"

"Up here," Niraya called from starboard. She waved a bronze spyglass. "I'm watching for dolphins. There's plenty to look for at sea, wildlings. On these dark waters, the ocean has as much a soul as you or I, and tonight, it's very much alive."

"That's a good thing, right?" Charlie asked. "Alive means good?"

Niraya didn't answer.

"Yes," I said. "She means good. She's just super focused right now." I said this like I knew, but really I was trying to make myself feel better.

"Don't speak." Niraya held up a hand, and then the waves went quiet—even the sails didn't seem to make any noise when they caught the wind. Almost like she'd commanded the sea. Niraya was Queen of the Ocean. "Listen and watch. Observe the waves. What do you see out there?"

A snowy-white bird squawked overhead, and a flock followed it into the horizon.

*Bloop.* Something bubbled in the water.

"Hey, sis," Charlie said. "Remember when we were trying to come up with an angry way to say bubbles? I just remembered that."

Charlie and I both burst into laughter.

"Shhh," Niraya hissed.

I had a feeling she could be scary if she got mad, so I quickly obeyed.

A trio of dolphins rocketed out of the water and tumbled in mid-air.

"Oh," I cried, pointing at the magnificent creatures.

The dolphins sliced into the sea and then disappeared.

The water bubbled again, and a glossy, gray matter brushed the surface. For a second, I thought

I'd hallucinated or that maybe it was a whale popping up for air. Until a long, slimy tentacle extended from the gray, writhing around as if reaching for a seagull. Disgusting.

Niraya crossed the ship, took the wheel, and gave it a hard spin to the right. "We don't want to be near that thing."

I wasn't gonna argue, but I was still curious about Niraya's reaction. All that peaceful serenity was fading from her expression.

"Why?" Charlie didn't look away from the tentacle. "What is it?"

"I need a minute." Niraya took a deep breath and squeezed the wheel's spokes, tapping her thumbs against the wood a few times.

"All the animals," I said, remembering the birds and the dolphins. "They're going the same way."

Niraya didn't answer. Her face reminded me of my mom when she was driving and trying to get through a nasty traffic jam.

"Could they be running from something?" Charlie asked.

My fears exactly.

The tentacle retreated, casting a silent ripple through the water.

"Are—are we almost there?" I asked.

As if to answer, nine more tentacles burst from the water's surface with a deafening splash, this time almost thirty times longer and uncomfortably close to the *Red Hood*.

"Kraken." Niraya adjusted her hat and raced away from the wheel. "Brace!"

Charlie and I had no idea what it meant to *brace* on a ship. When Niraya gave the order, it was like my feet put roots into the deck as the ship tipped beneath me. Charlie clutched his stomach like he might be sick. Niraya ripped her rusty dagger from her jacket pocket. She dropped to the deck as if doing a burpee, and I followed suit, scraping my knees on the rough wood.

The ship whirled like a malfunctioning carnival ride. I locked eyes with Niraya, her teeth clenched so hard I could see a vein in her forehead. Long locks of her thick, dark hair whipped about in the growing wind, and when the ship tipped further, she slid a few feet. She jammed the tip of her dagger into a plank and gripped. I had no such anchor and slid toward her, catching my backpack when it almost rocketed past me. I kept my gaze on her as a focal point, feeling only a little safer knowing I was with her and Charlie.

*Whumph.*

A massive tentacle swatted starboard. Saltwater drenched my shirt.

"Hey." Niraya gritted her teeth. "Charlie, I told you to brace."

I rolled on my elbow and saw the worst thing I could imagine: Charlie leaning over the side and reaching into the water. "What are you doing?"

My brother didn't look up. He stood on his tiptoes and stretched his arms, wincing and leaning at a hard angle.

"My backpack . . ."

"Forget it." Niraya snapped her fingers and pounded the deck. "Drop to the deck. Now!"

Charlie ignored her, biting his lip and pulling himself up onto a rusty metal rail. "But Tío's diary."

My heart sank. If we never went home—if we never saw Uncle Diego again—that journal would've been the last we'd ever have of him. It had to be protected. I swallowed, tears prickling my eyes. "Just do what Niraya said. It's too late."

"We need it." Charlie teetered dangerously, knees knocking together. The leather pack bobbed just beyond arm's reach. "It's gonna tell us how to survive."

"We have Niraya for that," I snapped. But that diary had become a comfort for me, knowing that at any point we could open it up and read his words, smell his cologne, retrace his steps, and know his life. Indiana Jones had his hat. Captain America had his shield. Diego Rosas had his notes—his experiences—and I didn't want to see them get swept away. But we had no choice. "Charlie, just . . . just get down like Niraya said, and we'll figure everything else out later, okay?"

Five more tentacles sprouted from the water. One of them curled around the mast—all slime and scales and gooey suction cups—and shook the ship like a rattle, and the others flailed haphazardly in the air. Their putrid color, fishy odor, and slimy texture were enough to make me queasy, and the ship's loss of control added fuel to the fire.

"Stay calm," Niraya said.

And for a second, I did.

Until the kraken curled its flailing tentacle around my brother's ankle, binding him by his shoe.

My knees went weak as I screamed my brother's name.

Niraya pulled herself up, snatched the dagger out of the plank, and made a run for my brother. "Not on my ship."

But she was too late.

The kraken jerked on Charlie's ankle, throwing him off balance. He went over instantly with a splash, some frantic ripples, and then a frightening calm.

# CHARLIE

EW

·:————·:·

The water swallowed me first.

The kraken swallowed me second.

It all happened within one minute. I hit the ocean with a force I thought would shatter my bones, and a wave folded me under. The water knocked the wind out of me, drowned me in darkness, and stung with the cold pain of a thousand needles. I kicked and fought like a rabid monkey, certain I'd be dead in minutes.

One of the coolest things about the body is how our eyes adjust to the dark. That turned out to be a curse this time, and I wished I was blind. The monster in the water was a slimy mass of tentacles, gills, many enormous eyeballs, and a mouth the size of Niraya's ship. I couldn't even see the end of the beast. I screamed, and bubbles burst from my lips. The kraken's mouth opened like a pair of automatic doors, sucked me into a dark vacuum, and snapped shut behind me.

To my amazement and relief, I didn't die. Nothing chewed on me. I wasn't even sure the monster had teeth. I tumbled down a dark canal, like a slide at a toxic water park. The liquid receded until it was shallow enough for me to stick my head up and gulp down some air. Too bad that air tasted like a dead fish trapped in a football player's sock. Gag. After a while, I stopped on something wet and spongy, and a gentle stream of seawater trickled past me. I lay on my back and caught my breath, relieved, horrified, exhausted, and disgusted.

I summoned the strength to stand on slippery ground, hoping my vision would adjust again. Fun fact: there's zero light inside a thousand-foot sea creature that lives in dark waters. But I remembered I still had my phone in my pocket, and Uncle Diego asked me to save the battery life. Of course, battery life wouldn't matter if the thing wasn't waterproof, and I couldn't remember if waterproof was part of the description. But I fished it out of my pocket, blew on it as if that would've saved it from water damage, and pressed the switch, hoping for an early Christmas miracle.

Warm, glorious light filled the kraken. I could've kissed that stupid little apple.

"Yes. Hashtag blessed." I only had six percent battery left, but I would make it count if it was the last bit of light I ever had. I hit airplane mode, low power mode, dimmed the backlight, and everything else I could think of to stretch my minutes. If only I could've used that charger I stole from the train wreck.

I shined the phone in every direction. A long, round tunnel of pink muscle pulsed ahead and behind me, jittering like sick Jell-O.

Ew.

I sucked at biology, but I was pretty sure this was the kraken's throat.

*Now what do I do?*

I refused to acknowledge that after surviving an exploding train and a dragon attack that I was doomed to die inside a giant fish. Unacceptable. Insulting. I'd suspected for a while that I wouldn't survive this adventure, but I at least wanted "a hero's death," whatever that looked like in Florindale. Losing a sword fight against an evil queen? Falling off a crumbling rope bridge after ushering Karina and Niraya to the other side? Letting Verdoro fall on top me and impaling him with a sword? Any of those deaths would've had so much more dignity than starving inside a stupid kraken.

I would've poisoned myself first. This place stunk, and it was so gross it made The Grinch's home look clean. When I pointed the phone, individual shapes glowed along the walls, floor, and ceiling of the beast's esophagus. Wooden planks. Fish bones. Clamshells. Giant shimmering pearls gleamed all around, like untouched gems in a rancid mine. If only I had a pickaxe to hack my way out, I'd go home rich, too.

There had to be some way to make this jerk spit me out.

Another stream of water poured in behind me, curling past my feet and into the dark abyss ahead. I definitely didn't want to follow the water. Yes, I wanted out, but I refused to follow the natural path. Somehow, I had to go back the way I came.

I turned and followed the throat, moving upstream past a flopping school of fish, one of Niraya's fishing poles, and then . . .

"My backpack." I sank to my knees and whispered an exasperated, "Thank you."

I unzipped the pack and swirled my arm around inside, relieved to find Tio's journal. It was a little damp, but I was so happy I planted a kiss on the cover. *Never letting go of this thing again.* In another pocket, I found Zid's grapes, some granola bar wrappers, a damp pair of socks, and some bandages. Everything was still here.

I pinched my nose through my shirt. If starvation didn't kill me, the smell would do the trick. *Think, Charlie, think. What would Tio do?*

I sat down and flipped through my uncle's book, feeling ridiculous with every turn of the page. What could Tio have written that would save me from a kraken's digestive system? He never could've prepared for this.

And yet, the first page I flipped to was labeled: *Anatomy of a squid.*

I bet he ate one on his show.

So actually this was his fault. Thanks for the karma, Tio.

I stared at the diagram. For all I knew, krakens were just squids from hell. I found the mouth, actually labeled *beak*. So squids are half bird? Then came the esophagus, the long tunnel where I was stuck. Right above that was the brain.

*I'm that close to the brain? Gross.*

Even grosser: If I kept following the esophagus, the kraken's intestines were next. Absolutely not an option.

I turned the page. There was nothing else productive to glean from squid anatomy. What if I found the brain, shut the kraken down, and the beak wouldn't open, locking me inside forever like a doomed spaceship that lost all power?

On the following page, Tio had made a list of emergency protocols for various wild encounters:

+ Brown bear: Play dead.
+ Black bear: Get loud.
+ Shark: Fight. Aim for eyes, gills, snout.
+ Lion: Make yourself look bigger. Freeze.
+ Ostrich: Stand your ground or play dead.
+ Kangaroo: Distance self. Do not turn around.
+ Bees: Cover head and run for shelter (not water).
+ Wolf: Be big. Intimidate.
+ All: Respect the wild.

On one hand, I found the list fascinating. I would've paid to see my tio fight an ostrich, for example. On the other hand: not helpful. It said nothing about a giant squid, and it was classic Diego Rosas to end his list with *respect the wild*.

*Sure, Tio. Let me try this:*

*I respect you, Sir Kraken. Please spit me out now?*

I glanced at my phone. How did I lose four percent so fast?

Annoyed, I plunged my hand into my backpack, then chucked a grape in front of me. It bounced off the creature's throat and rolled back to me like a Ping-Pong ball. While I kept thinking, I tossed it up and down a few times. To my wonder, a soft pink bump appeared on the throat where the grape had hit. As an experiment, I lobbed it again. A second bump welted up next to the first.

*Weird.*

The welts were the size of my fist, each with the shape and hue of a mosquito bite. Karina had been covered in these earlier, which only happened when something bit her, or when she ate something she wasn't supposed to consume.

Like fish.

*Gotcha.* I returned Tio's book to my backpack and gathered all the grapes. Then I zipped up, strapped up, and tightened the pack on my shoulders, arms full of grapes. As for my phone, *may it rest in peace and be remembered for its service.* It flickered out a second later, and a new stream of water rushed in and carried it away forever.

But I knew what I needed to do, and there was only one direction to go.

I crushed all my fruity ammunition in my fists, marched into the darkness, and painted that kraken's throat red.

# KARINA

## SOMETHING THAT WAS *NOT* AWESOME

·◦─◦·

W hen my brother went overboard, I made a run for the railing, determined to follow. I'd already lost my uncle. I would not lose Charlie too.

I climbed up on the rail, prepared to jump, and then Niraya seized me from behind and locked my arms to my sides.

"Let me go," I screamed, bucking against her. "It took Charlie."

"Karina." It's a wonder I even heard Niraya over my screams and the sea monster's splashes. She spun me around so we faced each other, her grip like iron and her eyes filled with fire. "Stop. Listen to me."

"But that thing has him," I said. "How do I get him back, Niraya? How?"

Niraya held up one finger. "Take a breath. Bring it in." She drew her own deep breath as an example, and I mirrored her, filling my lungs with salty air. "And let it out." We exhaled together, my breath shaky and uneven. "Do I have your attention yet?"

I nodded.

"Listen up. There's a fishing net below deck. Go down and grab it for me."

I wasted no time scurrying down into the hull, dim, musty, and packed with clutter. Newspapers, barrels, bottles, trinkets of assorted shapes and sizes, cannons, rowboats, and every type of pirate apparel from boots to breeches scattered the room with no obvious rhyme or reason. I ransacked the place, flipping barrels and tossing coats and trinkets over my shoulder. What did Niraya want a fishing net for anyway? There was no way she had anything big enough to trap the monster outside the ship.

I pried open a wooden chest with a broken lock, revealing a mountain of photographs inside. I had no intention of spending all my time looking at them, but the top one caught my eye, and I let my attention wander for about ten seconds. In the top picture, Zid stood with six other men about his height, pickaxes over their shoulders, and a tall, beautiful woman in a creamy-white dress smiled behind them. A second photograph showed a Chinese woman sparring with a handsome young man, swords crossed in an X. A third showed a boy hovering in the air and chasing his shadow. I wondered whether it was real magic or photo magic. Niraya didn't strike me as a Photoshop expert.

But every second I wasted, Charlie's chances of survival dwindled like a candlewick. I threw the photographs over my shoulder, and thankfully underneath them lay both the fishing net and a silver dagger. I tucked the dagger into my belt, grabbed the net, and spun around right as a long gray tentacle burst through the wood and blocked me from the stairs up to the deck.

I screamed, and as if the tentacle could hear, it curled toward me. I pressed my back to the wall, wishing I could stuff myself into the wooden chest. The *Red Hood* tipped and swayed, and water rushed into the hole the kraken made. I picked up the closest thing I could find, a dusty bottle of red wine, and threw it. I aimed a little too high, and the glass shattered near the ceiling. Wine dripped down, soaked the creature, and gathered into a puddle on the floor. But to my surprise, the tentacle turned an unhealthy shade of red, welts sprouting all the way to the tip.

Unfortunately, the attack only made the colossus angrier. Quick as a whip, it seized my ankle and yanked me off balance. My head smacked the planks, and my hair fanned out in a pool of wine and salt water. Now I was really ticked off. I reached for my new dagger and swiped, severing the end of the tentacle. The rest of the arm slithered back into the water. I peeled the writhing end off me, flung it over my shoulder, and ran upstairs.

Things were even worse on deck. A storm hit quicker than I could flip a light switch, nearly blinding me with wind and rainfall. Choppy waves battered the ship around like a punching bag, and thunder roared. Niraya, ever the warrior, was in the crow's nest, a glistening harpoon gun on her shoulder.

She fired the weapon and a harpoon sailed from her gun, raising a thin tower of water from the ocean's surface.

"What are you doing?" I raced toward the pole, wanting to shake her out of the crow's nest. "You could hit my brother."

Niraya didn't answer. She loaded the gun again, shut one eye, and took aim.

"Niraya," I yelled.

The pirate squeezed the trigger again.

This time, Niraya must have hit her target, because the kraken only got more aggressive. Part of the head poked out of the water, a harpoon below one eye, and the beast brought one of its massive arms down on the deck, cleaving a jagged crevasse through the planks and tearing a black sail from the mast. Crimson splinters flew everywhere.

I grabbed the mast for balance and dear life, putting on my mom stare. "You let my brother go."

"Oh, he'll let him go, all right," Niraya said. "One more shot'll do."

I waved the net over my head. "What am I supposed to do with this?"

"Tie one end to the rail," Niraya said. "Drop the other in the water, and go find the rowboat."

*Rowboat.* I didn't like the sound of that.

We were abandoning ship.

I did as the captain asked, casting the net into the water.

As soon as I turned around, the kraken made a terrible sound—something between a deep, painful moan and a roar that would've made Godzilla cower in fear. The hairs on my neck prickled. The creature wasn't writhing anymore. Instead, the arms retreated in the water, and the beast's head lurched a few times.

Its mouth slid open, and the kraken unleashed a powerful stream of water that blasted the side of the ship. Like a gun recoils after a shot, the kraken rocketed backward and covered the length of a football field, and Niraya fired the harpoon one more time.

I couldn't tell whether the weapon hit, but I did see the creature dip below the water. A single bubble popped on the surface, and the beast didn't come back up again.

I was livid. The monster still had my brother.

All was strangely quiet. Even the storm cleared away, unveiling ribbons of moonlight on the water and a gentle breeze that would have soothed me if I weren't so angry.

How dare the world be so calm when I had just lost another family member!

"Rina."

The call came from below.

I peered over the rail, and there, clinging to his backpack like a magnet, my brother had a grip on Niraya's fishing net.

"Charlie."

"Did you see that?" Charlie cried. "Dude. That thing's allergic to grapes, and it straight-up sneezed me out of its body. That was awesome."

I rested my forehead against the rail and shut my eyes. "I can't even right now. That was not awesome," I said under my breath.

With Niraya's help and a pair of her gloves to minimize hives from the fish water, I pulled Charlie up on the net, and he collapsed onto the deck with his arms spread out beside him.

I threw myself down and hugged him, noting that he was a little paler than usual, and I tried to ignore his fishy smell. "Are you hurt?"

He coughed and wrinkled his nose. "I wanna take a shower."

I clapped a palm to my forehead. *Of all the complaints. This* is *my brother.* "You need one."

"Excuse me?"

"None of us are ever showering again if we don't get that rowboat ready." Niraya gestured to the water climbing dangerously close to the deck.

I was so relieved to see Charlie again that for a second I forgot we were sinking.

"Get ready for a long trip, wildlings." Niraya planted her heel and yanked on a rope.

Charlie spat a piece of seaweed out of his mouth. "How much longer 'til we get there?"

"That depends." Niraya smirked. "How fast you can row?"

# CHARLIE

## I WORK ON MY
## ARM MUSCLES

·————·

The last thing I wanted right now was an arm workout. When we sat down in the rowboat, I thought about the Splash Mountain ride at Disneyland, where sometimes passengers sat knee-to-back—only on the rowboat, there was no individual seating to put buffers between us. It was gonna be a super tight squeeze, especially with our backpacks. Niraya took the front end, I took the back, and Karina sat sandwiched in the middle. *At least I'm not in the belly of a squid right now. Or a dragon. I'm with my sister. I'm alive.*

Maybe there was truth to Niraya's legend about Lady Fortune. So far, my sister and I were both the luckiest and the unluckiest kids ever to live.

Before we started rowing, we watched Niraya's ship sink into the silky waters, like a reflection receding in a dark mirror. The sinking happened slowly until the deck went under, and then the rest followed more quickly until the tip of a black sail bid adieu to the world above. A few barrels bobbed around behind us, along with Niraya's red-feathered hat. She fished that out with an oar before we left.

Poor Niraya. I didn't know how long she'd owned the ship, but she was no longer Captain of the *Red Hood*. She saluted her aquatic home and turned away.

Infinity surrounded us in every direction, a tapestry of stars above that reflected below. I couldn't buy into the beauty for long, though. Somewhere underneath us, there were things that hungered for human bones. Somewhere above us, there were fire-breathing, uncle-stealing monsters.

"All right, wildlings," Niraya plunged her oars into the water, "start rowing."

I didn't want to tell her that Rina and I didn't know how to row. We already made Niraya teach us to fish. So I watched her technique as she dipped her paddles in and out of the water, graceful like a butterfly. *Okay. I can do that.* She did tell me we were gonna work on my arm muscles. *Watch me turn that windlass now, Niraya. Mic drop.*

"So, let me get this straight," I said. "You had a fishing net the whole time, and we used poles to catch dinner? Doesn't that take longer?"

"Yes," Niraya said.

When Niraya didn't elaborate, Karina added, "So, why?"

"Because you need to be prepared to do things the hard way. There's value in having patience and being willing to work for what you want, or in this case, need."

In that spirit, I rowed harder.

Most of the night passed without much conversation. The burn in my arms pulled all the remaining energy from my brain, leaving me no will to talk. I didn't know how much time passed, but my shoulders grew weak and my eyelids drooped. Tension pulsed through my back, and my leg muscles cramped up from the uncomfortable sitting position. I willed myself to become a machine for a few hours, a metal bot that could row forever without feeling a thing.

"Hang on, James." Niraya's whisper cut through the silence, the words spoken so sincerely that I wondered if James could hear them somehow.

So I tried it myself. "Stay strong, Tio. We're coming for you."

Before the lavender glow appeared at the edge of the world, Karina fell asleep, her head bowed and the oars loose in her hands. I reached forward and collected them from her. I worried Niraya would wake her up or lecture us for not pulling our weight, but the pirate only shook her head, paused to take off her leather coat, and with a smile, she tucked the jacket over Karina's lap.

When Niraya faced forward again, she did the last thing I ever expected. She sang.

*"How strong you bloomed on fortune's bay,*
*and blossomed like a summer day.*
*Should autumn's breath lead you astray,*

*we'll say goodbye by winter's gray."*

Her voice was divine, sweet and light like fresh lemonade. I spent all night thinking about her song, wondering what she was singing for. For the *Red Hood*, maybe? For James? For Karina and me? Or maybe for herself.

Land appeared shortly after sunrise, an abundance of green rolling into a deep periwinkle tinged with white as broken forests morphed into mountain ranges. I had never been happier to see anything in my life, even if the final stretch seemed to take eighty years. The closer we got, the more I felt like each stroke of the oar did absolutely nothing. I started to get scared the island was getting farther away, like a rainbow.

"Kesterfall," Niraya said, the word like snow on my ears, cold and harsh and enchanting.

Like a spell, the word opened Karina's eyes.

"What?" she croaked.

"We're almost there," Niraya said. "We'll be docking in Jericho Harbor."

"And then hopefully I never see another body of water again," I said. My fingers were all pruned, blistered, and starting to peel.

Texture bloomed on the island. Beige dots became straw huts and wooden cabins. Rainbows of color dotted the rolling green—fruits. Bananas, oranges, and something teal I didn't recognize. But my attention was glued to two statues rising from the water like gods, a fifty-foot iron-gray man and a marble-white woman each armed with a spear and staring out toward the tiny rowboat.

"Here, there be giants." I made my voice sound deep and gruff like Zid's.

"And hopefully dragons," Karina said. "At least, the one we're looking for."

I nodded. "And only that one."

Niraya raised an eyebrow. "You'd do well to prepare yourself for more."

I scowled. "Can't you let me have this one wish? Why would there be more?"

"I'm not promising there will be. I'm only advising you to prepare for more."

Karina yawned and ran her fingers through her hair. "What else do you know that we need to know? For example, how do you plan to kill this thing?"

"With much caution."

"That's not a real answer," I groaned. "What are the chances Verdoro could have a fruit allergy?"

"Less than none. Let's say no more for now. We dock and find a place to rest."

I expected Karina to argue, but she was obviously still as tired as Niraya and I were. I would've given up Christmas for one hour in a real bed. For a decent meal. Hopefully one of those island huts was a barbecue stand, or like an island juice bar.

"Hey, look. She's waving us in." Karina pointed to a tall blonde woman in a navy-blue uniform. She stood on the boardwalk, waving a pair of orange flags at us.

"Row toward me, please."

When we rowed in, the woman tied the boat to the dock, and Niraya slipped her a coin. Karina and I scrambled onto dry land, so happy to be on solid ground that I could've kissed the dock. Karina actually did.

"Gross, sis," I said. "You don't know who's walked on this thing."

"I don't care." Karina wiped her lips with her sleeve and adjusted her backpack. "You couldn't pay me to get back in the water right now."

The blonde woman took our names, inspected backpacks, and asked the nature of our business.

"Family reunion," Niraya said. "We've just come from Florindale."

"Did you really row from Florindale Square for a reunion?"

"No. We encountered an active kraken out there. My ship, the *Red Hood*, went down in the middle of the Joringel."

"Kraken," the woman said. "Been awhile since I've heard about any of those. But we're happy you're here. Welcome to Jericho Harbor. You'll find some shops and taverns down that way. We advise that you steer clear of the forest and keep within the town borders. The woods and mountains aren't safe to explore unprepared."

"Wise words. Thanks for the tip." Niraya smiled, but as soon as we turned away and left, she rolled her eyes. "Take your own advice, princess."

Niraya sure could throw some shade.

We made our way to the village and deep into a crowd of fresh faces. The town had a rustic feel, but something here was different than Florindale Square's festive marketplace. For one thing, people paid much closer attention to us. It wasn't like we blended in, especially having come out of a storm, or a fish. But I could've sworn I even saw a boy drooling when we walked past him. Instinctively, I put my arm around Karina's shoulder and steered her ahead.

On the main street, we passed an observatory where a large telescope protruded from the roof. Next door, a fortune teller clothed in white sat in a rocking chair outside his shop, shuffling cards and nodding at us as though he'd already foreseen our arrival. The scent of smoked cinnamon cut through the air, light vapor trailing from a nearby candle shop. In a few places, piles of sticks or straw sat in place of a true cabin.

To my amazement, no posters offered a reward for Verdoro's hide. Was he tormenting Jericho Harbor as much as Florindale? Did Jericho Harbor even see the dragon as a problem? Or were they protecting him?

"Look," Karina whispered. With her elbow, she pointed into a thicket of rosebushes between two cabins. A pair of glowing eyes studied us from within the flora. "Is that a coyote?"

"That's a wolf," Niraya said. "Stick close to me, and don't go running into the bushes."

"Tio wrote about how to survive a wolf attack," I said. "He said to intimidate it if it comes after you. Whatever that means."

"I think he means try to assert yourself. Make yourself look big and get loud. It's not usually smart to run away from animals that are faster than you," Karina said.

"It's even smarter not to get yourself into situations you'd want to run from," Niraya said.

"What are *you* talking about?" I asked. "You're a pirate. You love another pirate. You live for danger. Don't lie."

Niraya chuckled. "Calculated danger, I suppose."

"Just like our uncle," Karina said, her chin high. "You'd like him."

"I'm sure."

Farther along the road, a painting caught my eye: a wheel. Six wedges with tiny orbs on the end of each spoke and the center of the circle. People really put a lot of belief in this legend.

Along with the woman painted on the wall.

"Check this out," I said. "Is that Lady—"

"Excuse me?"

Someone tapped my shoulder, and I turned to see a pale man with shiny blond hair and a finely sculpted beard. He wore a maroon tunic and dark breeches that were withered at the knees and held up by a cracked leather belt that matched his boots.

"Hello," he said.

"Can we help you?" Niraya asked. But her tone sounded more like she was asking if he had a problem.

"I'm sorry to bother. But I wondered if your party was looking for a place to rest?" The man tilted his head. "Forgive me for sounding intrusive. I have a keen nose for weary travelers, and, well, my colleague at the docks clued me in that we had three who rowed into Jericho Harbor today. Thought a group like that could use some hospitality. I do have a room open at my inn, if such a party were interested in the chance to rest before the family reunion."

I looked from Niraya to my sister. My arms throbbed, and I ached for a bed to lie down on. For a shower. For any way to refresh before we confronted Verdoro.

Niraya drummed her fingers on her elbows. "What's your rate?"

"Tonight would be on the house," the man said. "We can discuss rates if you wish to stay any longer."

"Then I suppose you're our divine intervention," Niraya said. "We only need one night at most. Maybe even a couple of hours. We accept your offer, sir."

"I'm happy to host you." The man bowed. "And please, call me Io. Sailing through the Joringel Sea in the stormy season isn't an easy accomplishment, let alone rowing through it. Come rest your heads and find peace at the Golden Gibbous, friends. You've earned that much."

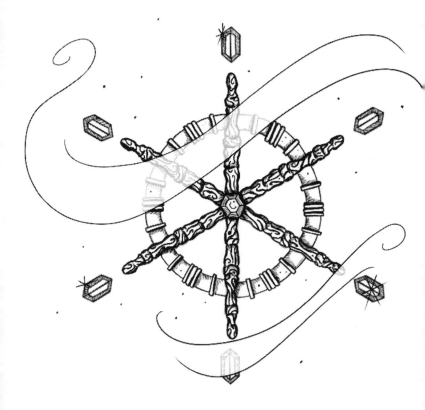

# PART THREE

THE CURSE
OF
JERICHO HARBOR

# KARINA

## A NIGHT AT
## THE GOLDEN GIBBOUS

·⊰───⊱·

"We most definitely earned this." The bed was like a warm, beautiful cloud hugging my bones, and I would never take it for granted. I wiggled my bare toes and shut my eyes. "This is gonna be the greatest nap ever."

"Yep." Charlie's voice was huskier than normal, indicating he was already half asleep on the bed across the room. He'd just had a bath, and the smile hadn't left his face since. Io had even been kind enough to bring us clean new clothes, which consisted of a cream-colored blouse for me; a dark, long-sleeved shirt for Charlie; and some pants and leather boots for both of us. We also had bowls of warm pumpkin soup and fresh bread. Sweet, cold milk.

I was immediately suspicious.

The hospitality here was too good, not that I had any desire to complain. The Golden Gibbous was pure paradise compared to what we'd come from.

Niraya peeled off her coat. "Enjoy this, wildlings." She checked the locks on the doors and windows then flopped onto the couch. "This is probably the last reprieve we'll see on the way to Verdoro's den. Jericho Harbor is one of the last places of civilization in Kesterfall. We're fortunate this inn took us."

*Fortunate indeed*, I thought.

Our room was simple—a pair of beds, a couch, a writing desk, and a picture window offering a view of the forest. I hadn't been expecting all the luxuries of, say, a five-star hotel in San Diego—spas, a fondue buffet, and movies on demand—and it wasn't like I would have wanted to use them. My body craved sleep. Sunlight kissed the room in all the right places, warming my toes but dodging my eyes as I drifted into the world of dreams.

And after such an otherworldly couple of days, I had quite a weird collection of images in my mind while I napped. I was glad to wake up when I did.

I mopped my sweaty forehead with my pillow and blinked the dreamy haze from my vision. Charlie's snores boomed through the air, and at some point, he'd flipped on his stomach, his arm hanging limp over the side of the bed.

"Pass the ball," he mumbled.

Go figure, I dream of monsters and he dreams of soccer.

Niraya slept with a lacy throw pillow hugged tight against her chest. The pillow rose up and down in a slow, steady rhythm, and her breaths didn't make a sound. She almost looked like a vampire, hands neatly folded on the pillow.

So much for our little nap, though. We'd officially slept the day away.

I rubbed my eyelids with my knuckles, shuffling over to the window. A titanic, glittering moon peeked over the tip of the mountain, throwing Jericho Harbor into a cool silver light I wished I could bottle up and carry home with me.

Even the forest didn't look as evil as the residents made it out to be. I considered waking Niraya and Charlie to ask if they were ready to take their chances in the woods. Somewhere beyond them, I knew a dragon was circling Mount Blackburn, and that's where we needed to be. I hated to think we were wasting valuable time in a cozy room while Uncle Diego . . . I squeezed my eyes shut. *Don't finish the thought, Karina. Stay positive.* I had to believe there was a chance he'd escaped, wandered into some unfamiliar jungle, and decided to treat it like his TV show. Somewhere out there, he was looking for us and documenting everything he found in this strange new world. One day, Diego Rosas would be the man who explored the land of dragons and lived to tell the tale.

*Yeah right. Nobody will ever believe this.*

Mind too full to sleep again, I slipped my new boots on, making sure to check them first like I'd been taught.

Then I grabbed Uncle Diego's book from Charlie's backpack and wandered into the common room. Dull pain still pulsed in my shoulders, and my brother and our new friend deserved to rest a little more. It would've been a disservice to continue on without properly functioning brains and bodies.

I slumped down by the fireplace and opened the journal to a random page in the middle. *Purifying salt water,* he'd written. I smiled because the book itself was still salty and damp. He would've joked about the irony if he were here.

"Can't sleep, Ms. Rosas?" Io, the caretaker, entered the room, startling me despite the low, calming timbre of his voice. "Did you enjoy your nap?"

I shut the book and wrapped the leather cord around it. "My sleep schedule's a little crazy right now," I said. "It's been a long trip. But yes, it's wonderful. Thank you."

"I'm glad to hear that." Io sat on the other side of the couch and stared into the fire. "We don't have guests often. I'm afraid most people don't visit Kesterfall anymore. The world's come to see it only as a hive for monsters. If only they would take the time to learn and see its natural beauty."

I curled my legs beneath me. "You must really love it here. Have you lived here long?"

"A while." Io smiled.

I had trouble guessing how old he might have been, but I knew one thing: I'd go stir crazy staying in a tiny village for too long. Maybe that's why Uncle Diego traveled. Wanderlust was in our blood.

I thought for a minute. "I was taught you can go anywhere and do anything if you set your mind to it."

"If Lady Fortune favors you," Io said. Before I could ask him to explain, he added, "Might I ask you a question in return?"

"Sure." I shrugged.

"Why are you really here?"

Suddenly I wanted Niraya to wake up. Back at the docks, she told the worker we were in town for a family reunion. Did Niraya not want people to know the real reason we were here? I didn't want to be the one to blow whatever cover she had in mind. *What am I supposed to say?*

But Io offered us shelter and rest, polite conversation, food, even new clothes. Would it really be that bad if he knew the truth? Would he even believe it?

I sighed. "Okay. It's a long story, but the truth is we need to rescue my uncle from the dragon of Kesterfall." *Don't say anymore,* my brain urged me. And then my mouth defied me. "Verdoro."

Io nodded. "Thank you for your honesty. Unless you were explorers or mapmakers, one might have guessed your party—like many others before you—had business with Verdoro. You won't find much civilization beyond Jericho Harbor. The plagues, curses, wars, and the dragon itself drove everyone overseas. Only a percentage of our village stayed home."

"Does the dragon leave you alone?" I asked. "What happened to the other groups who came for Verdoro?"

Io stood and smoothed the wrinkles in the couch cushions. When he bent over, I thought it might have been a trick of my imagination, but a very familiar teardrop pendant spilled out of the neckline of Io's tunic. I tried to be subtle, but I looked down at my throat to see if my own necklace still hung there. I definitely didn't remember taking it off before I took my nap.

And my heart skipped a beat when I didn't find the pendant on me.

Did the caretaker steal Uncle Diego's pendant? Even worse: Did he take it from me while I'd slept? This was why he was so eager to let us stay here. Somehow he knew I had a potential orb from the Lady Fortune legend. *There are people who would poison your goblets for that*, Niraya had warned.

Io stoked the fire, and I was glad he had his back to me, because I don't think I did a good job hiding my anger or surprise. "Verdoro doesn't take much interest in us anymore," he said. "We see him fly in and out from time to time, cloaked in flame. But he passes over us, and he doesn't look down. Not at us. One wonders why, but we stopped questioning it long ago. Still, I wish you much luck. We would celebrate—we would feast—if Verdoro did not cast his shadow on Jericho Harbor again."

I stared into the flames. *Maybe he has a necklace that looks like mine. Maybe Charlie has it, and Io just has similar taste in jewelry.*

When Io turned back around, the pendant was tucked into the neckline of his tunic. *He saw me looking. He definitely didn't have that on before.*

*I have to get it back somehow.*

"As for your other question . . ." Io gestured to the window. Moonlight coated the floor in a warm glow. "The forest prevents most parties from reaching Mount Blackburn. It's the birthing ground to a curse, and one many of us here suffer from. In its full essence, it actually forbids many of us from leaving, drawing a boundary at the edge of the mountains. We sometimes debate over what's worse: the main affliction . . . or the side effects."

*Curse? Side effects?* I thought I'd seen and heard everything. Krakens, curses, and Lady Luck. At this rate, I wouldn't be surprised if we encountered vampires in Kesterfall. My mind buzzed like a beehive. What did Io mean by curse? Did he have the curse? It seemed rude to ask, like prying into a medical issue.

On the other hand, it was pretty terrible of him to steal my uncle's pendant. I let Io go on while I concocted a way to get it back.

"We all learn our lesson when we catch it, of course. The enchantress of the wood makes sure of that. The good people who had nothing left to learn? They come and go as they please. I wasn't so fortunate. I've been waiting for a curse breaker to come along and reverse the Wheel of Fortune ever since." He sighed. "Forgive me for being intrusive. I can see you're feeling troubled and . . . I didn't intend to burden."

"No," I said a little too quickly. "Don't worry. I'm really sorry to hear all this."

Io bowed. "Don't trouble yourself, Ms. Rosas. As it turns out, I've recently found the perfect remedy. I trust all will be resolved quite soon. But I should leave you to your reading. Although you're welcome to stay as long as you like, I'm sure you're eager to save your family.

You may slip away in the morning—no need to notify me of your departure. Please take the utmost care."

"Thanks." I refused to let this be the end of the conversation. He wasn't going to walk away this easily. "Um, would you mind grabbing one more blanket for me? I think I might try to get some more sleep before the others wake up, but it's a little chilly."

"Yes, of course."

Io dipped out of the room for a few minutes and then returned with a dark fleece blanket folded into squares. When he handed it to me, my heart was pounding. This probably wasn't going to end well.

"Thank you for taking us in tonight, Io." I extended my hand, palm coated in sweat.

"Of course. But is it really so cool in here? You're sweating."

When Io went to shake my hand, I reached up and yanked Uncle Diego's pendant off the caretaker's neck with one smooth tug.

Io's eyes widened as though I'd slapped him, and for a second, I was afraid maybe he'd slap me. It wasn't my nature to do something like this, so I stood rooted in shock for a second.

But instead of getting angry or even reacting at all, Io doubled over in a terrible hacking cough, like I'd smoke bombed him instead of taken a simple piece of jewelry that didn't belong to him.

I took a giant step back, pocketing the necklace. "Io?"

The caretaker looked up at me, but something in his irises changed. The icy blue became liquid gold, and somehow his eyes looked angrier. "I let you in . . . offered you shelter." Io lunged forward, making a dive for my pocket, but he toppled to the floor and landed on his elbow with a harsh thud. He clawed his hands into his hair, and when he pulled them away, his canine teeth extended from his gums, growing longer and sharper like knives. Weirder still, his fine blond hair was sprouting all over his face now, then his arms. He rolled toward the window, his gaze locked on the moon, a full disc above the mountain now.

"Io . . ." My mouth dried up like cotton. I wrung my hands.

His bones contorted and swelled in his body, every joint a growing bulge. Io's boots came apart in patches, exposing dark claws and wolfish feet. He flipped onto his stomach, digging his growing thumbnails into the wooden floor while he howled in pain. His shirt burst into tattered shreds and fell in ribbons around his body.

My heart raced against my chest. Had I harmed him somehow? Should I have given the pendant back? I dropped my hand to my pocket and closed my fingers protectively over the necklace, letting it cool my palm.

*Niraya was right. People are going crazy for this thing. What does it really do?*

I had a feeling I wasn't meant to find out. If Niraya was right, Uncle Diego's stone shouldn't be passed to any other hands. I wasn't even sure he was supposed to have it in the first place.

*I should run. I really need to run.* But the fear was like concrete in my veins.

Io buried his claws in the floor, tore out a plank, and crushed it in his massive, furry new hands. When I snuck another look at him, he was no longer the kind caretaker but a seven-foot beast clawing the walls and drooling at the moon.

I screamed and bolted for my room, Io flying after me in a blur.

"Niraya, Charlie, wake up. We have to get out of here!" I knocked down everything I could see in the path to my room, from statues to trashcans, hoping to create obstacles for the monster behind me, but Io's growls only grew louder and more aggressive. I could even feel his hot breath on the back of my neck.

When I reached my room, I jammed the key in the lock, flung the door open, and then slammed it behind me, holding it shut as the doorknob jiggled.

Io pounded on the door and snarled. I knew my own weight wouldn't be enough to contain a monster that could tear wooden planks like paper.

"Karina?" Charlie sprung out of bed, his hair in matted clumps. "What happened? What's that sound?"

"Io's a . . . a . . ." I couldn't even finish the sentence. "He's after Uncle Diego's necklace."

The beast hammered against the door, the wood shuddering against my back.

"A thousand curses. I should've known." Fully alert, Niraya sprung from the couch and grabbed the dagger inside her coat. "Karina, get away from the door."

Charlie took my hand and pulled me away from the door as a portion of the top half fractured into splinters. We huddled behind Niraya.

"A werewolf," she said. "Our host is a shifter."

And the moon was quite full.

# CHARLIE

## THE FOREST
## GIVES US AN EXAM

·:—•—:·

In all my young life, I'd never had a ruder wake-up call. A werewolf shredding through the door while I was sleeping. Goose bumps erupted down my arms.

"What do we do?" I cried.

The wolf's face appeared in the hole in the door, its eyes vaguely human. I swore there was actual pain in those gold irises, a haunting sense that the man was still conscious in there. But it could have been hunger. Or both. I didn't plan on becoming a werewolf to find out.

"Werewolves," Niraya said. "Never in my life . . ."

Karina and I dragged the wooden chair from the writing desk and jammed it under the doorknob.

"All the traveling you've done, and you've never seen a werewolf?" I asked. "That's like the most basic mythical creature."

"Basic?" Niraya clapped her hand to her temple. "No. If werewolves are so basic, perhaps you can enlighten us on how to defeat them. They are not common in these lands."

"Silver bullet to the heart," Karina said. "Everybody knows. Where's your gun?"

Niraya let out an exhausted laugh. "Well, that's endearing. Ye of little imagination, when man turns to wolf, his heart turns to silver. You can thank years of evolution for rendering your silver bullets completely useless."

"You're useless." I regretted my snark right away, but I was moody and didn't have a filter. "How are we supposed to kill that thing then?"

"That thing is still a man, and killing isn't how we do this. Not today, with you younglings present. We're going to grab our things, open that window, and run."

Or not. As if Niraya had jinxed the room, the window shattered. Niraya, Karina, and I threw our arms over our faces. Glass sprayed the floor, and a second wolf sprang through the broken window and landed on two hind feet.

Before I could scream, Niraya flung me aside and onto the bed, brandishing her dagger in the other hand. "So the big bad wolves have come to tango."

I glanced at the hulking creature snarling at Niraya, who nearly had it matched for size. She stared the creature down, her feet spread apart and her free hand in a tight fist.

"I don't think it wants to dance," I said.

"Karina," Niraya said, not taking her eyes off the monster, "listen closely. I want you to put your uncle's pendant in my back pocket. And when I tell you, you're both going to climb out the window and run. You will make your way into the forest. You will not stop running until you're far away from this village. Have I made myself clear?"

"Leave the pendant?" Karina said.

"Run into the forest?" I repeated. "Really? Everyone around here's more afraid of the forest than they are of anything else."

"I don't have time to argue with you," Niraya said. "These things want your uncle's necklace, and I want you to escape. As long as you're holding it, you can't have both."

For a minute, I considered Niraya might've been tricking us. After all, she didn't want our company in the first place. Maybe all along she was one of the crazed fortune hunters, determined to plunder the necklace and break away. But she'd gotten us this far, hadn't she? She'd sailed and rowed me and Karina all the way across the sea and made a pretty convincing case for her hatred of the dragon. I had to trust her.

Another chunk of wood burst from the door. Io's snout poked through the hole, teeth gnashing like scissors.

"Hurry." Niraya's knuckles whitened on her blade. "Get out of Jericho Harbor. I'll catch up with you again."

"And if you don't?" Karina said.

"And if I don't . . . then you'll have to climb on without me."

No shame here: I almost started sobbing. "We don't know how to defend ourselves."

"You'll learn as you go," Niraya said. "You'd be surprised what you can do when you have no other choice."

With a hesitant step forward, Karina dropped her hand into her pocket and withdrew Tio's necklace. The wolf drooled like it had smelled a piece of meat, and another chunk of the door exploded into toothpicks. Karina gulped, opened her hand, and dropped the pendant into Niraya's back pocket.

"Karina, Carlos . . ." Niraya whispered. "Save my James. Go."

When Niraya yelled go, several things happened at once.

The rest of the door cracked into three pieces and fell to the ground.

I flung my backpack on my shoulder.

Karina did the same with her own bag, and with her free hand, she jerked me toward the window.

And the second werewolf pounced for Niraya's throat. Luckily, she was ready. She countered with a high kick that hit the wolf squarely in the chest, giving her enough distance and time to roll onto her back, lift her knees, and propel the monster's momentum behind her.

Karina and I didn't stay to see how the encounter ended. Instead, we obeyed Niraya's orders and climbed out the window.

"Come on, Charlie. Don't look back." Karina pulled me over the ledge and into the wild grass below that was brimming with millions of star-shaped flowers and the cursed roses that withered and bloomed in endless cycles.

We raced for the forest, a moonlit abyss waiting to swallow us on the edge of the harbor. A growl tore through the air, and I snuck a glance behind me. The wolf at the door, apparently our mild-mannered caretaker who'd given me bread and sweet new duds, was hot on our heels.

"I wanna get back in the water," I yelled, pumping my legs as fast as they would carry me. My backpack bounced on my shoulders. Silently, I thanked my soccer coach for prepping me for this adventure.

"No you don't, Charlie," Karina said through clenched teeth.

"But look at the chompers on that thing! At least the stupid kraken was cool enough to swallow me whole." Was I seriously arguing that being eaten by a sea monster was not the worst thing that ever happened to me? Talk about fifty shades of cray.

With a gust of wind, something bounded out of a rosebush and sprinted ahead of me. The sudden movement sent a wave of terror shooting through my veins, but my emotions softened when I got a closer look. "Look, Rina. That's the wolf from on the road. It's just a baby."

*And it's actually sorta cute. Run, little guy.*

The wolf reminded me of the husky we had when we were younger. The pup had the same silvery-gray fur with black-rimmed ears and little white feet. My heart melted for it. Was Io chasing it, too?

When the baby wolf entered the woods, it disappeared, and I was grateful to believe it might've gotten away. Karina and I quickened our pace and leapt into the forest.

All it took was a few steps for the dark woods to swallow us completely, barring any sound from the rest of Jericho Harbor. All we heard now were our boots on the ground and our lungs fighting for air, taking in the smell of cedar and dirt. Silver moonlight lit up the forest like a city of steel, bathing leaves in pearls and the ground in gold. But my attention wandered immediately to the crystal lake dividing two separate paths.

A woman in a silver gown emerged from the lake like a dolphin. She soared into the air until her feet were inches above water and then froze with a snap of her fingers.

"Stop," she commanded in perfect sync with her snap.

Time stood still, even freezing the woman's long flowing hair into a wild, impossible pose. The wind stopped, and I noticed a single leaf hovering above the lake. We paused as the woman commanded, rooted by wonder. We were the only life in the forest.

"Freaky," I said.

Karina rubbed her eyes. "What just happened?"

The woman spread her arms above her head and gestured to the trees. "I am Lady Constance, Spirit of the Broken Forest. I stand to offer you a test," she said. "Carlos and Karina, your actions at this juncture shall determine the fate of your journey—one many have made before you and failed. Countless journeys end here. Will you reach your kin and save him in time, or will we mark your graves in Kesterfall? Lady Fortune's wheel lies in ruins. You alone steer your fates."

I looked over my shoulder, expecting Io to spring from the trees. "We were being chased—"

"Your opponent will resume his hunt after I leave you," Lady Constance said. "But first, you must choose one of the two paths you see before you."

I studied the trails. Neither looked easier than the other. I expected an easy one and a hard one—one riddled with thorns and a steep incline, the other flat and paved with bunnies and pretty, edible flowers. But the choice wasn't obvious at all. "What's the difference?"

Lady Constance gestured to her left, and the moon brightened the first path like a spotlight. "This trail shall lead you directly out of Jericho Harbor and to the base of Mount Blackburn. One might call it a shortcut. Take this path, and the beasts confined to the forest have little time to catch you. You are likely to escape your foe."

"We want that one," I said without missing a beat. I turned on my heel and started toward the mountain. "Duh."

Karina shot her hand out and caught my elbow. "Wait. I think we should keep listening."

*She's no fun sometimes.*

Lady Constance swiveled and pointed to her right, and the moonlight followed. "But down this path, an innocent life requires your help, greatly misunderstood by many. There will be pain with no guarantee of healing. Your predator is certain to catch up to you. You will take much longer to reach your destination." I waited for the but, the something that would make this horrible path sound enticing. But Lady Constance was done. She clasped her hands at her waist. "Now you'll choose."

I shrugged. "I still like Option A. B just sounds like death."

Karina bit her lip, turning her head from side to side and studying the two trails. "Um, Lady Constance, ma'am, if we take the shortcut, what happens to that innocent life you talked about?"

The Spirit of the Broken Forest shook her head, and the trees shook off some of their dead leaves. "It is not for me to say."

Karina fidgeted with a strap on her backpack. "Charlie, Io told me something before he turned. Something in the woods cursed them all. I think maybe they had this same test, and they chose wrong."

"Is that why they're monsters?" That sounded supremely unfair to me. "So there's a wrong way to choose, and we could be cursed forever? It sounds rigged. Either way, our safety isn't guaranteed. If we take the shortcut, we escape the werewolf. We probably get to Tio faster, too."

"Something on the other path needs our help, too," Karina said. "Wouldn't it feel wrong?"

"The innocent life is in danger anyway," I said. "We have Niraya and Tio to think about. What do you think this test is measuring? Loyalty to family? Survival instincts? Because if it's either one of those, we have to take the shortcut." I massaged my temples. This was starting to hurt my brain. Maybe I did inherit the family migraines.

Tears swam in Karina's eyes. "Carlos, a perfect stranger sailed us across the ocean and volunteered to hold the werewolves back for us. She's sacrificing everything to give us a chance to live. I don't know how Niraya would answer this test, but if we have any chance to pay it forward and help somebody . . ." She blinked the tears back and stared up at Lady Constance. Without looking away, Karina opened her backpack and pulled out the dagger she claimed on the *Red Hood*. "Then that's the path we choose."

Lady Constance nodded, her expression like stone. A toaster oven would've shown more emotion. "You are certain, Karina Rosas? As you travel together, you must decide together. Carlos, which path will you choose?"

No pressure or anything. None at all.

I brushed a rock aside with my foot. "All right. Fine," I said. "I agree with my sister."

Honestly, I didn't agree, but sometimes familia is about stopping and seeing things from another point of view. Karina believed with all her heart that we needed to take the long way. As little sense as it made to me, I respected her beliefs.

"Then may the light be with you, children. I suggest you keep running."

Lady Constance plummeted back into the water and time resumed. The leaves fell. The wind blew. A tree toppled unprovoked and barred the shortcut, sealing our decision and fate.

I blinked a few times, wondering if I had dreamed the encounter. "Did we pass the test?"

"I don't know." Karina grabbed my sleeve. "Let's go. We can't waste any time."

The trail around the lake twisted and wound through hulking trees, and at every corner, wildlife bounded toward the mountain path. A white-spotted doe, a frantic bear cub, and several squirrels raced along the ground, bats and crows and owls tore through the skies, and then two long howls pierced the broken forest. The first came from somewhere behind us, low, guttural, and hungry, quickening my pace. Twice I stumbled, once I fell, and Karina pulled me back to my feet. The second howl was softer, higher, and sounded from up ahead. My heart broke to hear the whimper in the second howl, clearly a cry for help.

"I think I hear our baby wolf friend," I said.

We turned a corner, and the small gray wolf cowered in the middle of the trail, whimpering in a rusty cage.

"And I think I see our innocent life."

# KARINA

## CURSED
## WILD

·◆·——————·◆·

My heart was a puddle on the ground, dripping at the sight of the injured wolf in the trap.

"That poor thing." I jogged toward the pup, and Charlie followed behind. "This was our test, Charlie. We need to help it."

"It looks so much like Scrappy. Remember her?"

Oh, Scrappy. Thinking about how much I used to love that stupid dog, I took a knee next to the wolf. "Hey, sweetie. We're gonna get you out of this, okay?"

The wolf flashed all its canines at me and growled, breaking my heart into smaller pieces. I stepped back, unsure how to proceed.

"Hey, be careful," Charlie warned. "It's still a wild animal. We can't just touch it and expect it to snuggle us."

A deep, low howl sounded in the trees again, this time much longer than before. I gulped and looked up at the birds soaring away from the mountain and back toward the harbor. This forest gave me the creeps.

"We should probably keep going, Rina," Charlie whispered.

I kicked a pebble into the bushes. "Well, we can't leave this wolf here. It'll die like this."

"What do you suggest we do? There's a monster out there sniffing for our blood, and I don't think this little guy wants us touching him."

I threw my backpack on the ground. "We're not leaving him."

The decision tied my belly in knots, but I also knew I'd regret leaving this poor creature to die.

"This looks like one of those traps they set up to catch raccoons." My brother sighed and put his hands on his hips, his expression softening. "Any idea how to open it?"

"I thought maybe you'd know," I confessed.

"Me? Why? Because I catch so many raccoons every day?"

I gritted my teeth. "It was worth asking, at least. I don't know, maybe you've seen a how-to video or something." I reached out to pet the wolf, but it only snarled again, snapping its jaws at me. "I don't know what to do. It doesn't trust us."

Charlie sprang into an upright position and made himself look taller by standing on his tiptoes. He took three giant steps toward the baby wolf and puffed his chest. "Hey!" He clapped. "Calm down. We're trying to help you."

The wolf's growls softened a bit, but it still bared its teeth.

"Hey, quiet. Behave!" Charlie beat his hands together a few times and took another stomping stride toward the wolf. "Now."

The animal lowered its head on its front paws and simmered to a dull whimper.

And I thought my heart couldn't break into any more pieces. "What are you doing? Don't be mean. Don't yell at him."

"Remember what I told you? I just thought about it. Tio wrote in his journal that if a wolf wants to attack you, you're supposed to get louder and larger. We have to prove we're the alphas." Charlie got back on his knees and scooted closer. To my relief, the pup didn't counter. It looked so sad whining with its head on its paws, and I could hardly stand it. Inch by inch, Charlie extended his hand, and finally, he stuck one finger in the cage, able to reach just deep enough to touch the wolf behind the ears. "I'm sorry. We'll get you out, okay?"

He'd done it. He gained the wolf's trust. My heart mended itself and soared with pride. "You did it. It worked."

My brother smirked at me. "Duh."

I rolled my eyes. I actually thought he'd stopped saying that. And then a scarier thought hit me. All that screaming and clapping was bound to give us away. "Oh my gosh. The noise."

Charlie smacked his forehead, growling at himself. "You don't think that thing would have sniffed us out either way?"

Jinx. The howl pierced the air again. The baby wolf whined, and even the trees trembled. This whole forest was alive.

"We can run, you know," my brother said. "We can get out of here and be that much closer."

I squeezed the handle of my dagger, my heart galloping in my chest. "Get that wolf out of the trap. I know how much you love to tinker."

Charlie gave the trap our famous Rosas stare. "Wanna try to help me with it? Or are you gonna stand there?"

I ignored Charlie. As much as I wanted to help, someone had to be on full alert when the werewolf found us. I turned in a circle, watching for movement in the bushes.

"Wait a minute. This is spring-loaded, isn't it?" Charlie poked the contraption with a stick. "Maybe if I push down on these things hard enough, I can loosen the doors until—*Rina*."

Io charged into our path, front paws extended and claws ready to maul.

He came in a blur. I tried to slide out of the way, but I wasn't fast enough to fully evade the attack. Io dug his claws into my upper arm, sending a fiery pain through my muscles. Black stars exploded in my vision. I dropped the dagger by my toe, and the pup's cries echoed in my ears. I clapped a hand over my injured shoulder and gritted my teeth.

"Leave her alone, fuzz face. That's my sister." Charlie picked up a rock and chucked it, conking Io in the head.

Io turned and lunged for my brother. With the werewolf distracted, I leapt onto his back and put him in a chokehold. He flung me around like a bucking bronco, but I only pressed my arm harder against his throat. I was no ninja or athlete, but Jorge taught me some basic self-defense when he married my mom, and even though I'd hoped I'd never use it, I had those secret fantasies of being able to take down the bad guys. Charlie picked up another rock and hurled it at Io, only this time the rock hit me instead.

"Watch it, Charlie." I gritted my teeth, stars dancing in my vision.

"Sorry!"

Io dropped to the ground back-first, pinning me beneath him. And man, he was heavy.

I cried out and kicked at his legs. "Leave us alone. We did nothing to you."

Io flipped over so we were knee-to-knee, his paws locking my neck against the ground. Saliva gathered on his teeth. His breath seared my face, and for a second, I tried to imagine I was back in Tucson during the hottest part of the year. *Mind over matter.* But Tucson didn't smell nearly as foul.

"Get off her." Charlie sprung from the side, but his movements were too obvious for the werewolf. With hardly any effort, Io swung his massive paw and swatted Charlie in the stomach, knocking him on his back.

Hearing my brother cry out in pain, coupled with the cries of the pup, set a raging fire in me. Nobody was allowed to mess with my family. I curled my toes and tensed my shoulders. I reached to my side, snatched the dagger I'd dropped, then buried the blade in Io's shoulder.

The howl was horrible.

I ripped out the knife and seized my chance to roll over and throw him off me. Trying not to look at the blood or even really think about it, I wiped the dagger on my pants. Hot iron coated my stomach with the knowledge I'd injured somebody who took me and my brother in for shelter, even if it probably was just to steal my uncle's pendant. Was Io a good person when the moon wasn't full? I'd probably never know. I just didn't want to hurt anyone.

And sure enough, he didn't stay down for long.

The survival instinct kicked in and I scrambled into a tree, channeling my gym classes where I'd been forced to climb the rock wall. I moved like I had a sixth sense, finding all the branches and footholds without looking down. However, my shoulder throbbed like a billion sunburns. It took everything to hang on. In the back of my mind, Uncle Diego's voice pestered me.

*If you ever need to get away from something, don't climb a tree. Your predator can climb better than you.*

I wished I would've remembered that before I started.

Io sank his claws into the tree and followed me with the grace of a panther, cornering me. I moved up and looked for something I could drop on him. A beehive. A loose branch. A pinecone. Anything.

"Go, Rina." Charlie bounced on his toes.

My foot missed a knot on the tree trunk and I slid down, screaming until I caught a lower branch. Then my foot slammed into something plushier than the tree knots—something that howled. I snuck a glance down. I'd driven my boot heel into Io's nose, throwing him on the ground.

I closed my eyes and whispered a silent thank you.

But Io sprang onto his hind legs and leapt up, this time jumping twice as high and burying his claws in my ankle, setting it ablaze with pain. I kicked down, and the two of us tumbled off the tree and collided in a heap by the trunk. Time slowed, and my vision darkened like someone had placed a thin black veil over my eyes. I could still feel Io's claws around my ankle, and his hungry growls purred in my ears. I didn't have the energy to fight him anymore. I was going to black out. "Charlie . . ."

The rusty screech of metal squealed through the air, and then Charlie said, "Go, boy."

Our baby wolf zipped into view and sank its teeth into Io's tail.

"You freed it," I said.

Charlie took my sweaty hand and pulled me up. "Come on. We need to go."

Io whirled around in an attempt to get the pup off his tail, but the baby wolf clung to him like a living bear trap.

He was trying to protect us.

"Rina," Charlie pleaded. "Come on."

I held up a hand. "Wait."

When the baby wolf couldn't hang on any longer, it rolled into a rosebush with a light yelp.

Io threw his head back and cried at the moon again, and I couldn't help but think it was a battle cry. Shivers rolled down my back. He charged the baby wolf with a flying leap, entangling himself in a cluster of thorns and roses. While the pup was small enough to hide in the bush and maneuver freely, Io was too bulky to claw his way through. He wrestled the bush in vain, snapping his jaws while the pup whimpered.

I almost ended it right there. I knew where the dagger needed to go.

But before I could charge, something else entered the field: a flash of gunmetal gray and snowy white, a wolf much larger than our pup, but not quite as big as Io. The newcomer pounced on Io from the side, and the two rolled away from the rosebush.

Charlie gasped. "That looks like the baby's parent."

I sheathed the knife, my heart full at the sight of the new wolf's entrance. My brother was right. The baby and the new wolf were almost identical except for their size. The dark-rimmed ears, the beautiful eyes, the fluffy white paws. "I bet it's the mom."

The mother wolf bit, clawed, and snapped until she had Io pinned into submission, standing above his throat and rumbling with feral rage. Charlie shook his head in awe. "How did she know to come running?"

"That's nature," I said. "You know how Mom always talks about 'mother's intuition?' Mama Wolf had a feeling, and maybe that was all she needed."

In the time it took me to speak those words, Io stopped writhing with a brittle growl, and the forest went silent.

Charlie and I exchanged nervous glances, our faces matted with sweat.

"Is he dead?" Charlie asked.

"I—I don't know."

The pup limped to its mother and snuggled up against her paw.

My brother and I huddled together and waited for Io to move again, having no words to share. When I rested my head on Charlie's shoulder, he pulled me into a warm, tight hug, and the tears rolled loose down my cheeks. My mind was foggy. When I really thought about it, I was sad for Io, because with every minute that passed, I didn't think he was getting up again.

I dried my eyes on my sleeve. "He was cursed. The forest tested him, and he chose wrong. This place turned him into a half man who could never leave."

Charlie dabbed his forehead, a thin line of blood running down his nose. "But that could've been me. That could be anybody."

I didn't believe Io was evil. Charlie and I had faced similar temptations in the name of survival. In the end, the only difference was that Io yielded to them.

But what did he want with my uncle's pendant? Was Io one of the crazed treasure hunters Niraya had warned us about, or did he somehow need it?

As if the wolves sensed my emotions, they trotted over and stood in front of me and Charlie, panting with their tongues hanging out of their mouths. The mother rested her head on my thigh. I rubbed her behind the ears. She was velvety, warm, and pure, like our old family dog.

"Charlie, they're so friendly," I said.

The pup curled into a ball on Charlie's lap. "Yeah. We saved the little guy, and the mom saved us. We're friends now."

I was already growing attached. It had been a long time since we owned a dog, and I felt like I owed a debt to the two wolves, almost as much as I owed one to Captain Storm.

"Do you think we should go back for Niraya?"

Charlie ran his thumb in a circle between the pup's ears. "You know I want to. But she specifically told us to go on without her. We already lost so much time here. Our quick nap turned into a full day in this stupid village. Niraya's strong, though. If there's any other way to beat the monsters, she'll catch up to us. If not . . . you and me, *hermana*. We got this. I'm worried about your ankle, though. What happens if a werewolf scratches you?"

"I don't know." While the dull burn shot through my leg, twin sheets of clouds meshed together like curtains, drawing a veil over the full moon, and I mouthed a silent wish that it would stay covered. "We should keep going."

Charlie and I helped each other up before the wolves could fall asleep on us, which was a good thing. If they had fallen asleep, I would've sat there with them forever. When we grabbed our backpacks, the two animals looked up with wide, sad eyes.

"Aw, man," Charlie said. "Don't be like that, please."

I pet the mother wolf and kissed the top of her head. "Thank you, sweet girl. You are mighty. Uncle Diego would love you."

Charlie turned away from the pup and tightened his backpack. "No sad goodbyes. It's too hard. Let's just go."

I understood. With a soft smile, I followed my brother down the trail. *Every step is closer,* I told myself. *We're on our way. We're closer than before.*

A guttural voice croaked behind us and startled me out of my thoughts. "You think you're the first to pass the test?"

I turned around, and Io lay broken and pale in his human form. The yellow, hungry spark in his eyes faded to cold, ice-blue defeat.

"I was one of you," Io said. "Sent from Florindale. Verdoro was my task, and it ended here, as most journeys do. But just because you've made it further than me doesn't mean you're the first. You still won't reach the dragon. I know what crawls in the northern wild. Keep wandering the mountain for a day. You'll return to Jericho Harbor begging Lady Constance to curse you."

"I'm not afraid," I said. "I'm not even mad at you. I just feel sorry for you."

"You did this to me," Io said. "For ages we sought the one artifact that would negate our curse, now so needlessly clinging to the hands of two younglings."

"Then you were out of luck anyway," Charlie said. "We gave it to Niraya. We don't even have it anymore and you attacked us anyway."

Io sneered. "You unafflicted humans always blame the man for the beast's appetite. And yet you still didn't help us. You're no better than Lady Constance or the dragon of Kesterfall. Your heart is black with greed." Io's chest rattled with a dark chuckle. "But one need not venture far to hear the stories about where you're going. They're enough to make one wish for death. And your uncle? He's probably wishing for it, too."

Now I knew why Io was so desperate for the necklace—why he changed when I ripped it away from him—and I had no idea how I should've felt about it. On one hand, he was right. What did I need with it? What did Uncle Diego need with it?

I started to wonder if there really was a Lord Falk, an evil man roaming the old world, hunting for pieces of the Wheel of Fortune.

Io struck such a guilty chord in me that even though he wounded my shoulder and ankle, I apologized and offered to help him back to the Golden Gibbous. *He was after the dragon, too.* But he wouldn't have it, and neither would Charlie. So we left Io there, and Charlie and I hardly said a word to each other as we continued on. Deep down, I hoped Io would be okay, and that one day the curse of Jericho Harbor would be broken. But I wasn't the right answer.

A warm sensation at my heels made me glance over my shoulder, where I found the two wolves padding behind us, tongues hanging out of their mouths as we limped out of the broken forest.

"Look, Rina," Charlie said. "They're following us. They didn't want us to leave them either."

I stopped to pick up the pup and held him to my chest. "Then we'll protect them. Do you think we should give them names?"

Charlie patted the baby wolf's head. "This one's definitely an Oliver. What about the mom?"

The name flew into my mind effortlessly, like it had been hovering there all along. "Nella."

"Oliver and Nella. I like that." My brother continued down the path to the mountain. "Maybe we're not really alone after all."

I repeated the thought in my head, desperate to believe it. And for the first time in a while, we had a sign of hope following us out of the forest. But after Jericho Harbor, darker thoughts followed like a storm cloud over my head. Thoughts like:

We left Niraya.

We aren't capable of saving Uncle Diego.

He may not have even survived.

I could turn into a werewolf tomorrow.

There are so many more dangers ahead of us.

That pendant cursed our journey.

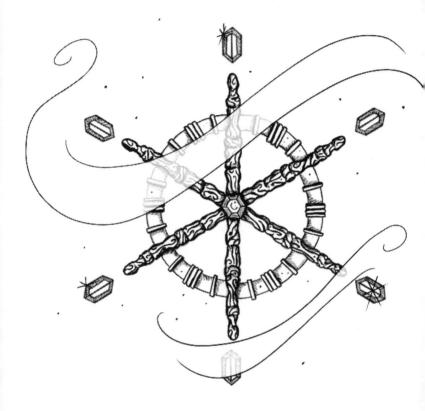

# PART
# FOUR

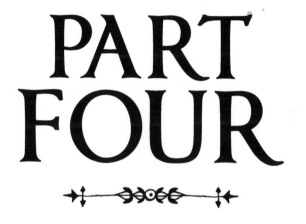

THE GHOSTS
OF
KESTERFALL

# CHARLIE

## COOKING WITH
## CHARLIE AND RINA

◈—◆—◈

If there was anything that could have made this adventure harder than it already was, it was definitely snow. All the snow for the two desert rats who broke out the jackets at sixty-eight degrees in sunny Tucson. Our poor sun-kissed bodies weren't prepared to handle the change in weather.

But this was no Winter Wonderland. It was like all color had been choked away from the world. Fern and shamrock turned to sage, emerald turned to ivory, and all traces of forest life withered away as we followed the mountain trail we'd been warned to stay away from. The chittering of bugs and grinding of dry leaves faded to nothing, masked by the whistling wind and the snow crunching under our boots. I paused for breath when the trail grew steeper, which might have been unnoticeable if the ground weren't slick with ice.

There was a time when snow would have been exciting for me and Rina. As Tucson kids, we'd dreamed of white winters and the chance to ice skate in the street after our tamale Christmas dinners. We begged Mom and Jorge to drive us up to Mt. Lemmon to play every time we had a view of a frosted peak. One year they finally did, and we enjoyed the snow for about an hour before we got sick of it—literally. My nose didn't stop running for days.

I jammed my hands into my pockets and rubbed my knuckles with my thumbs. My breath hovered in tiny clouds in front of me, and for the first time, it didn't feel appropriate to pretend to be a dragon, the way I always did when I could see my breath on cold days. With every step on the trail, it seemed like the temperature dipped another degree.

"We need to get warm somehow or we'll freeze," I said. I wished I'd seen Tio's Everest specials. Somehow, he didn't write much about seeking warmth in his diary. I checked cover-to-cover three times. So we improvised. We doubled up on socks, most of which we'd taken from random suitcases after the train wreck. I hoped they were clean.

"We need water," Karina said. "Just because it's not scorching out like home doesn't mean we shouldn't stay hydrated. The wolves, too."

One thing we had going for us was Oliver and Nella's company. They followed us like baby chicks, like shadows, straying only to sniff out rogue scents and returning when we called them. They padded around with their tongues hanging out and their paws leaving soft, tiny tracks in the snow. Not only were they nice to cuddle for our cold bodies, but they warmed our hearts, too.

Karina unzipped her backpack and pulled out a white fleece throw. "I forgot I took this blanket from one of the suitcases on the train."

All I had in my backpack for extra warmth was a book of matches. I wondered if they were any good after being eaten by a sea monster and then sneezed back into the ocean. If not, I'd have to learn to make fire Tío's way, with sticks and friction and a whole lot of patience.

"Do you think we can drink the snow?" I asked. "The fresh stuff?"

Karina scooped some into her hand. "We should probably boil it first."

I looked back on my footprints. We hadn't come terribly far since the forest, but we'd climbed high enough that we could look out over a layer of trees and see the harbor from where we stood. Odd rock formations rose around us on all sides, some piled like thin towers, some wide and sprawling like card houses, and some that looked like rock mansions, all blasted with a layer of frost.

"I think we need to find another place to rest soon," Karina said. "I don't want to waste any more time, but we're only equipped to handle so much at once, you know?"

Something about my sister's tone really bothered me. She was also a shade paler than usual. Thin rivulets of blood trickled from her shoulder and ankle. I had no idea how she'd come all this way without saying anything about her pain, or even cringing. "Yes, we need to stop. You're pale, and you're still bleeding."

"I'm fine. And you're bleeding too," Karina said. "Your forehead. Sit."

I obeyed and rested my head against one of the rock formations. Oliver curled up beside me while Karina dipped a clean sock into the snow, packed some ice into it, and dabbed it on my forehead. I winced when the cloth touched me, a cold burn screaming where I'd been cut, but Rina was able to scrape some of the dry blood away. I shut my eyes and imagined home. Warm sunlight. Taco trucks. Drinking fountains.

Crippling hunger. Physical exhaustion. Biting cold. Yeah, this visualization thing wasn't working out too well.

"Here." I tied the sock, rubbed it a couple times for warmth, and then dipped the clean end into the snow. "Let me get yours now."

After a few minutes of scrubbing, Karina pulled a stack of bandages from her backpack. They were the strips meant more for paper cuts and playground boo-boos than werewolf scratches, but they were small comforts. We applied them and crawled into a pocket of space—wide enough for the two of us and the wolves—that had been weathered out of the mountain.

"We can camp here for a bit," Karina said. "Let's start gathering sticks. Any shape, any size."

With Oliver at my heels, I gathered branches from the mountain trail. Because of all the snow around us, dry tinder was in short supply, but I did scrounge enough to make a small pile. I arranged the sticks in the center of our little burrow and tried out my matches.

"How are we alive today?" I asked. "How did the cavemen survive long enough to evolve and become us?" I scraped my third match against the booklet. Nothing happened. The ocean water had ruined our potential for fire. I chucked the booklet into the woods.

Karina took one of the largest sticks from the pile and held it perpendicular to the ground with both hands. She dug it into the pile and rubbed her hands together as fast as she could. "It's crazy to think about, isn't it? A time when people had no choice but to live like this, building their own fires, knowing which creatures to avoid, knowing which plants were poisonous . . . How did anybody survive without smartphones, heaters, and Target?"

"It might even be fun if we actually knew what we were doing." I frowned. "What if this is our lives now, Rina? What if we have to start from scratch with only these sticks and stones?"

Karina shook her head. "Nope. Don't talk like that. We're doing fine. If we can't get to Uncle Diego, all we have to do is make it back to Zid so the king can send us home. But we can't give up, Charlie." She gritted her teeth and rubbed her hands together faster. It took nine tries, but finally, a tiny plume of smoke oozed from the base of the woodpile. "Not. For. A minute."

A spark leapt from the stone, and warm, glorious fire ignited in our burrow.

I threw my arms up. "We got fire. Sweet, sweet fire. Burn, baby, burn!"

Karina burst into laughter. "We are fire ninjas. I didn't even know if that would work."

We grabbed hands and jumped up and down in ridiculous circles. The wolves probably thought we were crazy. We were.

After we had our moment, we sat back down and put our hands in front of the fire. Sensation melted through my limbs inch by inch, filling me with warmth and adrenaline. For a few minutes, we were invincible. Fire masters. Survival superheroes.

"And now, we can make a container, boil the snow, and have drinking water," Karina said. "We just need food."

I jerked my thumb toward Nella, who was padding around the trail in a crouched position, her gaze following something I couldn't see. She moved with the same cautious, calculated walk I used whenever I had a flyswatter. "Look at her."

"She's hunting something."

Then Oliver bounded into view and pounced on something I assumed was a tree branch. Nella trotted back into the burrow a few seconds later with a rabbit in her teeth, only this rabbit had two long antlers sticking out from between its ears.

Karina stared at the animal like it was a unicorn, her mouth in an O.

I scratched Nella under her chin. "Good girl." Seeing the shock on my sister's face, I added, "What?"

"That's weird, Charlie. It's a jackalope."

"So?"

"So, jackalopes aren't supposed to exist."

My sister was so weird sometimes. "What do you mean they don't exist? They're all over the desert, like in our own hometown. They're a thing, duh."

"Oh really? How many have you seen in person, then? Huh?"

I thought for a minute. "I don't know. They're just everywhere. It's not weird."

"I promise it's weird. They don't exist."

*Neither do dragons or werewolves.* I shrugged and took the jackalope by the antlers. "Well, doesn't matter now. We're about to eat one, and it sure looks real to me."

The next two hours were this disgusting ordeal in which I tried to teach myself to skin and gut a rabbit while Karina gathered snow to melt, boil, and collect as drinking water. Working with the rabbit was one of the hardest, grodiest tasks I'd ever had to do, and removing the fur was actually the easiest part. The rest was a slow struggle because I didn't want to do something wrong and contaminate the meat. Everything that looked questionable, I tossed aside. Karina certainly didn't make things any easier. She kept coming back thinking I was done, but then she would see me working and pretend to gag.

But obviously Rina was curious, because she watched the whole time she gagged.

"Ugh, *grossss*. Hurry up," she muttered.

"I'm not a hundred percent sure what I'm doing." This was stressful stuff, like doing surgery, but on

Gordon Ramsay's cooking show. To make myself feel better, I imagined the chef telling me my jackalope dinner was the best thing he'd ever tasted. "Chill out unless you want to do it."

"Ew, no, you. I'll do water."

"Yeah, you do water," I said. "And get a lot. I'm gonna have to clean this thing. And my hands. Like eighty-nine million times."

When I had the jackalope stripped down to clean chunks of meat that vaguely resembled shredded chicken, I cheered. For now, I could be proud of myself. Nobody was here to help me with this. Not Niraya, not Tio, not even YouTube, and yet I'd managed to get a decent wild dinner started. By the time I started roasting the jackalope over the fire, Karina had calmed down a bit and rejoined me in the burrow. She hugged her knees to her chest and stared at the fire in tired, droopy-eyed fascination.

"You're kind of good at this," she said.

*Heh, I know.* "Maybe we do have it in us," I said. "Some basic survival instinct or something."

"That's familia. It runs in our blood."

"Let's hope I did it right and we don't die." I forced a smile. "I'll take the first bite, 'kay?"

Before I could do anything, Karina ripped a chunk out of the jackalope meat. "Oh no you don't. I'm starving. I'll take the risk."

I grimaced as Karina popped the jackalope meat into her mouth. She wrinkled her brows as she chewed, analyzing the taste.

"Here goes nothing." I took the next bite, waiting to find out what made Karina wrinkle her brows. "Do you hate it?"

My sister swallowed, tapped her chin, and then took another bite. "I don't know yet."

"I don't either." I chewed the meat slowly and thoughtfully. The subtle taste of chicken filled my mouth, but there was a strange second flavor layered under the first, like notes of dirt and rain. I considered myself lucky I didn't feel any grains of sand crunching between my teeth, but it was still a little hard to swallow. "I don't hate it, but . . . meh."

I fed some tiny pieces to Oliver and Nella, who gulped them down like dog treats without any fuss, only to curl up and go to sleep after. They didn't come to me begging for more like Scrappy always used to do.

"They don't love it, either," Karina said with a smile.

"It just tastes weird. Gamey, I've heard Tio say. I can't complain about it, but I really want salt and pepper right now. Or hummus."

"Some shredded cheese," Karina suggested.

"Or Mom's famous salsa." Thinking of that divine concoction of tomato, garlic, cilantro, and jalapeno, I took another bite. Man I missed home.

"It's because you did it wrong and you suck at cooking." Karina stuck her tongue out.

"Aw, come on." I pouted.

"I'm kidding. Thanks for making dinner. It's way better than fish. And it's actually kind of filling. I'm not even that hungry anymore."

"You just don't like it," I teased. "Mean."

Karina doubled over in laughter. We were both so exhausted and stressed out the past few days that we had trouble remembering the simple things. Laughter. Smiling.

I took a breath. "We can do this, Rina. I know we'd both rather be home right now, but one step at a time, one fire, one jackalope, one sip of water . . . We can do this."

Karina nodded, staring at the shadows our dancing fire cast on the wall. The glow made us look so much bigger than we really were, so much mightier. It gave me hope.

"Yeah," she said. "One step, one fire, one sip at a time."

I picked at another piece of meat. "You forgot to mention the jackalope."

"Oh. Right." Karina made a face, her cheeks paler than ever. "Hopefully we'll find something else out there. Like a Culver's."

What I wouldn't have given for a Culver's. For a hike in the Tucson sun, bare-armed and comfy in shorts. I was so tired of the snow already. The cold made me tired.

Even though my eyelids were heavy, I didn't fall asleep as easily as Karina did. As proud as I was about our food win, I was scared for my sister. I checked her ankle. She wasn't bleeding anymore, but a thick patch of hair had sprouted from under the bandages.

Nothing ever seemed less fair to me. We chose the "right" path instead of the "easy" path even though it wasn't obvious. We did a good thing, and my sister was cursed anyway. Even though I was pretty sure Io's scratches were the cause, I still blamed Lady Constance. She may not have been the one to curse Rina— otherwise I should've been cursed, too—but the "Spirit of the Broken Forest" should've known she had given us a test that was impossible to win. Had we known that, we could've just taken the shortcut. Except then, maybe Nella and Oliver wouldn't have survived. Why couldn't this have just been simple? Unless somehow, we hadn't passed the test yet . . .

*We need to get her some help.* I wanted to turn back and demand that Lady Constance reverse the curse, but every minute we'd spend backtracking would just put Tio in more and more danger. Probably us, too.

I went back and forth and thought about this problem all night long, so much that all that stress spilled into my sleep a little bit later. I dreamed my sister went full werewolf and that I had to leave her behind.

We woke up with the Kesterfall sunrise and plowed on, winding through the mountain range for a couple more days and perfecting our mad wilderness skills. Nella and Oliver caught a few more jackalopes along the way, but they also caught squirrels. For the most part, I continued to cook, though Karina stepped in on the third day and decided it would be good to learn. In return, she taught me what she'd figured out about filtering water and boiling the snow. We built fires together and looked for places to rest. There we would sleep, peruse Tio's diary, and play with Nella and the pup. To my annoyance and Karina's amusement, it turned out Uncle Diego had diagrammed a rabbit toward the back of his journal and written down tips about how to cook basic wildlife. He also outlined methods for retrieving water from dry ground, filtering it, and building fires.

Maybe I hadn't looked cover-to-cover.

On the third or fourth day, Karina and I came to a turning point in the trail and started up a peak. Fatigue weighed us down like steel plates. It was all I could do just to keep my eyes open. My sister seemed to have it worse.

"You haven't said anything all day," I said.

Karina paused, crouched down, and hugged her belly.

I took her hand. "Come on. We're so close to the top of the peak, Rina. I can see it. Just a little farther."

"I'm so . . . tired."

"Let's play a game. We each take turns naming something we appreciate more now, like microwaves. It'll help us stay awake."

Karina closed her eyes and blew a foggy breath. "Oreos."

"What kind?" I prompted.

"Regular." Karina slowly straightened her back and stood upright again. "I don't like too much cream."

"Weirdo." I liked to lick the cream first. I already knew this about Karina, but I had to keep her talking. "I appreciate my room." My bed. The clean clothes in my closet, even if our mom had recently made us learn to do our own laundry.

Karina shuffled onward, and I walked beside, posed to steady her if she slipped.

"I appreciate Mom," she said. "Working and taking classes and still taking care of us."

I smiled. We were getting so close to the top of the peak. "I appreciate Jorge."

"Hot chocolate."

"Netflix."

"These wolves."

I took a deep breath. "Tio."

We were quiet for a few minutes, and as we approached the peak, Karina nodded. "That he invited us to spend his birthday with him. That he made the effort for us this time."

"That he . . . really does care," I said. "That he does stuff like this every day to teach people about the world."

Karina smiled. "And about themselves. How strong they are and what they can accomplish."

I even had to appreciate those dumb *Climb Your Mountain* posters at school. I took three big steps, and for the first time in my life, I finally got it.

Standing at the top of the world, there was no question of how far we'd come. I crouched down and hugged my knees, breathless and elated—until I looked ahead. My heart fell just as fast as it had soared.

Miles away, a much taller snow-capped mountain of rough black rock stabbed the sky. Nella started whining, and Oliver growled like the mountain was a stranger invading his mother's den.

Between the black mountain and where we stood, there was a deep basin—more like a canyon—and before that, a village of stone and marble, tall, sprawling, and as far as I could see completely deserted. It looked

like a city of tombstones and graves for giants, lifeless and monumental. I had to wonder what drove the civilization out of a place that probably used to be filled with wonder. Plague? Dragon? Something else?

All we knew for sure was that we'd have to go through that village—and whatever was in that basin—to get to the other peak. Rina and I didn't have to say a word to each other to know what that peak was. Speaking the name out loud seemed wrong. Like it could scar the roof of my mouth.

Because that was Mount Blackburn, where the dragon had our tio.

# DIEGO

## EPISODE
## III

⋅◆–◆⋅

This place was cursed. I'd never been surer of anything.

When James and I stepped outside the cave, we were shivering. We took no more than five steps into the jungle and the oppressive humidity smothered my skin, choking my pores and soaking my hair with moisture. This wasn't possible. There were patterns to these things, and a temperature change of fifty degrees in a matter of steps wasn't logical. In the cave, I wouldn't have been surprised to see a polar bear. In the jungle, boas coiled around the tree branches, and the air sizzled with heat and wildlife. If I closed my eyes,

I could pick out a number of birds—not all of which I recognized—and the buzzing of bugs.

Seriously, I hated jungles. Jungles are not playgrounds.

I took three deep breaths and addressed my new ally. "So, exactly how far do we need to hike to reach this ship?"

James appeared to do some mental math, squinting and rubbing his chin. "The other side of this basin is probably two to three days away if we hustle. But that beast dropped my ship somewhere between here and there, and that's what's certain. It could take hours to find. It could take days."

I bent over and rested my hands on my knees. *Days. Save me.* "And you're positive it's somewhere in the jungle?"

James threw his arms up. "Oh, no, forgive me. It's in the sky."

I was getting really tired of his snark. "You wanna step off?" I crossed my arms and locked eyes with the pirate. "I was only asking. This will go a lot faster and be much easier if we at least try to cooperate and make conversation."

James rolled his eyes and continued forward, ramming his shoulder into me along the way. I followed him with gritted teeth. *Don't antagonize him. Keep the peace.*

"Lad," he said, "I trained and fought alongside a woman in the Order who would disagree with you . . . best blasted warrior this world's ever known. A quiet, strong, no-nonsense type lass. If anyone had a shot at surviving out here, it'd be her. And she believed the less one said, the better. So I'm not going to make idle chatter with you just because you asked. I'm not your chum. All I want is to find that ship, set off the flare, and once we get out of here, I'm cracking open a bottle of rum and indulging until I forget everything about this purgatory. Even you."

I scoffed. "Oh, I'm sure we'll be best buds by the end of this."

"I don't think you heard me."

"You must not understand sarcasm very well."

I ducked under an intricate spider web strung between two trees. I didn't want to knock it down and kill its architect. James, however, had no such thought process and cleaved the web out of the air with a single swipe of his hook. The spider, a beige, hairless creature about the size of my thumb, dropped to the ground and scuttled away.

"So where are your ogres?"

James flicked a speck of dirt off his jacket collar then smoothed the pockets. "Oh, they're coming. Are you ready? Who's your favorite deity?"

I ignored the dramatics. "And when you talk about ogres, what exactly are we dealing with? Grunting, club-swinging trolls? Or something more intelligent, like *Shrek*?"

"Like who?" James asked. "I don't know who she is, but no. These are of the primitive, bull-headed variety. You got a weapon?"

I picked up a broken tree branch about as long as my arm. The leaves had already withered off, and thorns coated it from end to end. I slashed it back and forth a few times like I was fencing then turned around and aimed it at James's throat. "Good enough?"

James lowered the branch with his hand. "Careful where you point that thing." He raised an eyebrow. "Though if you plan on fighting with it, you might want to light it on fire or something. That's not going to fend off the ogres."

I tossed the branch aside. "Where's your weapon?"

"I am my weapon." James breathed on his hook and then wiped it on his coat sleeve. "Should have a firearm of some sort in the wreckage, though."

The deeper we went into the jungle, the more I had to keep an eye on the ground. Because of the rough, wild terrain, missteps or distractions meant the difference between solid footing and snakebites. Beetles descended from the trees and buzzed in my face. I waved them away with gentle swats, whereas James smacked, hacked, and stomped on them with swift, juicy crunches. I cringed every time the crisp sound of death crackled in my ears.

*If we run into a swarm of bees out here, please, let karma sting him first.*

I started to worry when James stumbled and tripped on his own feet. He caught himself on a tree trunk and wiped his brow. His face went pale, and his eyes took on the hollow color of a cloudy sky. One of his knees jerked. The man did not look good.

"Hey, you all right?" Without waiting for an answer, I braced him with one hand on each shoulder and sat him down against the tree trunk, ignoring his grumbles.

"You need food, or you're going to pass out. Can you wait here while I catch something?"

"I don't need this, lad," James said.

Pirates and their stupid pride. *As if I'm one to talk.* "I think you do, though. Let me guess: You're probably feeling a little light-headed. Next will come the headaches, which can be debilitating after days without food. Then you'll be throwing up, losing concentration, and—here's where I get concerned—slowing us down. Stay here. I'm going for food."

So for what I swore would only be a minute or two, I left the man on the ground and set off for something to eat. A bird, a snake—I could work with pretty much anything. I just hoped I wouldn't become food before the day was through. Of all the animals we could confront in the wild, the jungle had some of the worst. Once a lion marks its prey, for example, there's little one can do to escape.

I started by gathering leaves, shoots, and berries that looked fairly recognizable, the kind I was okay betting my safety on. In general, if they're the color of Lucky Charms, they're bad for you. It would've done us well to eat pretty much anything else, but the plants weren't going to be enough. We needed protein.

Leaves rustled in the distance, and a flash of black and burned orange darted between the trees. I crouched behind a fallen trunk and froze, sweat slick on my forehead. *All right, big guy. Come back out. Show yourself.* Although I really wasn't in a position to be taming tigers.

The bugs stopped rattling. Silence rolled through the forest, and I became very aware of how loud I was breathing. I closed my eyes and focused on slow, soft, even breaths.

The creature zipped between the trees again, almost too fast for me to perceive. But one thing was apparent when I saw the second blur: the creature was too tall to be a tiger. Whatever it was, it stood on two legs.

I shuffled a few feet to the right, trying to keep my footsteps silent. From my new angle, I could see the creature looming behind one of the palm trees. First I saw its tail, a long, orange whip with black stripes. I took another step, and the body appeared, painted with all the stripes of a standard tiger, but it stood more like a raptor, thin and awkward, with two bony arms sticking out from its chest. A long neck culminated in a pointed, narrow face with two horns that curled around the side, like a mountain goat. Two black, beady eyes stared back at me, studying me with quiet, hungry intensity.

On the plus side, I came up with a trivia question for my next show, something for viewers at home to puzzle out over the commercial break. Pop quiz: A tiger raptor mountain goat is staring at you like you're a Sonoran hot dog. What do you do?

A. Assert yourself. Don't let him push you around.
B. Play dead.
C. Man up and cry.
D. Ruuunnn!

In the real world, D is almost never the right choice, but I'd never seen a raptor mountain goat tiger before, and they're terrifying. For the first time ever, I picked D.

But before I could break away, a long, thin dart flew into view and pierced the beast's neck. The animal let out a bird-like screech, dead before it hit the ground. I pressed my palm against my mouth, forcing the shock back into my body. As the life faded from the animal's eyes, I felt sorry for it—angry, even. Where had the dart come from? I followed an imaginary trajectory, trying to reverse the path in my head. The tip definitely hit at a downward angle.

Meaning something was in the trees.

Probably watching me.

I crouched lower until I was almost on my chest, scanning the treetops. What was I even looking for? A human? A gorilla? A second tiger-raptor thing?

A purple beetle with shimmering wings fluttered onto my shoulder. I left the bug there for a minute, distracted by its color and anatomy, until a stinging sensation pricked my skin. The beetle's legs were glowing orange and burning through my shirt. I winced and flicked the beetle away, swatting the tiny plumes of smoke out of my sleeve.

Out of nowhere, another dart sailed over the trunk and embedded itself into the tree behind me. I turned, mortified to see that same beetle pinned to the trunk, tiny embers glowing on its wings.

What if I was next? I had to get back to James right away.

When I turned, a hulking figure with pallid yellow skin leapt out of the treetops and smashed into the ground about twenty yards from me. The trees shook upon impact, and even the earth beneath me trembled. The newcomer must've been ten feet tall, a lurchy sort of creature with more brawn than grace. Bulging, asymmetrical muscles protruded from its arms and legs. Its head was shaped like a pear, and it carried a hollow dart shooter in its massive hands. The monster landed on its knees—which is never recommended— and when I snuck another glance, it was already back on its feet.

This was not *Shrek*.

I backed away slowly, blissfully fortunate the thing hadn't shot me, and after a few steps, I sprinted back to James, who lay in a dreary daze on the ground.

I seized the pirate's collar and snapped him to his feet.

"Wegottago," I said in one breath.

James stumbled back to life, hanging onto the tree for support. "What? What did you see?"

"Your ogres are here." I shoved my hand in my pocket, ripped a handful of plant life out, and tossed it back to James. Somewhere along the run, I'd accidentally crushed the berries. The juice stained my fingers and jeans. "Here. Eat."

James caught the leaves and popped them into his mouth. "You're bad luck, Diego Rosas. You'll bring this whole jungle down on us."

He was probably right.

I shrugged. "Better the jungle than the dragon's jaws, right?"

Something bellowed from within the forest, followed by a series of hulking footsteps.

James sneered at me. "Wanna talk a little louder? I think the jungle just heard you."

More footsteps sounded in the distance, only these were much quicker, lighter, and drawing closer to me and James. Leaves rustled, grass whispered, and over all that, something breathed like Darth Vader.

I pulled on James's coat sleeve. "Get down. Something's coming."

James shook my hand off his sleeve, lips pursed together in an effort to silence his breathing. We huddled behind a bush. *If one of us sneezes, I swear . . .* I hugged my knees to my chest, trying to make myself as small and compact as possible. A tall shape leapt through the grass and into a vibrant bush smothered in dew.

I squinted to make out the shape. I only saw flashes of black and blue, though most of the skin was only slightly darker than a peach.

*Wait a minute. That's a human!*

The young man turned around, peering behind him for a few seconds before ducking back into the bush. His doe-eyed expression wasn't typical for hunters, but prey, on the other hand . . .

I couldn't imagine coming all this way alone. James wasn't exactly the best company to keep, but at least he was another pair of eyes, another body, and an accountability partner. I never thought I'd believe this, but I was glad I'd found the pirate in the den. I wanted to believe I would've found my own will to push myself into the rainforest, but I wouldn't have known what to expect. I would've been completely blindsided by the idea of ogres. Given a million guesses, I never would've thought a pirate ship in the jungle could be the key to my escape.

James scowled. "Who is this sea rat?" He brandished his hook. "This thundering mouth-breather will draw the ogres right back to us. He'll get us killed. I'm sending him to the Locker."

"Hey, no." I threw my arm across James like a seatbelt. "Cool it, man."

Another purple beetle buzzed around, steam coiling from its wings, and James flicked it out of his face. "Don't restrain me, Diego Rosas. You know this is for the best. You call yourself a survivalist? Then you need to prepare for hardship. You need to dirty your hands."

I lowered James's arm to his side. "Not like this."

The boy in the bushes popped back up, ran another twenty feet, and crawled into a hollow tree trunk. Then I realized something crazy:

I'd seen this person before.

Torn jeans, suede hiking boots, a black flannel shirt rolled up to expose a poorly designed tattoo on a hairy arm.

Except it wasn't tattoo ink—it was permanent marker, smudged and diffused from moisture.

*This has got to be a hallucination.* I tilted my head to the side, and the boy made eye contact.

"Evan?" I asked. My fan from the Fernweh Express.

I expected him to vanish like a mirage, but to my bewilderment, his jaw dropped, and he hissed, "Mr. Rosas?" Without waiting for me to answer, he clapped his hand to his forehead. "Whoa . . . Of all the people I could find out here. And you remembered my name."

"*Shh.*" I put a finger to my lips and looked around, listening for movement in the jungle.

James raised an eyebrow. "You know this scoundrel?"

I beckoned James to follow me. "Come here." We moved in a crouched position, closing the gap between us and the hollow trunk. I couldn't believe the luck. I took Evan by the shoulders and studied him. He'd lost a finger on his left hand. "What are you doing here? I haven't seen a single living person out here since the train."

Evan shrugged. "I dunno. I just woke up around here, missing a finger and everything. I've been wandering around ever since, looking for help, or at least some company. Did you see the trolls? They're huge, man. I think one of them saw me."

I turned in a full three-sixty, scanning the jungle for our enemies. "James here says they're ogres. James, meet Evan. He was, uh, on my train. The one that blasted me here."

"'Zat right?" James said. "Well, Kevin, let's not sit here and parlay all day. If that rock-head finds us, he'll blast us all."

Evan crawled out of the hollow log, and we ran. The leaves passed by us in a haze of green, and the other colors of the rainbow streaked overhead in the canopy. I couldn't tell how many of the colors were birds, which ones were butterflies, and whatever else might have been watching us. Our newcomer lagged behind a few paces, prompting me to slow down a little and make sure I didn't leave him behind. We caught our breath in a thicket of berry trees, the fruity scent pungent in my nostrils.

"This is absolutely crazy," I said. "You get that, right?"

Evan plucked a bramble out of the sole of his shoe and threw the thorn into a tree. "Oh, it's nutso, man. Like I said, I woke up here. Kept thinking it's a dream or some sick afterlife."

"You woke up here?" I asked. "On this island? Nothing brought you here? Because I woke up somewhere else, and then . . . then a dragon dropped me here. From across the ocean."

"That thing carried you?" Evan threw his hands over his head. "Whoa. I knew I saw a dragon flying above the jungle yesterday. Craziest thing I ever saw, man. I can't believe you actually touched it. Wicked cool."

*Okay, Evan.*

I waved off his comment. "Listen. I'm not sure if you already knew, but we're closed off in here. We're in a sort of ice basin. The mountains have us trapped in a bowl. James knows where we might be able to set off some flares and maybe catch some attention. So we're looking for a ship. Ringing any bells?"

Evan crossed his arms. "A ship. Huh." He stepped in front of James and looked him up and down, the same way I did when I first met him. Boots, rusty hook, earring. "Like a pirate ship?"

"Yep." Our whole situation seemed crazy until we discussed it out loud, and then it seemed insane. Evan probably thought we were losing it.

But he jerked his thumb and said, "The pirate ship's somewhere down that way. I saw it. Black flags, really big, statue of a cute mermaid on the front?"

James flashed a gold-toothed smile, light filling his eyes. "Ay, that'd be the one." He leaned forward and clapped his hand on Evan's shoulder. "It's that way? On your honor?"

"Mmhmm." Evan gave a thumbs up. "It's not too far, but you can't get there in a day. Maybe two or three. The thing's in about three different pieces though. Sorry to tell ya. Also, you probably shouldn't go inside. I was gonna hunker down in there myself, but the thing's crawling with those ogre trolls and some of the biggest spiders I've ever seen in my life."

Sweat beaded on my forehead. Of course there would be more ogres.

"Dandy," James said. "But I'll still be needing those flares under the deck. If we send one off, we increase the odds of rescue from this inferno. A royal shot in the dark, but I wager there's no other way out of here. Can you point the way, lad?"

Evan rubbed his chin for a minute, studying James as though he were a puzzle. "How 'bout I do you one better, man? I'll lead you there myself."

James swung his fist in front of him. "A most excellent plan. We'll need all the help—"

"Absolutely not," I interrupted. Yes, there was safety in numbers, and yes, Evan had survived this long on his own, but looking at him made me think of Charlie and Rina. I couldn't willingly lead him into more danger. "Point us in the right direction. Then lay low. If it's as dangerous as you say it is out there, you're not helping. You'll get yourself hurt."

"Come on." Evan went from peach to red in a matter of seconds. "How often does somebody get to go on an adventure with the great Diego Rosas? This is once-in-a-lifetime. I'm strong, I'm fast, and I can hold my own."

I hated to be the dream crusher, but this wasn't a negotiation. He was already missing a finger, and I hated to think of having his blood on my hands. James at least seemed accustomed to the danger. "It's not a game. If you get hurt, it's my conscience at stake. If you slow me down, it's my niece and nephew at stake. I don't mean to be brash, but—"

"You're not. You're just being a jerk." Yep, Evan went there. "Come on, man, you're my hero. Your show was everything to me when I was growing up. All this time I looked up to you, and when I finally get the chance to do you a favor, you stand there acting like a condescending jerk. Man, I feel sorry for all your fans who don't know the way you really are."

Sometimes words sting worse than scorpions.

With one last pleading glance, I turned to my pirate ally for support. "James? Back me up?"

James scraped under his fingernail with his hook, clearly disinterested. "Devon has a point."

"Thanks, bro." Evan jerked his thumb in James's direction. "See? Blackbeard gets it."

I kneaded at my temples, the aura of a migraine looming in my vision. "All      right, fine. But this isn't TV. It's life. If I tell you to do something, I really mean it. I'm in charge."

"Cool by me." Evan tightened the straps on his backpack and pointed straight ahead. "All right. We gotta go this way."

# KARINA

### STUPID
### LADY FORTUNE

:◦———◦:

Looking over the mountain ruins, I felt like I was the *Tomb Raider* lady and Charlie was Indiana Jones. With a view like that, I just knew there was cursed treasure hiding somewhere.

Down in the village, towers of red stone and white marble rose from the ground, some like dagger-nailed fingers scratching the sky, some swollen and stunted, but all mesmerizing. They had curved roofs with pointed tops, the corners curling up like flower petals holding scoops of fresh white snow. I started thinking about my mom's *raspados*, and the memory tied my heart in knots.

Was this a neighborhood? A town? A capital city of some sort? Did people eat, sleep, and raise families here? I wondered if some of the towers were once places of worship or government, because thirty-foot statues flanked their iron doors. Some were regal, bearded men of stone—like wizards—in earrings and ruffled robes. There were beautiful women with intricate hairstyles I could never pull off. I wouldn't say any looked happy, but they seemed dignified, lips tight and flat and eyes calmly focused. I kept staring at their massive stone hands. One clutched a thick brooch at her throat, another made a fist, and some spread their arms in mystical hand positions like they were conducting orchestras or casting spells.

"This place is incredible," I said.

"Word," Charlie said. "Who do you think the people are? The statues, I mean?"

"Gods and goddesses, maybe?" I put a palm over my eyes to shield the sun. With my other hand, I pointed to a woman with long wavy hair, a robe that swept her ankles, and a cryptic smile on her face. My sudden movement disturbed my bandages and sent pain biting through my shoulder. I winced and said, "I feel like I've seen her on a tarot card before. I just remembered there's a Wheel of Fortune card."

"Meh. I don't believe in tarot," Charlie said.

"I don't either. But now I'm questioning it. She's usually spinning a wheel, only she has people tied to it going round and round, like a clock."

Charlie cringed. "That sounds like straight-up torture. Maybe all these gods came down and smote the people who lived here."

I wouldn't have been surprised to learn that was true, especially after all Charlie and I had now seen.

We made our way down the hill and into the village, shuffling past a frozen water fountain: a nearly fifty-foot ice sculpture that hung in loops and curls over a dark marble disc. Looking at all this snow, I couldn't help but think of Uncle Diego's biggest challenge.

We were climbing our own personal Everest, locked in a prison of time and ice.

Watching Oliver and Nella prance around the snow was the cutest thing I'd seen in days. There was a time when I wondered what it would be like to be a wolf for a day. Carefree. Released from things like chores and homework. I used to think being a wolf would be the coolest adventure in the world.

Until the night Io scratched me.

I didn't tell Charlie, but ever since the forest, nights were torture. I could never eat enough to stay full, and hunger held me hostage for most of the day. I even craved the jackalopes after a few nights. My scratches were covered in coarse, dark hair. My headaches grew worse, and nothing could ward them away. If the moon weren't waning, I think Charlie and I would've been in serious trouble. I definitely needed to figure this out before the next full moon. My best medicine right now was my Rosas pride, refusing to slow my brother down, refusing to burden him, and refusing to turn back. Uncle Diego couldn't wait for my cure. He couldn't wait much longer at all.

We also couldn't wait much longer for warmth.

"Can we . . . can we go inside one of these buildings to warm up real quick?" Charlie asked. "I'm seriously f-freezing."

I was so glad he asked. The cold air stung my eyes. "Yes, please."

We picked a random tower, and Charlie covered his hand with his sleeve to turn the doorknob. It twisted, popped off the door, and then fell into the snow. From the hollow end, a moth the color of gunmetal crawled out and flew away.

The door swung inward with a hard creak, and a slice of wintery-gray light trickled into the building. Before we went in, we let the wolves sniff out the entrance. When neither of them growled or whined, I shoved the door open and we moseyed in.

Six round columns supported the ceiling of the circular room, each decorated with a marble sculpture. The tarot woman stared at me from the closest one. On the floor, a simple painting stretched between all six columns. The mural was a giant circle with six spokes dividing the room into colorful wedges. A thin ring of ice ran along the edges of the floor, almost a complete circle except for a thin space left to clear the doorway. Dark ivy climbed the walls, and I assumed it was unkempt until I looked in the spaces between the vines. In those spaces were six symbols I'd seen before. Rose. Tree. Teardrop. Flame. Sun. Moon. And a careful pile of wood sat in the middle of the floor and the hub of the painted wheel.

"Of course," I said. "I should have known when we first saw her. The statue is Lady Fortune."

"And she gave us firewood." Charlie sat cross-legged in front of the sticks. "We finally lucked out."

"Yes we did," I said. "Light it up so I can close the door."

It didn't take long for Charlie to get the fire going, which was a proud moment for me. After those few days we spent wandering the mountains, Charlie and I agreed we could audition for *Survivor* and win all the money. Or we could grow up and pick up Uncle Diego's show when he decided he didn't want to do it anymore. We could've continued a tradition.

While Charlie nurtured his mini bonfire, I walked in circles to study the symbols on the walls. What did they even mean anymore? It seemed the real legend Lady Fortune had been lost in time, warped and distorted like the world's longest game of telephone. *Did Io and those werewolves even know what they were looking for?*

I stopped and stared at the wedge with the crystal teardrop. When I shut my eyes, I pictured Uncle Diego's pendant, certain it was a perfect match.

"Can I tell you something?" Charlie asked, drawing me out of my thoughts.

I wrinkled my brows. "What?"

Charlie was bouncing his knee. "I noticed your ankle the other night. I know what's been going on with you since the forest."

A soup of mixed emotions trickled down my throat, and the strongest flavor was embarrassment. Even though my brother wasn't making fun of me, suddenly I was under a microscope. "Why would you bring that up?"

"Well, because I'm worried about you. Duh—"

"Stop saying that word." Heat flashed through my body, my muscles tense.

Charlie put his backpack in front of him like a shield. "I'm just saying. I feel like it's something we should talk about. Chill out."

"No." I took a big step forward, hands clenched into fists. "This isn't something we can look up in Uncle Diego's journal and solve with kindness to animals, Charlie. I'm . . . I'm basically mutating like some circus weirdo freak." Hot tears sprang to my eyes. "Unless we're still out here by the next full moon, this isn't your problem to solve. Okay?"

I turned away from Charlie and buried my face in my hands. As if my emotions triggered a chemical reaction, a thick layer of hair sprouted up my arms. I covered them with my sleeves before Charlie could see. *Bury your emotions, Rina.*

"We're familia," Charlie said softly. "Your problems are my problems, too."

And then neither of us said another word.

In the silence, the wolves started sniffing around, and when I opened my eyes again, they were pacing by the door.

"Someone's coming," Charlie whispered. "Put the fire out."

When Nella growled, I scooted away from the door, silently regretting our decision to break into the tower. Maybe someone did live here after all. That would explain the fresh pile of wood on the floor and the carefully trimmed ivy.

The door burst open, and the winter gray illuminated a frightening silhouette.

The wolves prepared to charge, but it was a good thing Charlie recognized the figure before they sprung. He called them down, and I caught a whiff of sun-kissed leather drifting over the fire.

"Niraya," Charlie breathed.

The fire illuminated a fresh cut above her left eye, like a crescent moon. Dark half circles rested above her cheeks, and her lips were chapped and pink. This wasn't the same infallible force of nature that whisked us to Kesterfall. But whatever she'd been through, she'd endured, and so did her red-feathered hat. She was a burning sun that couldn't be eclipsed.

I threw my arms around her with such force we both almost tumbled to the ground.

"Hello, wildlings." Niraya returned my hug and rocked me side to side a couple times before stepping back. She dipped her hand in and out of her pocket, held out her arms, and looped Uncle Diego's pendant back around my neck. "I believe this is yours."

I was positive the orb weighed more than the last time I'd held it. I kissed it and tucked it behind my shirt.

"We missed you," I said.

"It's good to see you fared well on your own." Niraya hooked her thumbs into her belt loops, the flames casting hollow shadows on her face.

"We weren't entirely alone." Charlie loosened his hold on Oliver. The pup walked a circle around Niraya, and I imagined him memorizing her scent, analyzing her, trying to understand her nature. "This is Oliver. The big one's Nella."

Niraya smiled, and thin dry cracks spread across her lips. "They're beautiful."

I sat by the fire and made a space for Niraya. "We're just so glad to have you back. You have no idea. How did you find us?"

Niraya jerked her thumb outside, reminding me I'd forgotten to close the door behind me. "You might start thinking about covering your tracks. As I told you, and as you've seen, there are people who want your uncle's trinket, and they will hound you until they get it. No pun intended, of course."

Charlie blew into his hands and rubbed them together. "And the ones who were after us before? What happened?"

"The werewolf that jumped through our window is currently locked in a wardrobe in the Golden Gibbous," Niraya said. "When she changes back and comes to her senses, she can unlock it from within and go back to the docks."

My heart lurched. "That woman sold us out? She seemed so nice."

"They always do until they find out you can give them something. Make no mistake, Karina. That charm on your neck? That's the stone that would have lifted the curse of Jericho Harbor."

As if she'd uttered a spell, the hair on my arms and ankles retreated into my skin, and the sharp pang of hunger in my stomach melted away.

I didn't have to fear the moon anymore. For now.

I should have been overjoyed, but an arrow of guilt pierced my heart. "I know." I tugged a loose string out of my blouse and blew the strand into our little fire. "Do you think maybe I should've—"

"No. You shouldn't have. Because, first, they'll collect one. The people of the harbor will celebrate and believe in their happiness. A couple years will go by, and then a new curse will consume them from within. The curse of greed. They'll decide they want to go looking for another orb. Then one more, then another, and yet another, until they reconstruct the entire wheel"— Niraya gestured to the mural on the floor—"or they destroy their village defending their pendants from others who wish to claim them."

In a way, Niraya's logic made sense. How many times had I promised myself I'd only eat one piece of chocolate, only to go back for five more?

"Humankind is not fit to wield such a power," Niraya said. "We will never be worthy of governing each other's fates. Let every man and woman steer one's own ship. Let virtue and skill be our compass and our wheel, and leave fortune to the winds. So no, Karina. Do not pity the shifters confined to their bodies. Pity what could happen to all people if one man such as Io—or Falk—governed our futures."

I pushed the goose bumps down on my arms and scooted closer to the fire. "Then why does Uncle Diego have this one? That's what I don't understand."

Niraya traced a pattern on the floor with her finger. "I suppose we all have our secrets."

We told Niraya everything that happened from the time we separated to the moment she found us, about the Spirit of the Broken Forest, about the battle with Io, our days catching jackalopes and building fires for survival. Her journey hadn't been much easier. Apparently, she'd been ambushed by bandits outside the forest, and that's where her scar had come from. And still, she pressed on. She came back for us. Or for James.

"So what happens now?" Charlie asked. "We're getting really close to the mountain. What happens between here and there?"

Niraya took off her hat and spun it on her finger. "I don't know. But let's be ready for anything, and let's proceed quickly. We're under Verdoro's flight path, and I don't like the ambiance of this place. The silence is anything but quiet."

I hated to admit it, but Niraya was right. In most quiet places, there's never really an absence of sound. Even when there's no traffic in the cities, you can kind of hear the neon lights, or the static on television, or the breeze between the trees. But here, besides the crackling fire and our steady breaths, the village in the mountains had this haunting, complete overarching silence, which was a random phobia of mine. It's why I usually slept with the TV or at least a fan running, even in the winter.

I wasn't my uncle, no expert on the wild, but I believed total silence meant one of two things. Maybe everything capable of making sound—even the birds and the bugs— was hiding from something big. That, or something was hunting right now, watching, sniffing, waiting.

# CHARLIE

## WE VISIT
## A HAUNTED HOUSE

·—◆—·

We moved through the village like ninjas, quick and quiet, and stopped for nothing until we came to the ruins of either a fallen castle or an epic mansion.

A moat had frozen around the walls, most of which had probably fallen away a long time ago and left a ghostly shell behind. Patches of carpet lay in the snow. The moisture warped a painting of an old man in a crown then congealed into clumps of ice where his beard should've been. A marble stairway wound up into nothing. Frost coated the walls that remained, like diamond glass. Some of the ice around us probably was diamond.

"Wow." A thick cloud of vapor escaped from my lips.

Karina nodded. "This is straight out of a bedtime story. I've written about places that look like this."

I had a feeling this tale didn't have a happy ending. I ran my hand over a half-wall scarred by burns. "I wonder what brought it down. Or who lived here."

"Could've been a number of things," Niraya said. "War is a likely explanation. Even before the Age of Avoria, kings didn't know how to compromise or share land. They always insisted on fighting for it. Perhaps time weathered this place back to its foundation. The inhabitants might have lived long, joyous lives, died and fallen to rest beneath our boots, and the world forgot they ever existed."

I picked up a green bottle filled with white powder, like the stuff that goes on funnel cakes. "Could there have been a plague?" I tipped the bottle, squinting to look at the faded label, and watched the white powder change into thick black fog. Before the smoke reached the cork, I put the bottle back down and took a giant step away from it. "Oops."

"Charlie," Karina hissed.

Niraya shook her head. "You want to be careful what you kick up around here. This is uncharted territory. Yes, it might've been a plague. Might've been a curse. A dragon."

I was starting to miss the simple tales of La Llorona, the crazy crying ghost who took bad kids away. Curses and plagues were too much for me. "I think I wanna go home now. We don't deal with plagues, dragons, and curses back home."

"You're conditioned not to notice or remember the curses and plagues in your land," Niraya said. "You may not know New York City played host to a war against an evil queen that invaded your world not so long ago. James fought in it. And none of you will ever remember it happened. I would hope you'll never remember this, either. You two and your uncle will go back to your normal lives and act as though your train never encountered so much as a ladybug on the tracks."

Okay, now she was talking crazy. A war against a queen? Please.

Karina frowned. "What if we want to remember all this?"

"What if we don't succeed?" I added.

"Stop it." Karina glared at me. "We're so close, Charlie."

"Doesn't feel like that mountain's getting any closer." I looked toward the peak, dark and ominous. "Tell me I'm wrong."

Niraya used her finger to doodle on the frosted layer of one of the walls. "We will get there," she said. "Come hell or high tides, we will get there."

Only we barely escaped the werewolves, kraken, and the first encounter with Verdoro. What skills did we possess that could help us fight the ultimate monster? We weren't ready.

"Ch-Charlie," Karina whispered, her voice shaky and weak. "Look up."

I followed my sister's finger to the fractured second story of the ruins, where a fuzzy white shape hovered at the top of the staircase. At first I thought I was imagining it, but whatever it was, even Niraya looked dumbfounded to see it. Slowly, she reached for her knife.

The shape was made of fresh snow, floating and clumping in odd formations in midair, like it framed an invisible statue. There was enough space between patches and flakes that I could tell nothing was there, but when I squinted, the snow formed a hooked nose, a cleft chin, two big ears, and a billowing cluster that I imagined might have been hair.

Then I made out the shallow lines of a grown man's chest muscles, rising and falling like the snow had lungs.

This was something human, or formerly human.

"Not possible," Niraya breathed.

"What . . . what is that?" Karina asked.

Nella took a protective stance in front of me and Karina. Little Oliver bared all his teeth at the snow figure.

The hollow man took a step, the snow disintegrating and reforming around his invisible foot, on which I could see the individual toes. He crossed his arms and bowed his head so he was looking directly at me. "You are intruding on my resting place and disturbing my slumber." His voice was mostly wind, empty and cold, but it had a masculine undertone, deep notes booming somewhere in the back of my mind. "Why have you set foot in my burial ground?"

*Burial ground?* I swallowed a mouthful of cold air. "You're a ghost?"

"Well, this is the first time I've awakened since my death, so yes, I suppose I must be." The snow ghost examined his chest then his fingers. "Strange. I thought I would be colder."

"Filbert?"

Another snow phantom appeared near the castle entrance. This one was a woman, and she wore a star-shaped crown of snow upon her head. She stood with her hands on her hips and scowled at the man upstairs.

The man clapped his hands to his cheeks, and a handful of snowflakes fell out of his invisible hair like dandruff. "Agatha?"

"Why are you awake?" The woman sneered then looked at her ankles. "Why am I awake? What is this?"

"I think we're ghosts now. My stars, Agatha, it has been ages, and yet you look so radiant. What a joy to be reunited." Filbert floated down to the ground floor and passed through me on his path to reach Agatha. Goose bumps rocketed down my arms. The snow that made up his body melted on my skin, and a fresh wisp of white flakes gathered from the ground up to recreate the ghost. Filbert pointed to me. "Did you invite them?"

"I thought you invited these people." Agatha tapped her foot. "You know how I feel about dogs and pirates in the castle."

"They're wolves," Niraya said, ignoring the pirate comment. "We apologize for waking you. We weren't aware this was a burial ground. Where are your gravestones?"

Agatha and Filbert exchanged glances. "Gravestones?" Filbert repeated. "*Where are our gravestones*, she asks us. Would you ask a stranger where he makes his bed?"

Niraya rolled her eyes.

Filbert went on. "Nay. We haven't the luxury of gravestones. Only our scattered bones."

I figured it would be rude to ask what killed them.

"How did you two die?" Niraya asked.

I cringed.

Agatha swelled three times her size and hurled a ball of ice in Niraya's direction. The pirate slid out of the way and cleaved the snowball with her dagger. The two halves exploded into icy dust.

"*How did you perish*, she asks. The nerve! Filbert, hold my purse. Wait, where—"

Filbert grasped the snow lady's hand and kissed her wrist. "We shall take pity, my lady. They haven't learned proper manners because they haven't greeted Lady Death. Not yet."

Karina took a step forward, so much bolder than me. "Did the dragon get you? He did, didn't he?"

Agatha turned her back to us and busied herself shaking snow out of a knight's helmet. "We assign the greatest blame to the greed of man. Filbert?"

The male ghost passed through Karina this time, sending a wild shiver through her body. I didn't know if the cold was more about the fact that he was a ghost or that he was made of snow. Karina rubbed her arms, and Filbert materialized again in the center of the ruin.

He gave us all a smirking glance as if to ask if we were ready. And without waiting for an answer, he snapped his fingers. A wall of ice cascaded through the ruins and towered above our heads, a rainbow of color pouring down the sides and painting the castle back to life. Within seconds, the ruins transformed into a magnificent stronghold with ivy-coated walls, blue-flamed torches, and a ruby chandelier. Everything about the place looked stunningly real.

"We lived in peace for centuries." Agatha's voice echoed off the walls. "And this was the home we built for ourselves . . . me, Filbert, our court jester Gavin, our weaver Mirabelle, and those who harvested our crops, cooked, and tended to our laundry."

The light of the sun opened into human shapes in random poses. Some scrubbed the floors and whistled tunes. A boy and his mother carried a basket of corn and walked it to a wooden table, upon which a crooked-nosed man stood and danced around like a fool. I assumed he was the court jester, clad in crimson-and-white garb and curved footwear with little bells that reminded me of elf shoes.

"*I'm a chicken. A funny chicken. I'm a silly, goofy, funny little chicken,*" he squawked. "*Bakawww!*"

When the boy set his corn on the table, he clapped for the court jester. Agatha and Filbert laughed and brushed tears from their eyes.

But Gavin the Jester wasn't paying attention to anyone except the beautiful young woman in the corner of the room who sat spinning a loom with a sweet half-smile on her face. I looked from Gavin to Mirabelle then back to the jester. When I looked back to the weaver again, something else caught my eye.

Seven precious stones had been set into her loom, and one of them belonged on Tio's neck.

I tugged on Karina's sleeve. "Look."

"I know," Karina whispered.

"Life in the castle was pleasant," Agatha said. "Happy. I might even confess that I had fun most days."

A montage of days played out in fast forward. An orchestra performed at a royal ball while Agatha, Filbert, Gavin, Mirabelle, and the castle dwellers swept each other in circles. A portly man set a large cooked turkey on the table while the residents tucked into their steaming dinner. And Mirabelle wove. Agatha cradled a newborn child in her arms while Filbert watched over her shoulder. A magician stirred powders into wines and served them to the royalty. And Mirabelle wove. Gavin danced his jigs, told his jokes, and wore goofy costumes. Agatha's newborn grew into a dashing young dude and learned to wield a sword. His tutor taught him how to read. And Mirabelle . . . Yeah, she wove.

Over time, the weaver and the jester fell in love. Even being young and naive, I didn't need any more hints than the gleams in their eyes and the evolution of Mirabelle's smile, which progressed from a sly half-smirk to a bright, full-on Cheshire Cat grin. At the end of the montage, Gavin approached her, and they touched hands.

"And this is the moment all our luck went up in flames," Filbert said.

The light changed.

The castle drank in darkness. The door crashed open, and a mountain of a man in silver armor stomped into the room and drove his spear into the ground. He put two big dirty fingers in his mouth and whistled. An army stormed in behind him. The hulking man seemed to stare right through my soul, his gaze like bullets, his body a volcano of muscle ready to unleash its strength.

Villains gonna vill, I guess.

"The man you see before you is Lord Falk." Agatha watched the scene unfold from above, shaking her head with a maternal frown on her face. The mention of the big man's name tied my innards in knots. We were watching Niraya's legend in high definition right now. "And Falk had quite the particular interest in our Mirabelle and her enchanted spindle. Our weaver of worlds and preserver of fortune . . . Oh, what we wouldn't've sacrificed to protect her."

The servants, guards, and royals marched into the foyer, armed and united, and formed a wall of protection around Mirabelle.

Gavin, suited in his own coat of armor that curled and spiked like his jester outfits, took the weaver in his arms and attempted to sneak out through a passage in the walls. "This way, my lady."

"But the wheel." Mirabelle halted, her face pale. "I shan't leave it."

Falk thrust a spear in the air. "Stop them!" he roared, his voice like thunder. "Lady Mirabelle and her gift are mine. My fortune. And if Kesterfall isn't willing to give her over, this land will feel the curse of Falk and perish in my wrath."

Arrows flew.

Spears soared.

Swords stormed, and daggers danced.

Even knowing this wasn't happening in real time, I pressed my back against the wall and found myself trying to dodge the illusions of blades coming at me.

The court magician waved a wand, enchanting the dining hall table, the chairs, the empty suits of armor, and the carpet. They all sprang to life. The rugs bucked like broncos, throwing Falk's army into the walls, where the suits of armor pummeled the soldiers and broke china over their heads. Falk careened through the crowd, swatting his enemies around like bowling pins. Enchanted chairs slid along the floor and glided toward the man with the speed of race cars, but while they had the momentum to knock some of his lackeys over, Falk was simply too large. Every chair that attacked him burst into splinters on impact.

Karina covered her mouth with one hand. Niraya clenched her fists at her sides, and the wolves pounced about the room, attempting to attack the image of Falk, only to soar right through him and become confused.

"This is awful," my sister said. "All this over a wheel."

"The greed," Agatha said. "Unbridled, toxic ambition. It was the darkest day. Our people were slaughtered by Falk's army—the wheel destroyed. Mirabelle did that herself to protect the fate of the people, for in Falk's hands, I cannot imagine what would have become of our land."

*Like a deserted wasteland smothered in ice? I'm sure it could be so much worse.*

I'd been wondering about the dragon when the roof blew off the castle, revealing our flying death lizard in all his villainous glory.

Karina and I huddled closer to Niraya. I tried to remember this wasn't real—that it was just a memory of the past, probably way before we were born—but none of those thoughts eased my fears.

A column of flame burst from Verdoro's throat, engulfing the ghosts of the past in a river of fire. I could almost feel the heat pooling around us. I didn't know if it was the fire or the stress commanding the beads of sweat to gather on my forehead.

"So Verdoro was Falk's dragon?" Niraya breathed. "We've had the legend all wrong. The Wheel of Fortune was a spindle, and Falk wanted it for himself. So he sent the beast to help him conquer the people of Kesterfall and claim the spindle for himself."

"No." Filbert shook his head, the snow trickling off the ends of his hair. "Look closer."

Falk climbed out of a mountain of flame, pulling the fire apart like curtains and emerging unscathed. He unhooked a leather whip from his back and snapped it against the floor. Footsteps shook the mountain from somewhere outside the castle.

The windows burst, and three hairy beasts the color of ash crawled into the castle. They were unlike anything I had ever seen, only vaguely humanoid but close to ten feet tall, smothered in long hair, and hulking like gorillas. The three creatures roared until the chandelier shook, and then they split up. One ran toward Mirabelle and Gavin. Another stood and protected Falk's blind spot. And the third ran for the dragon.

It was the court magician who stepped between the death gorilla and the death lizard, throwing his arms at his sides, almost like he was protecting Verdoro. "He is not to be touched."

That was the last thing I saw. The memory ended mid-scene, reducing our surroundings back to rubble and ice. The ghostly visions of Agatha and Filbert stood in front of us once again, and my heart crashed against my bones. I'd seen enough.

"Falk didn't bring Verdoro to kill you all," Karina said.

Thinking about the magician's protective stance and the yetis running for the dragon, I slowly connected the dots. "He was your dragon, wasn't he? He was on your side. He was . . . good?"

# KARINA

## SNOW SCOURGE

:•———————•:

My mind continuously looped what I'd seen. The snow phantoms had just unleashed visions of war scarring the crumbling walls, forcing me and my brother to watch a castle fall to a madman. As for the dragon . . .

"You were Verdoro's masters," I said.

"His family," Filbert said. "We raised Verdoro from his hatching to the day Lord Falk snuffed out our lives. I know little of what became of our darling dragon, but I should say Falk's snow beasts—his yetis—were monstrous. I also know Mirabelle destroyed her spindle during the battle. I watched the pieces scatter far beyond our reach, some disappearing outside Kesterfall. This, of course, was a blessing. In Falk's hands, those pieces would be our downfall. He claimed one piece before he left the ruins, and then he chained our Mirabelle—our Lady Fortune—to the clouds, where she watches him search for the rest. I know nothing of what became of Gavin."

Charlie shook his head. "Falk killed you . . ."

"Spare us your pity," Filbert said. "Save it for yourselves. Don't think you fool anybody as you stand before me. You are no descendants of Florindale. You're here because one of those pieces brought you here."

"No," I said, not nearly as sure as I sounded. "Impossible. We're here because a train blew up and blasted us clear across the world. I have one of those pieces. It was my uncle's." I ripped the pendant out of my pocket and held it out for the ghosts to observe. "The werewolves tried to take this one from me. But it didn't bring us here."

Agatha swirled around me like a mermaid in water, studying the pendant from different angles. "Hmm, no, this one didn't. But locomotives alone haven't the power to transport you across worlds, youngling. This particular orb did not send you to Kesterfall, but I bet my afterlife another one did. There was a stone made for that, you see. And you encountered it."

I didn't think Agatha was right, but if she were, I would never trust another piece of jewelry.

"Well, there's one thing we do know." Charlie crossed his arms. "Your dragon took my uncle away. We need to know how to get him back. Is there any chance—"

"Our dragon would do no such thing." A blizzard rained over Agatha's body, or lack thereof. She leaned within inches of Charlie's nose, and her cold aura bit at my ears. "Our dragon was good. Gentle. A protector. He wouldn't have swallowed a fly if it flew between his jaws. Either you are mistaken, or you lie. Which offense rings true?"

Oliver and Nella crouched into defensive poses, low growls rumbling from their throats.

Niraya put a hand on Nella's neck, soothing the animal. "Easy, Nella."

I was proud of my brother for holding his ground. He stood tall and spoke confidently. "I know what I saw. We all do. I'm sorry you don't believe me, but your dragon's gone wild. He has my tío. He has Niraya's friend. He might even have other people. We need to make sure they don't get hurt. Only you can help us with that."

Agatha pointed her nose in the air and soared above the ground, hovering in circles around us. "If our baby abducted your friends, they surely deserved it. Verdoro never attacks unless he's threatened."

This wasn't looking good. I had a feeling Agatha wasn't changing her mind. "Well, could it be that he broke free after the battle and sorta went wild after that? All those years without a master, needing to start feeding himself?" The idea actually made me a little sad. "We wouldn't blame him if that's true, and we don't want to hurt him. We just want to rescue our uncle. Please. What if he had Mirabelle? Or someone you loved?"

Filbert grew ten feet, snowflakes storming around his body. "She told you he wouldn't do that. He is gentle, unlike the beasts of Kesterfall. You mean to put a target on his head."

I opened my mouth to argue, but dozens of wanted posters in Florindale would've made a liar out of me. So would Io and every other bounty hunter that set out for the gold and failed.

Niraya threw her arms out to her sides. "We have nothing to hide from you. We've come a long way. We're tired. We're hungry. And when I'm in this mood, I'm not someone to tango with. Know my intention is not to harm your dragon, but I will reach my James one way or another. So once again: How do I get past Verdoro? If I have to put you down a second time for an answer, I welcome the challenge."

"We were deceived by too many of your kind in our lives, pirate, and we will not be fooled by your dishonesty in death. We know our dragon, and if he's truly turned on you, then you—and anyone who travels with you—deserve your fate. You'll never reach him." A haunting grin flashed across Agatha's face, and she lowered her voice. "The yetis will tear you limb from limb. They're everywhere. And you can lay your bones next to mine. We can share a graveyard."

Filbert leaned over the ruined walls of the castle, a palm to his forehead to shield his eyes from the blade of sunlight slicing through the clouds. "They're coming. Agatha, love, let's disappear."

The words were a hot iron to my nerves. *They're coming?* "Who? Who do you mean?"

But I had a feeling I already knew the answer. Because when I looked over the broken walls, two furry dots moved through the trees and beelined their way through the village.

The yetis.

The snow rolled off Agatha's body and fell to the ground in soft clumps, leaving nothing but empty air where she stood as she whispered, "We'll see you soon."

Filbert made a flashier departure, whirling around in a full circle that shook all the ice off him in a single turn.

Panic bubbled in my chest. "Aren't they going to help us?"

"They're gone. Good-for-nothing snow scourge. We'll kill your dragon." Niraya beckoned me and Charlie to follow her, and the wolves leapt the wall and led us deeper into the village. "We won't be able to outrun those things for long, wildlings. Start thinking about how you're going to fight."

"How?" Charlie asked.

I had similar questions. Did Niraya miss the part where the snow beasts tore down an entire castle guarded by the same dragon that destroyed our lives?

"Stay close," Niraya said. "Be quick, and be quiet."

My mind raced as Niraya pulled us deeper into the village, an increasingly complex labyrinth of towers, statues, stairs, tunnels, bridges, and ruins, all half-buried in thick layers of snow. A hand-painted sign forbade passerby from fishing or swimming in a lake I guessed we were probably sliding on right now.

Beside the frozen lake, a glistening palace rose from the icy hills, as barren as every other building in the village, but much grander and promising a greater chance of hiding from the yetis. Niraya must've had the same idea, because she sprinted for the temple, kicked the doors open, and waved me and Charlie in front of her.

"In here. Hurry."

We ran inside, daunted by stairs that spiraled up several floors. Sunlight cut in through the broken windows. Niraya threw the doors shut, and we barricaded the entrance with a stone statue of a dwarfish figure who looked a lot like Zid. We raced up the stairs without a word.

Haunting moans and growls penetrated the walls. I didn't even want to imagine what a yeti could do if it got its claws on us. What kind of senses did a yeti have, and could it sniff us out even if we found a decent hiding spot? The werewolves had been scary enough, but I imagined these snow beasts had to be even worse. Somewhere deep down, Io had a shred of humanity. The things I saw in Filbert's vision were driven by primitive instinct.

More disturbing: In that same vision, Lord Falk was commanding the yetis. Was it possible after all these years that Lord Falk was still alive, hunting pendants and commanding beasts to attack anyone who stood in his way?

*No. It's a myth from many years ago. Lord Falk isn't alive, and nobody is commanding monsters. It's just us versus them, and after we rescue our uncle, it can just be us again.*

At the top of the stairs, we pushed through a set of golden doors that revealed a bedroom fit for a king.

My bones felt like iron, begging me to sink into the shining pool of satin in the center of the room, though the film of dust told me the canopy bed hadn't been touched in years. Neither had the large ivory mirror on the wall, the wide-brimmed leather hat hanging on the door, the boots by the bed, the velvet ottoman, or the ornate wooden chest tucked in the corner. The room was everything I wanted right now and everything we didn't have time for.

Niraya put a hand to her throat, catching her breath. "Help . . . help me move the bed. We need to block the beasts."

We hadn't even touched the bed when the doors thundered open downstairs, and stone crackled.

A feral roar trumpeted from the stairwell.

My heart leapt into my throat. "How did they find us so fast? I don't understand."

Niraya bared her teeth. "Grab a weapon. Anything will do. Stars above, I hate this island."

I grabbed the dagger I'd snatched from the *Red Hood*, while Niraya went straight for a crossbow in the corner of the room. Charlie didn't grab anything but walked straight up to the ivory mirror and ran his hands along the wall behind it.

"Charlie?" I said. "Not the time to admire the walls."

"Haven't you ever watched *Scooby Doo*? There's a door here," Charlie said. "You can see the cracks. This temple was built into the mountain. Maybe there's a tunnel out of here that can get us closer to Tio."

"Or maybe," Niraya said, "it'll throw us in the path of more wretched sasquatches."

"We're already in their path." Charlie banged on the wall a few times, loosening dust and exposing cracks behind the mirror. "There's gotta be a switch somewhere."

Footsteps boomed outside the door, and a guttural roar shook the walls. I tightened my grip on the dagger, my heart pounding faster than ever. "No. We can't waste time rubbing the walls. They're closing in on us."

And then the golden doors burst open.

# DIEGO

MY
SERIES FINALE

·:•———•:·

This adventure was going to be the end of me. It was official.

I vowed to reach the shipwreck no matter what, but under all confidence and charisma I put on for the cameras, I prepared for the possibility that James's flares might not even exist, that they'd malfunctioned when the ship crashed, or perhaps the most heartbreaking possibility: no one would even see our distress signal. Who would choose to make their home on this crazy island?

Then again, by a stroke of good luck, I'd found some good companions for the ride. James and Evan proved to be decent company. Could there be other people out here, stranded in the dragon's vicinity and waiting for someone to get them out, or at least someone to talk to?

"Hey, Diego," Evan said. "How does this compare to your other adventures? Everest? Sonora? Borneo? Is this tougher?"

I had to smile. Evan really was a loyal fan. He'd been rattling off location names and various tips he'd learned from the show ever since he arrived, a habit that made James roll his eyes and mumble something about mangy brownnosers. But I actually found it all flattering. I told him this was infinitely scarier, that it wasn't every day I'm dropped somewhere and expected to fight off a flying, fire-breathing monster.

"Kid stuff," James scoffed. "You wouldn't last one day in the Order, my friend."

He mumbled a lot about his Order, a group of heroes who ran around beating up evil *brujas* and dispelling curses, knocking evil kings off their thrones, or scientists who let toxic ambition corrupt their minds . . . "We were quite a team back in the day. Blasted dragon would've been on the ground with its head cut off like that." James snapped his fingers for emphasis. "Never thought I'd be down here running from one, babysitting two blubbering idiots."

Like we were enjoying this any more than he was.

But I felt for the guy. He told me a little more about Niraya. It turns out they'd been on his vessel together when the dragon plucked it out of the water. She and the rest of his crew opted to jump ship before they soared too high. James, apparently, cared too much about the boat to abandon it. So the dragon carried the pirate away while the crew and the poor woman who loved him swam to safety. He tells this story like he's the brave one, but really, I think this Niraya was the smart one.

Evan asked us what we're going to do when this was all over. A nice thought. The idea that there's life after this.

All James wanted was "a quiet life far from bratty children, snobby rulers, and dragons." He made sure we knew it, stomping his foot as he told us. "When we get out of here, I'm taking Niraya and we're moving to the New World. You don't have these problems over there."

I explained that yes, we did have to deal with terrible leaders and bratty children. And we may not have had dragons, but he'd never seen a desert scorpion. Our world wasn't perfect. That was part of the beauty of it all.

"What about you, Diego?" Evan asked. "Will you make more shows? You could do a spin-off about life in the wild in fairy-tale land. Oh man, imagine your ratings, the money you'd make, the ladies that would line up at your door . . ."

Except I didn't care about any of that. If I did get home, I might even call it all quits. Move back to Arizona to be closer to Karina and Charlie, settle down and write a book, start traveling to experience culture instead of thrills. Maybe this was a sign for me to slow down and enjoy life. Assuming I got to keep living it outside this jungle.

Evan was the opposite. "Surviving a train crash and exploring uncharted territory with Diego Rosas? I feel infinite right now. What am I not gonna do when I get home?" He pumped a fist in the air.

"Hey, Devon," James said. "How much longer 'til we reach my ship?"

In response, a deafening screech pierced the air, and wind rattled the trees from their leaves to their roots. My hair fluttered like I'd been caught in a storm, and the sound raised the goose bumps on my arms. A flash of emerald-gold glided above the canopy.

On instinct, I dove to the ground and rolled into a hollow pocket of earth tucked beneath a tree. "Get down."

James tumbled in next to me. "A thousand curses."

Evan clapped a hand to his forehead and gawked at the treetops. "Whoa. The dragon came back."

"Evan," I growled. "Get—down. Get over here."

But it was like he'd been put under a trance. He didn't move. He just stared. "Awesome . . ."

I had to climb back out and tug on his collar to get him to move. I tore through his shirt a little but finally managed to snatch his attention as we ducked back into the hollow.

"Hey, you listen to me from now on." I jabbed his shoulder with a finger.

James massaged the space between his eyebrows while Evan caught his breath.

"I'm sorry, guys," Evan said.

I put a finger to my lips.

The dragon stopped and hovered in place, treading air like a hummingbird. Again, I could see the eyes, the individual scales on its throat . . . the talons. At least it had come back empty-handed. Unless it ate its prey along the way. The beast scanned the ground like a cat prowls for mice, gaze sweeping from side to side. Was it looking for me? Coming back to finish the job? I pressed my finger tighter to my lips and gave Evan a warning glare. *Don't. Move. A muscle.*

An enormous hairy spider dropped from the trees, detached the thread of silk from its body, and scuttled into the distance. Seven more followed, looking like a tribe of freak acrobats rehearsing for a performance in Hell. They tied my stomach in knots. I'd seen some weird things in Australia, but this island had them all beat.

"Don't let the demon bug army come over here," James said. "Let the dragon take me instead. I surrender!"

"Will you hush?" I mouthed.

The ogres came next, stampeding full-speed through the jungle in a symphony of grunts, battle cries, and heavy footsteps. Their feet pounded within inches of the hollow, kicking gobs of dirt into my face with their long, unclipped toenails. I turned away and threw my arm over my eyes. A worm wriggled its way up my neck, and I waited until the crowd of ogres passed before I flicked the squirming larva off my skin.

Everything was trying to get away from the dragon. Beast versus the jungle.

A bird with crimson feathers soared above the canopy and taunted the monster, circling the dragon with a series of swoops and caws. I thought of those old *Tom and Jerry* cartoons where the mouse messes with the cat, because the bird was exponentially smaller and less equipped to fight. The dragon whipped at the air with his tail and tried to snatch the bird out of the sky, but the smaller creature was quick and wily. It zigzagged around and even pecked the dragon on the nose. I had to admit it was a funny sight, but I almost wished the bird would stop.

*You're gonna make it angry. Don't get cocky.*

Sure enough, the bird burst into flames a few seconds later.

I gasped, covering my mouth and hoping the beast didn't hear me. I hadn't even seen the dragon spit fire. "How did . . . how did that . . ."

"It's what they do, mate." James nudged me with his elbow. "You never saw a phoenix before, did you? The little one had the last word. And he'll be back, too."

I watched the ashes drift from the sky to the ground, like a thin, hot snowfall.

Angry and rabid, the dragon curled into a ball, spit a column of flame into the air, then poked his head into the canopy, scanning the ground.

I forced myself to freeze. *We are statues. We are rocks. We're made of stone.* The dragon grunted and snorted, its hot breath close enough to ruffle my shirt, and I was positive we'd already been spotted. *Just a matter of seconds now.*

The dragon dipped deeper, and with another snap and a sickening crunch, he snatched an ogre off the ground and crushed it in his jaws.

James turned away from us and vomited.

Evan shook his head slowly, his mouth hanging open.

"Gross," he whispered.

The vomit or the dragon's meal? Either way, understatement of the year.

A thought came to me: the dragon was distracted. It took a lot of mental power to tune out the sounds, the grinding of bones and cracking of cartilage. Once James collected himself, I pointed in the direction we'd been running, my whispers feather-light. "We need that flare. This is our chance to run."

"And follow the demon bugs and troll things?" James's voice was raspy with bile.

"Pick your poison," I said. "This is not getting any better if we stay here. You wanna see your girlfriend again? Then help me."

Evan nodded. "I'm with you, Diego."

Flames swallowed a patch of trees near the hollow as the beast roared, the heat licking my face. Through the warped, hot air, more creatures charged through the jungle and scattered in various directions before the dragon rose above the canopy, flapped his wings, and soared back toward his peak beyond the jungle.

I leapt out of the hollow, reached for Evan's and James's hands, and pulled them out of the ground, masking my face with my shirt. Smoke billowed from the trees and fire danced from trunk to trunk, painting the emerald jungle with flames.

"It's trying to smoke us out. This jungle's coming down on us with or without that flare," I said. But there was a silver lining. "That smoke's bound to grab someone's attention. Let's see if we can't hold it. Evan, get us to that ship."

We sprinted, leapt, and climbed, racing against the fire. If I glanced up for even a second, I could make out the snow drifting from the sky, melting when it touched the treetops. For a second, the image mesmerized me, causing me to trip on a wild root.

My elbows hit the mud, bringing me face to face with a monstrous spider barreling toward me from the side.

"Humans in Kesterfall," a gravelly voice mused. "We haven't tasted meat so sweet in ages." The spider's pincers clicked in such a rhythm that I realized the beast was speaking.

I hated this place.

I screamed something I'd never be allowed to say on my show, rolled like a log, and kicked out, my stomach heaving when my leg brushed against something furry.

"Back off." Evan swung a tree branch at the spider's abdomen.

The spider rolled into a ball and careened toward the fire, igniting in a cocoon of orange flame.

Evan grabbed my hand, both of us plastered in sweat. "Come on. We're almost there."

"I see it." James tore ahead of us.

Relief nearly brought me to my knees when the hulking structure of jagged wood appeared in front of us. A mermaid figurehead carved in polished cedar towered over the jungle like a queen, trident in her hands and crown upon her head. A smug smile breached her lips. If only she were real so she could zap me back home.

But as Evan warned, something had beaten us to the shipwreck. A web hung between the figurehead and a palm tree, where two more spiders clung to each other and spun an unseen creature into a silky wrap. I noted where the ship had cracked into three pieces. The mermaid's section was the biggest, whereas the middle and back lay with splinters face-up, clawing at the sky. Ogres climbed the barnacle-crusted bottom and into the dark shelter.

James sank to his knees and groaned, as if he were finally coming to terms with a truth he'd been avoiding. "My ship . . . my lovely, aquatic home. Ruined."

"We're doomed, right?" I asked. "Which piece is your flare in?"

"Could be any. Could be on the ground somewhere, much like the dark fragments of my heart right now." He shook a fist at the swarm of monsters. "Any final ideas, Diego Rosas?"

I shook my head. "I really hoped that would be you. What would your Order do?"

"Distract," James said. "No sense having all three of us stampede into a fire. It's mindless suicide. I suggest one of us draw the beasts away from the shipwreck then send the other two in to retrieve the flare. It's the most logical plan."

I hated to admit it, but the pirate was right. Someone had to lure the ogres and spiders away, because there was no chance of rushing in and out of their mobs alive. The three of us couldn't take on a whole army of beasts by ourselves. Unfortunately, luring the monsters away also had its own share of complications. The act would be certain death for whoever volunteered.

Evan raised his hand. "I'll draw the things away if you want. I'm pretty fast, so I doubt they'll catch me. I ran track in high school."

"Absolutely not," I said. "If I leave you alone and those things catch you, I'll . . . I don't know. It's just off the table, all right? I'm not letting you be the bait. James, you go."

The pirate sneered. "I've been on this island longer than both of you. I've been through enough. And in case you missed it, that's my ship. I should be the one to go inside and retrieve the flare. I won't have the two of you poking about my quarters. Last thing I need is you raiding my breeches." Like we wanted to. "What about you, Diego? Aren't you the hero where you're from? What's stopping you from volunteering?"

I turned away and stared into the orange glow. We probably only had a few more hours before the fire swallowed the ship. I shut my eyes and made peace with the fact that I was going to be the bait, and it wasn't going to end well. Even being reasonably fit, I wasn't an Olympian. There was no way I'd be fast enough to outrun those freak spiders or tough enough to take a beating from the dirty ogres cluttering the jungle. The only thing I could do was run like heck and hope it would buy Evan and James enough time to call for rescue.

I thought of the night the train blew past my house with its own orange glow and its monstrous moans, how it frightened little Karina and Carlos. How I promised them they had nothing to worry about, that I'd always be there for them, and that the dragon would never hurt them. I'd failed them on all counts. How would they remember me?

"I'll do it." My voice went down an octave. "I volunteer."

To my surprise, the scowl melted off James's face, and I thought I saw sadness there. The pirate walked over, looked me in the eye, and pulled me into a tight hug. "Lad, of all the people I could've been stranded with, by Lady Fortune's grace, I got a true warrior. What a fine addition to the Order you might've been." He pulled away and clapped his hand on my shoulder. "Given time, we might have even been friends."

I managed a smile. "Yeah. At least frenemies, I'm sure."

Evan stood with his hands in his pockets and the saddest look on his face, like a child that was about to part with his favorite stuffed animal. He didn't say a word; he just looked at the ground.

"But give me fifteen minutes," I said. "Fifteen, then you can sweep the ship. I have one last thing I need to do."

In the time I was given, I took the notebook from my backpack and scribbled my parting words.

Maybe one day, someone else would find my notebook. I hoped if I never came back to my family from off the beaten path, my *sobrinos* would still know I cared.

# CHARLIE

### WE PLAY
### *TEMPLE RUN*

·◆——◆·

There was a reason the legend of La Llorona stuck with me all those years: because we knew exactly when she was nearby. Any time a monsoon came to Tucson and the wind was powerful enough to throw the screen door open, my mom made sure we knew it wasn't really the wind. La Llorona liked to open doors. "She's heeere . . . Better go hide."

Yeah, Mom knew how to keep us in line.

I thought I'd outgrown that story's effects, but when the golden temple doors opened, all that fear came rushing back. Not because I feared the crazy crying ghost lady, but because I feared the snow phantoms in the mountains—and the yetis.

Niraya aimed her crossbow at the entrance.

The hairiest thing I'd ever seen stood at the door, and Karina and I both screamed bloody murder. "Yeti!"

Only our intruder wasn't really a yeti. It was a burly man with an amazing Jesus beard. He couldn't really blame us. We were conditioned to expect the worst, until we recognized the sweaty man in front of us.

My cheeks flushed. "Zid?"

"Shut the doors," the dwarf commanded. We obeyed and threw all our weight against the doors while Zid caught his breath. He carried two rusty swords crossed behind his back and a leather bag strapped over them.

He reached into his pocket and tossed Karina a vial of thick gold liquid. "Heard about your injury from Lady Constance. She sent this for you for being pure of heart. That pendant merely suppresses the curse until the wearer removes the charm. Essence of sunlight is what you want. Cheers."

Karina caught the vial, forced the drink down her throat, and puckered her face when she finished. "Thank you, Zid."

Niraya gripped the dwarf by his shoulder. "What are you doing here?"

"Pleased to see you, too, Captain Storm. Come now, that's the first thing you're going to ask me when I just saved this girl's life and there are yetis marching through this temple?" Zid shook his head. "Surely you didn't think I'd let you all go chasing dragons alone?"

Niraya jerked her hand away, her lips pursed into a thin line. "Yes. For a while there, I did."

Nella growled at Zid, and I put a hand on her neck to calm her down. "It's okay, girl."

Zid took a breath. "Okay, I almost did. But the king wouldn't have it. He sent me straight away and asked that I aid you. I'm still convinced the best way to do that is to change your mind." He pointed out the window, where the dark mountain loomed. We'd been running for so long that I hadn't stopped to consider how close we were. "I implore you. We have time to turn around. You cannot hope to survive what's in there. Don't you see? If I can't tame a dragon, then it's far too dangerous to approach. It's all madness."

Niraya pounded a fist on the dusty writing desk. "You don't get it, Zid. What's madness is that you led the yetis right to us." Grunts and roars poured in from behind the door. "We could have been rid of those beasts if somebody else hadn't been following us."

Zid grew two inches taller when he stood on his tiptoes, still having to look up at Niraya as he shook his fist. "I'm about to save your life. And the younglings to boot. Come home, Captain Storm. I'll see to it that you're well-fed."

"I'm not leaving him again." Niraya massaged her temples. "You don't get to swoop in and pluck me off the trail when I'm this close. I deserve more respect than that, and so do these kids."

Zid leaned in closer. "But the king—"

"Tell the king to go carve something, for all I care. If he really wants to help, he'll come out here and lend a hand. But we don't need him."

"The king has a thousand things to do, so it's my duty to talk reason into your tiny minds," Zid said. "What have you seen in Kesterfall? Werewolves, yetis, and apparitions. Not a single human soul walking around. You think you'll be the first to survive?"

The tension in the room was thick enough to bounce on. I dropped my hand to my pocket then remembered the kraken ate my phone. Gone were the days where I could pretend to text people or check the time during awkward situations. Stupid Hell Squid.

So I stepped in. "We care enough about the people we love that we're willing to take a risk. If we turn into ghosts, at least we died trying."

"Let's see if your optimism lasts." Zid stepped away from the door, unstrapped the swords at his back, and then held one out to me. "You'll want something to defend yourself. That's no teddy bear on the other side of the door."

In the reflection of the blades, I noticed my hair was all wild and crazy, and thin patches of dirt masked my cheeks, tracing a map of all the struggles I'd had since the Fernweh Express.

The sword was cool to look at with its crisscrossing leather straps and a polished stone in the handle, but my attention was at the rusty tip. I took a step back. "Whoa, I can't take that. I don't know how to use one of these things."

"Insert sharp end into bad things and remove." Zid thrust the handle into my palm and closed my fingers. "Repeat as needed."

I was surprised by how light the blade was, enough that I could comfortably swing it with one hand and lift it again without much strain. Maybe that was why Zid carried two. But I still felt weird about holding it.

"Stop looking at it like that," Zid said. "You're not going to break it."

"It's not the sword I'm worried about."

I was worried about me, obviously.

But I had bigger problems. Our yetis had found us.

A shaggy white monster with eyes like coal burst through the door, howling like the wind. If I stood on Karina's shoulders, I may have been eye-to-eye with the yeti. If Karina and I stood shoulder-to-shoulder, we may have been as wide as the beast. But alas, Karina, Niraya, Zid, and I were all much punier than the hulking creature that towered into the chamber.

Nella and Oliver sprang into action right away, clawing at the yeti's leg. The monster bent down, swiped, and sent both mother and pup flying into the wall where they yelped in pain and lay injured in a pile.

Tightening my fists, I brandished the sword and leapt forward with a jab.

Zid did the same with his own blade, but stabbing the yeti was like trying to cut through iron. The blade wouldn't give. The impact jolted my elbow, and the sword recoiled against the creature's fur.

The yeti pounded its chest like a gorilla, leaned forward with a deep roar, and the next thing I knew, I was five feet off the ground and struggling to escape from the monster's hands around my ribs. A vile scent assaulted my nostrils, and I saw the end of the world in the yeti's eyes, darker and hollower than the deepest cavern. The monster pinned my arms to my sides, and all I could do was kick out and squirm.

Karina screamed my name.

A hard *kathunk* sounded from behind me, and a silver bolt hit the yeti's chest.

The beast threw its head back, and after a mighty roar that shook the ceiling, the yeti raised me above its head and tossed me aside like a toy. Pain exploded through my bones, and something pulsed in my arm. I didn't hear anything crack, but darkness took my vision for a few seconds. When it faded, two more monsters entered the room, and one of them barreled straight toward me.

"Get off our land." A gust of snow swirled into the room and gathered in the shape of an elderly man, stepping in the path between me and the yeti. The snow ghost spread his arms, holding a staff in a sort of warning pose.

The yeti stopped, apparently confused by the apparition. But after a brief pause, the monster lunged and swiped the ghost out of the air. In that short pocket of time, my sister climbed up on the bed and threw herself onto the yeti's back, dagger in hand. She hooked her arms around the beast's neck, causing it to spin around and squirm with rage.

Meanwhile, Niraya and Zid had engaged the other two beasts. Zid ran around whacking the monsters with his blade, whereas Niraya kept her distance and furiously cycled bolts out of the crossbow, loading and shooting and loading again.

Sitting on the floor like that with a weapon that didn't seem to do any good, I was running out of options. I did a quick scan of my surroundings. Within a few feet of me there were three choices: a pair of boots, a velvet ottoman, and a jar of creamy-white powder I guessed was meant for wigs or makeup in this world.

"Close your eyes, Rina," I said. I picked up the jar, unscrewed the lid, and then hurled a scoop of white powder at the yeti's face, coating its dark, beady eyes. It flailed around and rubbed its face, squirming until Karina slid off its fur and gave it a hard shove. While she took a step back and mopped the powder from her eyelids, the yeti stumbled, and for a second, I thought it would fall out the window and leave us alone. That certainly didn't happen, but in its stumble, it kicked one of the empty boots over, and a shining lavender beetle flew out of the shaft. The bug zipped around the air, steam emerging from the wings, until it latched onto the yeti's arm.

The bug scuttled all around the yeti's body, and everywhere the beetle stepped, tiny red embers appeared and oozed wisps of smoke. When the yeti had enough and finally squashed the poor bug, its shell burst into flames and ignited the yeti's fur.

I realized two things. First, Uncle Diego was right about checking his boots for bugs, and I would never ignore that advice again. Second, apparently yetis are super flammable, because about a minute after our beast crushed the bug, we had an enormous shaggy fireball waddling around the room and igniting everything it touched, including one of the other snow monsters. This was a problem.

Smoke clouded the room, and heat welded the door shut.

Here's a commercial break quiz for Tio's next episode, or better yet, for the first episode of *The Adventures of Charlie and Rina*: You're sealed in the penthouse of an ancient temple with three other people, two wolves, and three abominable snowmen, two of which are pretending to be birthday candles. What do you do?

Well, I was always taught to keep low when there's a fire. Crouch down, stay below the smoke, and feel the doors with the back of a hand. So I started to crawl, but considering there were ten-foot beasts after us, I had to crawl on turbo speed, which wasn't fun for knees or throbbing arms, which were already forming bruises.

"We have to jump out the window," Niraya cried.

Maybe she was a ninja who knew how to land on her feet unharmed from a five-story drop, but I definitely wasn't, so I wasn't taking Niraya's advice. She picked up the velvet ottoman and hurled it out the window, shattering the glass and releasing some of the smoke around us.

And in my unique position—being the guy on the floor—I finally saw the ottoman's glorious purpose. Sure, somebody might have enjoyed sitting on it or propping their feet up, but when Niraya lifted it, a black button sat in the middle of the floor. It was like something out of an old mystery, where the secret lever opens a hidden passage from the lounge to the conservatory. Heck, if I were crazy rich and living in a haunted mountain, I'd install hideaways in every single room of my ritzy palace.

I had to press the button.

I smacked it with my entire fist, which royally hurt my arm, but as I'd hoped, the wall behind the mirror slid up to reveal a dark passage into the tunnel through the hill.

"I told you all." I grabbed Zid's sword and scrambled for the hole in the wall. "Come on."

Niraya was already halfway out the window, but Zid grabbed her leg and pulled her back into the room. "You're not a cat, Storm. The fall is suicide. You come with us."

Nella and Oliver limped at my heels. Karina grabbed her dagger and sprinted after me. The burning yetis didn't follow, but the healthy one did.

So that left four of us, two wolves, and one abominable snowman clamoring after us in a dark tunnel like a rabid bear. Every few steps, Niraya would whirl around and fire a bolt from her crossbow. I had no such bravery, functional weapon, or hand-eye coordination. I only knew I planned to survive another day, and that's what kept me moving.

The tunnel's steep decline and the adrenaline in my body propelled me forward. I thought of what Niraya had said earlier: "You'd be surprised what you can do when you have no other choice." Like run when every inch of my body wanted to crumble and give up. I had this weird sense we would be coming to the end of our journey pretty soon. Whether that meant we were going to free Tio or become yeti kibble, I had no idea, but I saw no third option.

All along the tunnel, more snow ghosts materialized in our path and whispered through the winds. Some encouraged us, but I think most of them were mad. After all, we left a burning ancient palace behind us, and the damage was bound to disturb some spirits.

When the end of the tunnel opened into view, the slope steepened, and I had to take smaller steps. Staying upright was hard on my calves.

Niraya fell, hit her chin, and rolled onto the snowy ground of the outside world. We'd come to the end, not only of the tunnel, but the entire village, finishing in a steep cliff with a vertical drop.

Karina helped Niraya to her feet while Zid and I faced the incoming yeti. Behind the monster and not too far above us, the temple glowed orange, and melting snow and falling debris rolled down the hill.

Zid and I were prepared to smack the white demon with our swords for all they were worth, but we didn't have to. As soon as the monster charged out of the tunnel, a boatload of snow rolled off the hill like an avalanche, sealing the passageway behind us and burying the hairy jerk in a mountain of ice.

I crouched down and caught my breath.

Five seconds too late, and that could've been us packed under the slush.

Thank you, Lady Fortune?

Just to be sure the yeti would stay down, I drove Zid's sword into the fallen snow and left it there.

"That was a treat," Zid said.

Niraya dusted the snow off herself and pointed to the dark mountain. "We're nearly there. We need to keep moving."

There was one big problem, though: move where?

The only way forward was down. As in jumping. This was the edge of a near-vertical drop that led into a jungle, the only thing left that separated us from Tio. We must've spent five minutes looking for an easier way down, but it wasn't going to happen. We were basically looking into a giant cauldron with a creepy, dark mountain poking straight out of the center.

I finally understood how defeated we were. We'd never have what it took to finish the quest.

Now here was the final nail in the coffin.

While I stared out at the mountain, another phantom hovered up from the jungle, this time made of dirt and leaves. At first, it didn't look like much, but as it climbed, it accumulated vines and the form became stronger. It took its time ascending, looking around like it was admiring the view until it reached our level.

And then I realized I had seen the face before. Looking at it this way made my blood turn cold.

"Karina," I whispered. "Is that . . ."

I didn't have to finish my sentence. Karina already knew what I was thinking. She saw it, too, and she knew the face as well as I did. We'd known it for years.

It was Uncle Diego, and I was already screaming his name.

# KARINA

## UNCLE DIEGO'S FAREWELL

·—•—·

Seeing the ghost of Uncle Diego shred my heart into tiny grains of sand, lit them all on fire, and then crushed the ashes with a steamroller. I was devastated. My knees were weak, my stomach was hard, and my throat was tight. The worst had happened.

We were too late. We didn't save him.

"No." I rushed and put my arms out to hug my uncle, but my body passed straight through him. The snow melted on my chest, and his ghostly form showed up again behind me. "Uncle Diego, no. No. It's not true!"

I vaguely heard Niraya and Zid speaking behind me, but I tuned them out. Only one voice mattered.

"Rina. Charlie," Uncle Diego said, "it's time for you to turn around. You're already too late. You need to go home."

Tears assaulted my eyes, and my own breath choked me. "We tried, Uncle D. We were so close."

"I didn't want you to come." Uncle Diego's voice boomed much harsher and deeper than I had ever heard it before. "Turn back."

"What happened, Tío?" Charlie asked.

The snow phantom shrugged. "Nature won. I always knew I couldn't keep this going forever."

"Yes, you could have," I said. He was invincible. Immortal, even. There was no situation Diego Rosas wasn't equipped to handle. That's why we'd come all this way because deep down we knew he'd still be there when we arrived.

I sat down and buried my head in my hands, a headache frying my brain.

Niraya approached Uncle Diego, her hands clasped at her waist. "Mr. Rosas, I'm Captain Niraya Storm. I'm sorry to hear about your passing, sir," she said with a slight bow. "I hope it was painless and quick, and my heart breaks on behalf of these younglings. They spoke most highly of you. I only want to ask you one question. Was—was there another man with you when it happened? A man named James?"

I lifted my head, my vision blurred by tears. But I could see Niraya grasping for hope. And I knew no matter how crushed I was, I wanted her to have that hope. She was my friend. Even if Charlie and I had already lost our happy ending, Niraya deserved hers.

"I'm sorry," Uncle Diego said. "Turn around. Go home. Goodbye."

The snowflakes disappeared, and Uncle Diego blew away.

Gone forever, just like that.

Niraya crumbled to her knees.

I wanted to do the same, but I'd gone numb inside. My uncle would never tell somebody to shy away from a goal. Ever. He always talked about how people would try to talk him out of his adventures, out of climbing Everest, out of crossing the Sahara, out of doing this or that. *Turn back, Diego.* Those were his least favorite words. How could they have been his last ones? Did I even know him at all?

I crossed my arms, my teeth clenched, and my nostrils flaring. I'd gone so numb it took me forever to notice the orange glow in the jungle below. Fire was blooming, spitting red embers into the sky as further proof of our loss.

Zid put a hand on my back. "Miss Karina, I can only imagine . . . All that's happened to you and your brother since your arrival is an utter tragedy. It's madness."

"Yes, it has been," I said coldly. "I've wanted to go home for a while. I was in this for my uncle, and now I just saw him tell me to give up."

"You never should have been caught in the dragon's rampage," Zid said. "I cannot grieve hard enough for you, or for Captain Storm. If there's any way that I can ease your pain, tell me what I can do. Do you want gold? Do you want a monument for your uncle in Florindale?

I shall make arrangements with the king for whatever you need."

The offer gnawed at my pride. What good would gold do? What could Zid share that would fill this hole in our hearts? As for a monument, would Uncle Diego have wanted that? I wasn't sure I knew him quite well enough to say.

"Send us home, man," Charlie said. "We're done with this evil place. I was eaten. We've been attacked by one monster after another. My tío's gone. He wouldn't want his statue here, and neither do we."

The pain and the lack of warmth in my brother's voice broke my heart into even tinier pieces, like black sand. I could barely look him in the eye. "I think I agree," I said. "Just tell the king we want to go home now."

Zid bowed and clasped his hands. "The offer was always there. And I deem it the wisest decision you could have made. Let's get you home."

Hearing him acknowledge our wishes confirmed everything. Our uncle was gone, the dragon had won, and we were giving up. We were going home one man short, and we would have to explain everything to our mom. But of course, we'd never be able to prove anything, and Diego Rosas was a household name, so the tabloids would paint our faces on every newsstand. He'd be declared missing, and we'd be interrogated. A lie might send us to juvie. The truth would send us to a mental facility. There was no winning. Lady Fortune's last bit of luck for us had run dry.

Zid nodded at Niraya, whose eyes were red and wet. "Come along, Niraya. We'll return to Florindale and feast in honor of Captain James. We'll sing shanties and light fireworks and—"

*Pop-ffft! Boom!*

I snapped my attention toward a commotion in the jungle. A pink star shot up in the air, pulsing like fire, and then it exploded into seven pieces and arched back toward the ground in an umbrella of black smoke.

I gasped. "An emergency flare."

"Someone's still out there," Charlie said.

Niraya pushed past us, a gleam returning to her eyes. "It's James. He's still alive. I know it."

Zid shook his head. "I must insist that we turn back. I'm terribly sorry, but it's too late."

"Somebody needs help down there," I said. "If that were you, would you go through all that trouble to send up a flare and hope somebody would ignore it? Who else would see it?"

"We have to help," Charlie said. "It's what our uncle would've done."

Niraya picked up her crossbow. "Zid, did the king really send you to help us? If so, now's your chance."

Zid mopped his forehead and growled.

One of my favorite things about Niraya Storm was that she didn't tell me and Charlie we could turn back, or that we "didn't have to do this." Of course we didn't, and we knew we could've turned back if we wanted to. But we wouldn't have accepted such an offer if she made one, and she knew that. She was our friend, and even if we weren't going to find Uncle Diego at the bottom, we were going to do something that would make him proud.

This was in our blood.

I made a mental note of where the flare went off. Could we trace it back to the right place?

Charlie threw an arm around my shoulder. In the scariest moment of my life, my brother was there. We were together.

"Hey wildlings," Niraya said. "Wanna go slay a dragon? I'll race you there."

Without waiting for our answer, she took a deep breath and jumped.

# PART FIVE

HERE
THERE BE
DRAGONS

# KARINA

## WILD
## ONES

·◆———◆·

It was all I could do to stop screaming when Niraya took the plunge, hitting an icy slope and rocketing down into the dark jungle of the dragon's land. I could've sworn I heard her laugh like a maniac when she started to slide, but when she disappeared, silence followed.

Zid took one look at me and Charlie. "She's going to get there first. You lost the race."

Charlie tugged at his hair, breathing wildly like he needed a paper bag.

"I need a minute," I said.

"You know the best way to get over your fear, younglings?" Zid said.

I was immediately suspicious of the grin on his face.

Zid charged me, scooped me in his impossibly strong arms, and my heart rushed to meet my stomach as he tossed me over the edge. "You take the plunge, m'dear."

The scream I'd been suppressing burst from my lungs as I hit the slope, and the incline carried me down the mountain with frightening momentum.

Charlie's scream came next, but once he hit the slope, it morphed from a cry of terror to a "Geronimooo!" Somewhere above me, the wolves were yelping, too. I hoped they followed.

"Right behind you," Zid boomed. "Close your eyes if it helps you feel better."

I squeezed my eyelids shut, but more because the wind was like knives on my face. My eyeballs took the worst of it, a rush of bone-dry air colder than the Arctic Circle. Bits of snow frosted the tips of my hair as I careened faster and faster down the slope.

After a certain point, the wind roared like a highway in my ears. Even Zid's voice didn't reach me anymore. We were on a roller coaster to the underworld.

I opened my eyes and peeked a few times, enduring the sting of the wind as I took in fragments of ice tunnels, open sky, and finally, the approaching ground. I tucked my chin to my chest and braced for a hard stop. The impact was more like the awkward jolt of someone braking too hard in a car, throwing my upper body forward and propelling me head-over-heels until I lay face-down in a blanket of mud, my backpack thrown over my head. My breath escaped me, and my face stung like I'd been slapped. I pushed myself to my knees, muscles protesting every move, and blinked until the blur cleared away from my vision.

I found my brother sitting cross-legged in the mud and massaging his shoulder, his backpack a few feet away from him.

Zid tumbled in next, inadvertently head-butting me in the back of the knee and forcing me down again before he erupted in a fit of grumbles and complaints. "A thousand curses on this place! *Harumph.*"

I considered my surroundings. A frozen river circled the area, a mass of frosty white and electric blue only loosely distinguishable from the rest of the ground. If I squinted, I could make out schools of little red fish and strange plant life frozen in time beneath the surface.

The mountain peak towered over us, a dark landform coated in ice.

And in the center of the ring, a massive rainforest stood against the snow, untouched by the crazy weather. I imagined a thin boundary around the trees. The ice built up around the ring and grazed the circle, but everything inside was dry and untouched.

Except for the smoke pouring from the center and the orange glow that lit up the sky.

"Rina," Charlie breathed. "The fire. That's where the flare went up. The death lizard's in there with someone who needs our help. Come on."

I hooked my fingers in Charlie's sleeve. "Wait, please think for a second. We run into the jungle, we find Verdoro, and then what do we do? We don't know how to kill the dragon."

"We don't have to. This isn't a murder mission. It's a rescue."

"So how do we get out of here once we save whoever's down here?" I gestured to where we'd come from. "We can't climb that."

Suddenly I realized what a terrible idea all of this was.

"One thing at a time, wildlings."

I'd almost forgotten about Niraya, but there she stood in front of us, hands on her hips and surveying our surroundings: the fire, the living jungle, the chattering and growling coming from deep within the trees. "I really don't like this place."

"They don't either. Rina . . . Look at the wolves."

I spun around. My brother was pointing at our two wolves that lay with their heads on their paws at the edge of the jungle. Oliver was whimpering.

"I don't think they want to go in with us." Charlie took a knee and rubbed Nella behind the ears. "It's gonna be okay, girl. Come on in with us, please? We need you in there."

Zid clapped a stocky hand on Charlie's shoulder. "This may be the place to say goodbye. They do not wish to continue. 'Tis unwise to force them."

"Please." Charlie took Nella's paw and gave it a half-hearted shake.

A low rumble sounded from Nella's throat.

"Carlos," I whispered. "I think we should go."

In true Rosas pride fashion, he only tapped harder on Nella's paw.

"I'm telling you, boy," Zid said. "Let her go."

"Charlie." Niraya's voice had venom in it.

The rumble in Nella's throat crescendoed to a full growl until she sprung to her feet and snapped her teeth together inches away from Charlie's nose.

My brother cried out and fell on his back, and Nella pounced on top of his chest, growling in his face.

I reached for my dagger, my nerves lighting up like a Christmas tree.

"Nella," Charlie whispered. "*Shh*. Hey. You know me."

Zid stepped forward and made a grand sweeping motion with his arms. He clicked his tongue against the roof of his mouth. "Get off the boy. Be gone, beast." He thrust his foot out. "Go."

But Uncle Diego's suggestion to be assertive didn't work this time.

Nella pointed her snout toward Zid, every one of her teeth showing.

Zid must have been expecting a different reaction, because his Adam's apple bobbed when he swallowed. Sweat beaded on his forehead. "Any ideas, Miss Karina?"

Before I could open my mouth, Nella made a mad leap for Zid. The dwarf ducked, caught the wolf's front paws, and swung her behind him. She landed with cat-like grace on all fours, rounding on me.

I spread my feet and raised my dagger, locking eyes with the wolf. "Nella," I whispered. "Don't make me do this."

Behind me, mechanical clicks echoed as Niraya loaded her crossbow.

"Make no sudden moves," Niraya warned. "I'm going to put her down."

In unison, Charlie and I shouted, "No!"

Zid shook his head at me. "She has to, Miss Karina. This wolf is your friend no longer. You must see this. If she doesn't attack you now, she'll chew your eyeballs out when you sleep tonight. I know you have an attachment to this creature, but she is eyeing you like a hot breakfast."

"Maybe she's trying to protect us from something," Charlie said, "or maybe she's trying to tell us something, or—"

"No," Niraya said. "I'm a friend to nature as you are, Charlie, but once a beast turns on you . . . there is little you can do." She squeezed one eye shut and took aim.

And she let the bolt fly.

# CHARLIE

## DRAGON
## HUNTERS

---

I shut my eyes, and when Niraya squeezed the trigger, the crossbow sounded more like a gun, harsh, thundering, and final. I assumed maybe the noise was louder in my head because I feared for the wolves' lives.

But when I opened my eyes, my heart galloping, Oliver and Nella were gone, replaced by a trail of paw prints leading out of the forest. "Where did they go?"

"They ran. That sound . . ." Niraya inspected her weapon.

"We're not alone." Zid sprang back to his feet and turned in a full circle.

Niraya reloaded the crossbow, shut one eye, and mirrored Zid's turns. "Who's out there?" She cocked her head slightly, as if to beckon me and Karina closer to her. We took our cue and scrambled to her side, huddling back-to-back. "Show yourself."

My breath hung in my throat. *Is something hunting us? Are we the next shot?* Every shadow in the jungle made me a little warier. In a land of dragons and krakens, it was almost insulting to think we might fall prey to a rogue hunter lurking in the jungle.

"Lads, had that been me, I might have simply said thank you."

Niraya's jaw dropped, revealing genuine surprise for the first time I could remember. "That voice," she said. "It can't be real."

A lanky, masculine figure trudged through the shrubs, veiled by the shadows. His leather coat fanned out behind him like a cape, and a thin ribbon of smoke curled above him. He stopped, blew the smoke away, and then slipped a blunderbuss into his coat pocket.

Zid aimed his sword at the bushes. "Are you the scoundrel who tried to shoot our wolf?"

"Correct me if I'm wrong, but I had ventured the guess you were trying to fire an arrow into her head. The more humane thing to do was to make a sound loud enough to scare her away. I'm no friend of nature, but wolves, on the other hand . . ." The figure emerged from the shadows, revealing a bearded man with a hook for a hand. If Niraya was a pirate, then this guy was the king of them all. He looked Niraya up and down. "And I'm especially a friend to this fair lady. Are you real?"

Our friend dropped the crossbow and rushed into the newcomer's arms.

He needed no more introduction than that.

A smile spread across Zid's face. "It's been far too long."

The man planted a kiss on Niraya's cheek, took her hand, and gave her a twirl like they were in a ballroom. "And so we meet again, Captain Storm."

Niraya slapped him on the face. "That's for worrying me." She kissed him. "And that's because I love you."

Ew.

I cleared my throat, obnoxiously. "Um. James?"

The pirate man swiveled around. "I see you've heard of me." He bowed. "Wish I could say the same of you, but . . . who the devil are you two? Niraya, what are those?"

"We're dragon hunters," I said. "At least, we are today."

"Dragon hunters." James scoffed. "Charming. Zid, explain yourself."

"We traveled all through Kesterfall in hopes we might find you alive. You set off that flare?"

James nodded. "Aye. Risked our lives looking for the blasted thing. Wagered nobody would see it. I suppose we got lucky." He pulled Niraya closer. "Lucky as can be."

I narrowed my eyes. "We?"

"Aye. So before you take us out of here, there's a cave nearby we need to get to. I promised my companions I'd check for them there before we leave."

I glanced at my feet, considering James's words. *Before you take us out of here . . .* This man trusted Karina, Zid, Niraya, and me to get him home, but I had a sickening feeling we were all as trapped as James now.

"Um, James?" my sister said. "Who exactly are you traveling with?"

"Awkward, lanky sort of lad who seems far too excited to be here, and a man who . . ." James looked down and turned away. "Never mind. I don't expect I'll ever see the other one again."

"Our Uncle Diego," I blurted. "That's who you're talking about, isn't it? Was he here?"

James pulled away from Niraya, rushed up to me, and clapped his hand and hook on my shoulder. Immediately, I caught a whiff of leather and wet dirt, and his grip sent pain shooting down my sore arm. "Stars, you two are the niece and nephew I had to listen to him blabber on about?" He whirled around and took Karina's shoulders now. "You've come all this way."

"Just tell us what happened to him," I said. "We already know he's dead. We saw him in the mountains, and he told us to turn back."

The pirate man raised an eyebrow. "Huh. You saw him?"

"There are apparitions in the mountains," Zid said. "We saw people of the past out there. And among them was Mr. Rosas. He told the younglings it was too late and asked that they abandon their journey, a sentiment I shared with him. This venture is much too dangerous, and would I be wrong in assuming you won't be saying thank you?"

James shook his head. "You can't believe everything you see in the mountains. Our king claims he saw his own ghost there not so long ago. The mountains know your minds. They heighten your fears and spin stories in them. Come back to the cave with me. Oh, and keep your weapons ready. There are worse things in the jungle than your rabid wolves."

*Poor Oliver and Nella,* I thought. We'd probably never see them again. I hoped they'd be okay as we followed James deeper into the jungle, where a monstrous symphony of grunts filled the air.

And then the source came barreling after us.

# KARINA

### DEAD
### END

⋅•———————•⋅

Shrieking sounds filled the jungle from almost every direction, making it impossible to know where the cries came from.

I stood with Charlie, Niraya, Zid, and James, all of us back to back with weapons in hand. The leaves shook. The ground rumbled. The whole place was alive.

"The beast is here," Zid whispered. "Verdoro."

"Verdoro? So evil has a name." James flipped his blunderbuss into the air and loaded it with gunpowder from his jacket pocket. "They're all here. No need to worry about the dragon if the ogres and the spiders get us first."

My heart dropped into my stomach. "Spiders?"

"Just keep that lovely dagger of yours handy, lass. If something comes at you—dragon or ogre—bury that blade in its heart and run."

Charlie cracked his knuckles. "Sounds like great advice to me."

"No unnecessary heroics," Zid said. "You stay close to me and the pirates. If we get split up and you find a way out of here, take it. With all due respect, I won't hesitate to do the same. After all this time I've been offering—"

"Just take us to the caves," I said. "Please."

James rolled up one sleeve. "Naturally."

And then the ogres and spiders flooded our path from the side, cementing my heart with terror.

The eight-legged monstrosities were far more terrifying than any image James conveyed by calling them spiders. He wasn't wrong, but I had wicked arachnophobia, and I wouldn't even touch the tiniest of spiders with a ten-foot pole. I'd rather burn down the house—or the jungle.

I swear they were tarantulas that crawled out of some freak lab experiment, and one of them scuttled straight for me with pincers clicking. I swore it even spoke to me, growling something about fresh dinner. With every ounce of willpower I had, I swallowed a scream and thrust my knife into one of the spider's eyes. Unfortunately, a stab to the eye wasn't enough to kill the beast—only to inflame its fury. I ripped the blade out of the spider and ran. The beast followed, matching my pace until Zid intervened and swung his sword into the spider's abdomen. After a sickening crunch like dry cereal, the monster shriveled into a ball and rolled on its side.

"Oh man, I'm gonna be sick." Charlie puffed his cheeks. "I really am."

"Be sick in the cave, mate," James called back.

Charlie stumbled and leaned into a shrub.

"Don't stop." I pulled my brother out of the bush at the same time an ogre tore through it. The oaf beat its chest a few times and grunted a phrase full of nonsense, much like baby talk. He swung a long tube around that looked a lot like a blow dart shooter.

I'd finally had enough.

With pounding in my ears and adrenaline rushing through my body, I turned around, my vision tunneling until all I could see was the ogre. My nostrils flared, and I marched up to the ogre with dagger in hand. With a tug that caught him off guard, I pried the shooter out of his grip. "No!" I slapped his leathery hand. "No."

The ogre seemed to understand me, which I hadn't expected. He wrinkled his nose and jumped up and down a few times, scratching his sides like a monkey.

"No, I said." I shook my finger. "You leave us alone. Go away."

The ogre drew his brows together. "Not . . . play?"

My jaw dropped. *Did I imagine that? Did he just talk to me?* Did these things actually think we were having fun? I shook my head. "No. Not play." I pointed to him then back to myself. "You play. Me, no. Not play."

The ogre beat his fists on a tree three times, like he was throwing a massive monster tantrum, and another demonic spider toppled from the branches. The ogre picked it up by one leg, spun around a bunch of times, and flung the terrible creature like a Frisbee so it sailed far into the burning edges of the jungle. Then he ran away crying, and I actually started to feel bad.

Until the ogre came back with five buddies behind him, and they looked absolutely livid. I pocketed the dart shooter and bolted.

I had to give this every last ounce of my energy or die trying. If the monsters of Kesterfall weren't going to catch us, the fire would bring the jungle down on our heads. There was no reasoning with fire. No slapping its hand and telling it no.

As I was running for my life in the jungle, all I saw was a stringy, chaotic blur of forest-green rays devoured by orange blobs, beige hairy beasts racing past, and brown clumps of earth rushing to meet me every time I stumbled. The race through the jungle was the most nightmarish, impossible moment of my life. Everything burned, and everything terrified me.

Near the moonlit base of Mount Blackburn, I tripped on my shoelaces, hit the ground, and prepared to die.

"Up, lass. You're not finished yet." James hoisted me to my feet, slashed at something behind me, and then guided me into a hole in the mountain, where the rest of our group was beginning a descent into a dark cave. We'd made it at last.

We moved through the dark tunnel, eager to escape the grunts and groans amplifying behind us. James helped us navigate, calling out cues. "There's a dip ahead. Watch your step here. Crouch down low."

The tight squeeze tapped into my anxiety around cramped spaces, but I hoped it would be just enough to keep the hulking ogres away from us. I tried to imagine the power and strength those things possessed. Seeing one hurl a massive tarantula over the jungle canopy was proof enough that I didn't want one of those ogres touching me.

My heart raced when a new sound echoed somewhere in front of us, but thankfully it turned out to be the guy James had been looking for. He looked a lot different after all his time in the wild. I'm sure Charlie and I did, too.

"Tevin," James said. "You made it. We got separated in the ship, and I thought I'd lost you."

"His name's Evan," I said. "I remember you. How are you here?"

"I could ask you the same question," Evan said. "Aren't you Diego Rosas's family? Who's the lady and the short guy? Did you find Diego out there?"

"We're not sure Diego made it, mate," James said. "The evidence is bleak."

An invisible hand squeezed my lungs again.

"I've come to collect you so we can make our escape. I don't know about you, but I'm ready to get out of here."

Evan rubbed his forehead, eyes screwed up like he was about to cry. "You came back for me." He studied the smudged makeshift tattoo on his arm. "But Diego . . . I don't believe this."

"Let's talk about it later," I snapped. My blood boiled again. This random fan did not deserve all my sympathy for losing his favorite reality TV star. Not when Charlie and I lost an uncle. I crossed my arms. "How do we get out of here?"

We all stopped to listen. The moans and groans didn't get any softer, like a thousand heavy feet were drumming through the cave. Somehow, all the fiends of the wilderness found a way to push through the narrow crawlspaces and dodge the rock formations.

We'd done nothing to evade them.

James reached into his pocket. "I have . . . one shot left in this blunderbuss."

"I have one bolt," Niraya said.

Zid, Charlie, and I all had blades, and I had the dart shooter in my pocket. But did we really have enough to make it past the army in the caves? More importantly, did we have any other choice?

We exchanged glances, and the imaginary storm cloud spread over our heads. We were cornered. Unprepared. We had no chance of getting out of here alive.

James pressed his forehead against Niraya's. "No matter how vast the oceans, sometimes two ships meet, and there I met you, Niraya Storm. Thank you for coming back for me. We've, uh . . . had quite a voyage together, no?" Casting a glance at the group of us, he added, "Have the rest of you made amends with your favorite deities?"

"Wildlings." Niraya removed her red-feathered hat and clutched it to her chest. "For what it's worth, I apologize for all that's happened to you and for this foolish decision of mine. We've come farther than anyone together. Mighty roses, our thorns have protected us." She took James's hand and sang. *"How strong you bloomed on fortune's bay . . ."*

James shut his eyes. *"And blossomed like a summer day . . ."*

As they sang, we closed the gap between us and huddled against the wall, with Zid attempting to form a human shield in front of us by puffing his chest. Though he wore his best brave expression, his lip trembled. "The beasts will have to go through me first."

Evan slumped down against the wall and drew his knees against his chest.

I rested my forehead on Charlie's shoulder and pulled him into a tight hug. "Charlie," I said. "I'm sorry I was so horrible to you when you tried to help me with the werewolf scratch. I—"

"Shh." Charlie hugged me back, a half-embrace because of his weak, bruised up arm, and we didn't let go. "It's gonna be okay, all right? Don't be afraid. Just . . . just close your eyes."

I obeyed, desperate to tune out the sounds of the spiders' legs on icy ground and the grunts of the ogres echoing through the caves. Charlie must've had the same idea, because he started singing to himself mindlessly.

The ogre grunts and footsteps grew louder and louder until I guessed they were only feet away. Charlie squeezed my hand until I thought my bones might pop.

Zid's breaths quickened. Standing in the right place, each of his breaths sounded like a hundred. The acoustics of the cave threw everything back at us over and over again. One man alone would've sounded like an army.

But then all the grunts and footsteps stopped.

*That's it. Cut to black. Our lives just ended.*

I opened my eyes, expecting pearly gates— hopefully not fire and pitchforks—or maybe even some end credits about my life hovering around. *Directed by Karina Rosas. Made by Her Parents. Music by Hans Zimmer.* If only.

Only instead of opening my eyes to pearly gates or end credits, I got to see my Uncle Diego, and nothing could have made me happier.

# CHARLIE

## A LEGENDARY
## REUNION

·:—◆—:·

K arina and I rushed our tio full force, realizing a
second later that it took all his strength to stand
on his own. We held him up, basking in his warmth and
the dirt and soot caked on his arms, his natural musky
scent. If the man before us were another ghost of some
sort, he couldn't have been more convincing.

Tio steadied his balance and wrapped one arm
around each of us. "What are you two locos doing here?"
He kissed the top of Karina's head and then planted
his forehead on my shoulder. "You have no idea how
worried I've been."

Karina pulled away, wiped a tear from her eye, and
smiled. "Oh, I think we have a pretty good idea."

We shared another hug, three dusty desert rats wrapped in family love.

"We thought you were dead, Tio. We saw your ghost in the mountains."

"My ghost? How long have you two been wandering around?" He pressed the back of his hand to my forehead, smearing it with dirt. "You running a fever or something?"

"We really did," Karina said. "You told us to turn around and give up. We thought you were already dead. The thing is . . ."

Tio slumped down against the wall and wrapped his arms around his knees, finishing Karina's thought. "I would never tell you to give up on something."

"As I told you, the mountains can't always be trusted. The wind plays on your thoughts, desires, and feelings. You feared losing your uncle, so the winds fanned your anxieties. But those fears might very well have come true if Mr. Rosas here hadn't experienced a healthy dose of good fortune." James clapped his hand on Tio's shoulder. "Glad you made it back, mate."

Uncle Diego rubbed his face, his eyes red and lips chapped. "Yeah. Me too. I was pretty close to death out there, but then you pulled the flare and I was so sure I heard Karina's scream. Nothing gives you a second wind like hearing your family in danger, you know? So why did you two come all this way? Didn't you know how dangerous this would be?" He tilted his head toward the mouth of the cave. "There's a dragon out there. I don't know how to kill it, I don't know how to escape it, and I don't know how we're getting out of this alive. You should've just gone home."

"I thought you'd never tell us to give up," I said.

"Don't begrudge the children." Niraya extended her arm and shook Tio's hand. "Niraya, by the way. I should tell you I didn't want these two to come with me. I thought they'd slow me down, be holes in the sails. But they insisted, and they held their own like nobody I've ever seen. Charlie and Karina came to Zid here"— the dwarf nodded and waved—"and we made a pact to rescue you and James."

Tio clasped both Niraya's hands in gratitude. "Niraya, huh? I heard a lot about you." I had trouble reading the look he gave me and Karina afterward. Shock? Exhaustion? I liked to think it was pride. "Thanks for looking after my family."

"And now that we're all safe here, let's do what we set out to do." Zid brandished his fist. "Escape."

"And how do we intend to do that?" James asked.

Nobody said a word. The question we'd all been dreading.

Zid tapped his fingertips together and scraped the ground with the ball of his foot. "Well, um, you see, the thing is that we uhh . . . We—"

James's lips curled into a scowl. "Go on, lad. We haven't got anywhere else important to be, have we?"

The pirate's response only worsened Zid's awkward stumbles. His face reddened under his beard, which he tugged on in alternating pulls again. "I should tell you that what we meant to do was, uh, perhaps"—Zid stopped pulling on his beard and balled his fists at his sides—"Oh, curse you, seadog! Where are your ideas? Mister Order of the Bell?"

"You came down here with no means of getting back out?" James did a half-turn and swung his fist into the cave wall. "Ten thousand curses on you, dwarf. And a hundred more to the younglings you brought with you. Not you, Niraya, never on you—"

"Hey," Tio said in his deepest, scariest voice. It was awesome. "That's my familia you're cursing."

James stood nose-to-nose with Uncle Diego. "Then curse you too, Diego Rosas, and every salty bone in your body. I told you you were sour luck."

"Leave my tio alone." The cave amplified my voice.

Karina massaged her temples. "Can we stop now?"

"Silence, codfish. Grown men are talking."

Zid gave James a light shove. "They have every right to partake of your senseless banter. The things they endured to get here and listen to you blubber and snivel, you . . . you scoundrel!"

Like a genie out of a bottle, chaos broke loose. James dealt out cheap insults and complaints like playing cards. Tio jabbed a finger in the pirate's chest. Zid launched into a long list of complaints about the yetis and the cold, and about James himself. Karina and Niraya tried to shove the arguing men apart, but they might as well have tried to separate a pair of canyon walls. With all the sounds bouncing around the cave, I could barely pick out a word.

Was this part of Dante's Inferno? Standing in a frozen cave with a bunch of grown men arguing forever or until a flying death lizard ate us all?

But like thunder, one phrase shattered through all the rest and ended the banter.

"I have an idea."

Silence. Everybody turned to stare at Evan the Fanboy. I'd almost forgotten he existed. How long had he been sitting there listening to us all before he decided to chime in?

James raised an eyebrow. "You have an idea, Kevin?"

Tio blinked and shook his head as if snapping out of a hypnotic trance. "You have an idea. Well, let's hear it, buddy. I'm all ears."

Evan grinned and stood, dusting the snow off his back. "I have to admit it sounds like a stretch. It's not going to sound like the best idea at first, but hear me out, cool?"

"Of course," Tio said.

After a full, deep breath, Evan pointed at my sister and said, "First, I need what's on Karina's neck."

*No.*

Rina stepped back and hid the necklace in her shirt.

My stomach twisted. Where was he going with this?

"Absolutely not," I said.

Evan threw his hands up. "I told you to hear me out."

"No." I stepped in front of my sister. This was going to turn into Jericho Harbor all over again. "We don't want to hear your idea."

"Charlie," Tio scolded.

"What's the big deal? You're not even giving me a chance to prove myself. What if I told you I can get all of us out of here and that I'm probably your last hope, huh? What if all of this"—Evan gestured broadly at everything around him—"and everything about this moment was destiny? Are you really just going to brush me aside before I can finish telling you my idea?"

"Yes—"

"No, go on," Tio said.

Evan made an immature *haha* playground sort of sneer at me, boiling my blood. He'd seemed so nice on the train, but seriously, what a jerk.

"Just let me see the pendant. I'll explain everything."

Karina bit her lip. "I don't know. I probably shouldn't. I'm protective of it because it's made from a super rare gem, hard to find anywhere else. If you dropped it or anything, I'd be really upset and I don't know if I would ever forgive you or myself. I'm sorry."

I cheered in my head. *Way to go, Rina.*

"It's just a necklace," Evan said. "If it's really that important to you, I won't do anything stupid. I promise. Isn't it worth it if it can get us out of here?"

"Rina, he's right. It's just a necklace," Tio chimed in. "Evan, I'm not sure where you're going with this, but if you think you have a plan . . . We all want to get out of here alive. Hand it over to him. If I never see it again, I'm not going to cry over it."

"I wouldn't, Diego," Niraya said.

Alarms pulsed in my bones. This guy wasn't just a jerk—there was something far more off about him, in the same way things were off in Jericho Harbor. Off like Nella's behavior when we reached the edge of the jungle. He was one of the crazed hunters looking for the Wheel of Fortune.

"Tio," I said, "you don't understand. I'm sorry, Evan, but the last thing I'm going to do is let my sister give you that pendant. Not without you telling us exactly why you want it first."

"Charlie," Tio said, "why are you acting like a child? I don't understand."

Evan smirked, looking like a sly crocodile. "No, Mr. Rosas. You wouldn't understand."

Tio wrinkled his brows. "Come again?"

"Since your family is being so difficult, I'll tell you exactly why I need that pendant." Evan tilted his head to the side and took a step closer to me, his voice growing deep and guttural. "Or how about I show you all instead?"

Evan scrunched his eyes shut, made two fists, and concentrated with an intensity that turned his skin red. For an actual second, I thought he might explode or something. Instead, he underwent a gruesome Jekyll-and-Hyde transformation. His shoulders swelled, his thighs contorted, and his face bulged in patches that would haunt my nightmares. Even his eyes changed colors from iron blue to liquid gold. He cried out in pain as his bones popped and adjusted themselves to a new structure, his skin stretched over them, and his red hair sprouted from his scalp like it'd been pushed up through his skull.

*Creepy.* I took a step back and shielded Karina and Tio with spread arms, my heart thrashing against my ribs. "What's happening to him?"

Rina swallowed. "He's . . . he's—"

Niraya clenched her fists. "A shifter."

Sure enough, a brand new man knelt in front of us, a massive pair of knees on the ice and a thick head of black hair covering the new face. He dug his wide, hairy knuckles into the ground and took deep, Darth Vader-like breaths.

Karina, Zid, Niraya, Uncle Diego, and I stood speechless at what we had witnessed. James broke the silence, taking a cautious step with his hands up, fugitive-style.

"Mate? You all right?"

Instead of answering James's question, Evan kept his head down and continued to wheeze, apparently recovering from whatever pain the transformation had brought on.

Then, with a toss of his hair, Evan lifted his head and revealed a new face, an uncannily familiar sight that chilled my bones. A new voice came out of his throat, deep and raspy. "Surprise."

"Evan?" Tio's voice was flecked with doubt. The brute in front of us wasn't even kind of the same person we met on the train to Switzerland. Tio's signature still blurred the man's skin, but Evan didn't share the same ears, fingernails, or even the same attitude as this new stranger.

The man rose to his feet, and I had to tilt my chin up to see him. He was a mountain. I knew I'd never seen him in my own world, but I was starting to remember why he looked so familiar.

"What is this sorcery?" Zid marched up to the new Evan and jabbed his gut with a thick finger. "What are you trying to pull, youngling? You think to have a good laugh making fun of a dwarf's stature? *Harumph.* I demand you change back at once."

"This isn't a youngling," Karina said. "He's nowhere near our age."

"It's Lord Falk," I said.

Every legend I'd heard in Kesterfall and in Florindale was based at least partially in truth. And now we knew why the boy we thought was Evan was so intent on swiping Tio's necklace. After all these years, Falk was still hunting for Lady Fortune's wheel.

Lord Falk bowed, a crooked grin spreading across his face. "So my name has graced your ears already. I'm pleased to hear it."

"Lord Who?" James asked.

Zid wrinkled his brows, evidently just as confused as the pirate. "Explain yourself."

"Falk," the man said. "Time has molded my name into many shapes, just as Lady Fortune has molded my body. What other names have the whims of legend concocted for me?"

"I smell a rat," Zid said. "Falk is but a legend. We used to hear of him in the mines. Lord Bellamy tossed the name around like a boiled potato, threatening of a madman who would raid our domain to find hidden riches scattered from the Wheel of Fortune. All of us knew he was just trying to stop us from keeping what we found down there. There is no Wheel of Fortune, no orbs of destiny, and no Lord Falk."

"But there is," the man said. "And I am he. And I inch ever so close to finishing what I started, thanks to you, Diego Rosas, and your family."

Tio pulled me behind him. "Stay quiet," he said. "Me? What did I do? What are you?"

"Why, I'm the most powerful man who has ever lived," Lord Falk said. "Or so I will be when I have the Wheel of Fortune. You'll know it. Florindale will know it. Every world between will know it. Your luck, your world—your very destiny—will rise and fall with the stroke of my hand. The things I can give to you . . ." Moonlight flashed in his eyes. "Riches, fame, adventure, glory. And the things I could take away from you, if I so desire."

"I don't understand," Tio said. "Wheel of Fortune?"

Niraya raised her crossbow. "It's a very real thing, Mr. Rosas. But it doesn't belong to him."

"Save your bolt for the dragon, love," James said.

Karina clutched her necklace. "Uncle Diego, where did you get this? You stole it, didn't you? Before you believed in only taking pictures and leaving footprints?"

Tio turned away, cradling his temples with one hand.

"This thing's gotten us into a whole lot of trouble," I said. "Where?"

"Giza," he finally breathed. "A souvenir from one of the first places I ever explored. It's the only thing I've ever taken. On my honor."

Karina kicked the ground. "I knew it."

A thought clicked in my head. I turned to Lord Falk, trying to sound brave. "And you brought us here, didn't you? Not just to the cave. You wrecked our train and ripped us from our home and . . . This is all you." I shook my head. "What happened to everyone else?"

Lord Falk answered with a slow clap. "I wondered when you'd weave the threads together. Do you see the tapestry before you now?" He clasped his hands behind his back and paced the cavern. "Worry not, little roses. Somewhere in your world, the real Fernweh Express is whole and intact, and all its passengers remember is little more than a hiccup. All of them but you, of course.

"When I found the first of Lady Fortune's stones, I wasted not a minute learning to harness its power and turn the tides of my own fortune. How can one resist giving me what I want when I can be"—he scrunched his eyes shut, and his body contorted into a more slender figure with inky-dark hair and bright eyes—"the king of Florindale? Or perhaps"—he shifted again and became shorter, a bit darker, feminine—"his radiant queen? Stars, if I wanted, I could be your uncle." Lord Falk changed yet again, each transformation much smoother and quicker than the last, and fire pulsed in my lungs when a duplicate Uncle Diego stood in front of me.

"Get out of my body," Tio said.

Lord Falk laughed and returned to his hulking original form. "You do wear it better, Mr. Rosas. But I don't need to be you to get what I want. Not even you can command nature the way I can, thanks to this beauty." He drew a second shining stone from his pocket and squeezed it in his hand. The snow stopped, and the clouds cleared away in a matter of seconds. "I found that one in the bottom of the Joringel Sea. It was so fortunate that with the help of the first stone I could become a whale, or a krill, or the leviathan itself if I so desired."

I almost crawled out of my skin. I couldn't fathom the lengths—and the depths—this man had explored. He could've combed the ocean floor for decades in another form. What would that do to a man's sanity? What would my own brain look like if I'd spent decades as a jellyfish?

"The third fell from a cloud, if you must know," Lord Falk said. "I made it rain in Kesterfall for seven years before the stone finally popped me on the head as if from another world. And that other world was where I found you, Diego Rosas, so mindlessly clinging to the fourth orb. Lady Fortune had the bright idea to entrust you as its guardian. A god among warriors has to spend decades in the ocean and summon seven years of rain to touch one of these, but you? You saunter into a pyramid, crack the codes within, and you waltz out with the fourth stone as if plucking a flower. You. A mere mortal. The idea!"

"So you decided to take it from me," Tio said, "by slipping between worlds, crashing our train, and bringing it through to some fairy-tale world where you'd have us all to ourselves. I can't imagine being so obsessed with something that I would go to all that trouble."

"But you do it every day for nothing. In the name of adventure. I rummaged through your backpack when Verdoro brought you here. Imagine my ire when I didn't find what I was looking for. I should have killed you and the pirate then and there."

"So why didn't you?" James scowled. "I had no business here anyway. I never touched one of your stones!"

"It became your business when Storm, the dwarf, and the younglings latched on to each other and made this journey for you two scoundrels. Had she not taken them in, I would have ended you. One of them had to have the stone, and when I discovered them scuttling over here, I had a better idea. If you can pluck one stone from a pyramid and survive the beasts of Kesterfall, you can surely procure the other stones for me. You can help me, or you can die a meaningless death in a land where nobody knows your name. After all"—Falk held up his arm with Tio's smudged signature—"your signature bound you to me. If you run, if you take that pendant from me, I vow this: I will always find you, Diego Rosas. I will hunt you and your family eternally until I have that wheel."

Zid put up his fists and side-stepped in front of Tio. "How dare you threaten this man and his younglings!"

My bruised arm was hurting worse and worse now, and suddenly I was dizzy with understanding. "He's going to eat us. If you're a shifter, does that also mean . . . you're Verdoro?"

"That's where you're wrong." Lord Falk reached over his head and snapped his fingers, the crisp sound echoing through the cave.

An earth-shaking rumble cut through the air, rattling the cavern until one of the icicles fell from the walls and burst into white dust. Tio wrapped his arms around me and Karina and scooted back against the wall. James, Niraya, and Zid ducked and shielded their heads with their arms.

"I told you, thanks to one of these lovely gems, I control nature now. I'm not the dragon." Lord Falk laughed. "I merely command him."

# KARINA

## THE WEIGHT
## OF THE WORLD

·◦———◦·

The trembling earth clued me in on what was happening overhead. Rocks scraped together, tiny storms of dust and ice trickled from the cave ceiling, and the stalagmites vibrated like tuning forks. All the while, I couldn't block out the screeches and death cries of everything outside: the murderous call of a dragon, the beating of its wings, the cries of ogres who couldn't escape its fire, and the disintegration of the snow-capped mountain that once contained the beast. There was no doubt about it: Verdoro had returned. For a second, I actually thought we'd be able to pull off this rescue without confronting him again.

Lord Falk closed his eyes, raising his hand and pointing at the ceiling when a boom sounded above. "Can you hear it?" he asked as if the rest of us were deaf. "The sweet music of the dragon following his conductor? Verdoro plays his part so masterfully, doesn't he? He's my favorite performer. I must say I also rather enjoyed the final song of the poor wolves you dragged along with you. When I became aware of their attachment to you, I couldn't resist changing their tune. The best song is one that truly moves you and that makes you feel things, is it not? If only I could ensnare all of nature at once . . ."

My heart dropped into my stomach. No wonder Nella and Oliver had been acting so weird when we arrived. They'd fallen under Falk's control over nature, and because of him, we almost put them down. Who knew if they even survived the fire? I drew my dagger and lunged for Falk. "How dare you? Those wolves were our friends!"

Lord Falk swiped the dagger out of my hand and plunged the tip into the icy cavern wall. The metal sank into the ice too easily, like a knife in a cake. "Let's point that blade somewhere safer, foolish girl." With the back of his other hand, he swatted me across the face.

I think the cold numbed my cheeks too much to really feel anything, at least as far as pain went. But now I was livid. This man was a monster.

"That's my sister, Buzzard Face," Charlie said.

When I turned back around, Niraya's crossbow, Zid's sword, James's hook, and Uncle Diego's fists were all pointed at Lord Falk. The four of them could've melted all the ice with their expressions.

"Oh, this is endearing." Lord Falk chuckled. "A village full of warriors and dragons couldn't stop me, but you four mean to thwart the mean ol' bad guy? Let me put this to you simply, fools." He pointed to the ceiling, and the icicles trembled again. "Give me the pendant, or I'll bring this mountain down on your skulls. The only place you have to run, of course, is outside."

*Where Verdoro is.* A chill scuttled down my spine.

"Of course you could shoot me, but I'm the only thing holding this mountain over your heads right now. I'd hate to accidentally slip." On cue, an avalanche of snow and rock spilled from the wall behind Lord Falk's head, kicking up dust in a ghostly cloud.

"At least you'll go down with us," Niraya said.

"But will I?" Falk asked. "After all this time? I've lived centuries already."

Niraya lowered her crossbow. "You're mad."

"I prefer honest. And now you'll choose. Death by fire, death by avalanche, or will you accept Fortune's hand?" He extended an arm toward me, and everyone turned to meet my gaze. "Quickly now. You have about five seconds before my hand slips. Four."

"Miss Karina," Zid said. "Give him the pendant."

"Do it, lass," James said.

I had to save my family. I couldn't let these people die for a legend.

"Three . . . oh my, this mountain is heavy." A truck-sized mound of earth burst over Lord Falk's head, showering me with dirt.

Charlie grasped my shoulders. "Rina, no."

On the other hand, what if I tossed the pendant over and the world ended tomorrow? I would be responsible for that.

"Rina," Uncle Diego coughed, bringing his shirt up to cover his mouth from the dirt. "Do what you've gotta do, okay? No matter what, we're familia."

"Two . . . Verdoro, I hope you're getting hungry out there."

I couldn't take it anymore. Almost like a puppeteer was controlling my arm, I ripped the orb off its chain and chucked it at Falk.

And he caught it.

The mountain stopped trembling.

I blinked a tear out of my eye, unable to meet my family's gaze.

"You win," I whispered.

*What have I done?*

I would never forget now: Man is more dangerous than anything in the wild. Falk had just proven that to me.

The overlord cupped the pendant in his hands, eyes widening as if he'd discovered a precious metal. "*Gooood.*" He reached into the pouch at his side, withdrew three other gems, and shook them together like dice. "I knew you were smart. That makes four out of seven thanks to you, Diego Rosas. Perhaps you're good luck, after all." He plucked my dagger out of the cavern wall, slipped it in his pocket, and then beckoned us to follow him through the cave. "Now, come. I require your assistance."

# CHARLIE

## WRATH OF THE FLYING DEATH LIZARD

·•———•·

We found most of the jungle in charred ruins, an eerie wasteland of ash and snow. Only a thin strip of trees ran from mountain to mountain. The spiders—or as I called them in my head, nopes—lay in crispy black husks. While a few ogres ambled around mindlessly swinging their clubs, most lay motionless in the dragon's shadow.

The scene reminded me of something out of those *Jurassic Park* movies. Verdoro tromped around the broken jungle, slow and lazy. His massive feet covered the spiders' abdomens, making sickening crunching sounds that turned my stomach inside out. I froze in place at the mouth of the cave, James, Zid, Karina,

Niraya, and Tio huddled behind me. I wished I could learn a superpower and become invisible, fly my family off the island, or grow as big as Verdoro and have a chance at taking him on. Or better yet, I could put Falk in chains, shackle him to Verdoro's leg, and let the man spend eternity chained to his own flying death lizard.

Falk waltzed ahead of us, and I strongly considered tackling him from behind to reclaim the gems. But we couldn't attack him while he could still turn the beast on us. *How do we get out of this? We can't let Lord Falk claim the Wheel of Fortune.*

Lord Falk approached the dragon and produced a dark whip from his belt loop. "Verdoro. Say hello, my pet."

The man flung the leather strip, disturbing a row of gold-green scales on the dragon's leg. Falk wound the whip into a loose coil around his wrist as Verdoro turned his head toward me. Flames curled from his mouth.

Zid's jaw dropped. He looked at Verdoro the same way my sister did when she wandered into a bookstore. "Stars, I forgot how magnificent he is."

I wrinkled my nose at Zid.

"You should never abuse nature like that," Tio said. "It's wrong."

An impish grin crept across Falk's face. "I'm sorry. Did you tame this dragon with your cookies and sweet lullabies?"

Tio's temples bulged when he pressed his jaws together.

One of those stones controlled the dragon. And whichever one it was, we had to get it away from Falk.

Lord Falk spread his arms in a grand gesture. "Now, my wild friend." He marched over to Tio and tilted his chin up with two thick fingers. "Tell me where we begin our search. Escort me to the remaining orbs."

Tio stepped back and rubbed his chin where Lord Falk brushed him. "I can't do that. Even if I wanted to help you, I don't know where to go. The first one was an accident."

Lord Falk cracked the whip behind him. "Oh, Verdoro?"

Quick as a mousetrap, the death lizard lunged and snapped his teeth in Tio's face, eliciting a scream from all of us. Even steel-nerved Niraya didn't hold back.

Falk clapped his hands once. "That's close enough, my slave. At ease."

Verdoro retreated and fluttered his wings, shaking off a layer of ashes.

"Unfortunately for you, sir"—Lord Falk seized Tio's collar—"I wasn't asking. Because if you don't help me, I'll command Verdoro to eat you after you watch him devour your travel companions. And I assure you he's famished."

Tio swept his arm across his forehead, his shoulders slumped in defeat. "I don't know how to help you. I wish I did, but I'm not a treasure hunter. I'm just a man who took something off the beaten path. I'm . . . a wild rose who got caught in the dragon's den."

And to my great horror, my fearless uncle fell to his knees and lowered his hands on the ground.

"Tio, no . . ." I gasped, my heart sinking into my stomach. Tio had given up. After Sahara, Everest,

Borneo, and even dragons, The Great Diego Rosas had yielded.

A devious grin spread across Falk's face. He looked like one of the purple devil emojis on my dead phone.

Without looking up, Tio continued, "I'm begging you to leave my familia out of this. I'll help you look for the stone. You can chain me to your ankle or tie a rope around my waist and drag me around this inferno until I drop dead. But Rina and Charlie and James and his girlfriend and this dwarf have no part in this anymore. They've been through enough."

Eyes bright and cheerful, Lord Falk nodded and crossed his arms. He took two steps forward so his toes were directly beneath Tio's chin. "You impress me. Such loyalty." He shot me a glare. "Well? What are you all waiting for? This man sets an excellent example."

With my pride in shreds, I tucked one knee under me and knelt. Karina, Zid, Niraya, and James followed.

"Thank you," Falk said. "Diego, your request is denied. I want these people behind you every step of our journey until we find the Wheel of Fortune. I want them to know I'll always be watching. And I want you to remember that if you fail, I will use them to punish you."

I gritted my teeth, my breaths coming out in heavy bursts.

Apparently I'd been breathing really loud, because Falk turned his head and walked toward me, kicking up ashes with every step. He stopped in front of me and lowered his hands onto his knees. "I'm sorry, boy. Is there a problem?"

I gulped and lowered my gaze to his feet. "No."

A hot pain shot through my bones, and I fell sprawled on my back. Falk had kicked me in the chin. He chuckled and took a step forward, cracking his knuckles. "I didn't hear you."

I eyed the silver pouch hanging from his belt, just an arm's reach above my head.

"No."

"No, what? Speak up, boy." Lord Falk bent over and tilted his ear toward my face.

This was my chance. My heart raced as fast as a werewolf. I tried to keep my eyes down, nervous about drawing attention to what I really wanted. "I said . . ." I shot my arm up and ripped the silver pouch from Lord Falk's belt. "Tio, catch!"

Tio sprang to his feet, and I hurled the silver pouch at him. Football wasn't my strong suit—my throwing arm was okay—but the pouch was light and easy to chuck. No matter what, it was crucial that the orbs stay out of Lord Falk's hands. The man snarled, raised his leg, and brought his foot down on my chest, forcing the air out of my lungs.

Verdoro lurched, batted his wings, and snapped at the air as if suddenly unchained.

Tio caught the silver pouch, pulled Karina to her feet, and ran for the strip of jungle that still remained. "Rina, let's go."

"Go, Tio," I wheezed.

Zid thrust a fist in the air and stood again. "Way to go, Charlie. You've turned the tables. Your time has come, Falk!"

James breathed on his hook and wiped it on his jacket. "Ah, now we've got ourselves a proper brawl."

Lord Falk swatted James aside like a fly, knocking him on his shoulder. "I win."

"James." Niraya fired her crossbow at Lord Falk, and he slid away from the bolt with a single step. She tossed the crossbow on the ground and tended to James.

Lord Falk sneered and ran after Tio and Rina, his massive body gaining train-like momentum.

Free from his trance, Verdoro became a much different creature. Whereas his movements were robotic and lumbering before, now he was more graceful without Falk's control. The dragon whipped its tail around with more aggression and speed. He threw his head back and spit fire into the air, brighter and hotter than I remembered. The puppet had been cut from its strings, and he was angry. I didn't know if this was a good thing.

Smoke pouring from his nostrils, Verdoro batted his wings and screeched at Falk.

The overlord picked up speed, not looking back. "Never take that ungrateful tone with me. I am your master. I have gifted you glorious purpose!"

Verdoro unleashed a flame that came dangerously close to Falk's heels before the "master" disappeared into the jungle.

"We're not safe." Zid slapped my upper back. "We're not immune to the dragon's true nature. He's hungry, and he will not wait for Falk's command. We must hide."

I looked up at the dragon, a dangerous idea cooking in my brain. "What if we try something? Aren't you the famous dragon tamer? The man who can get any beast to listen to you?"

Zid stuck his nose in the air. "I won't try again. He's untamable."

"But he was under a trance! We may have broken it," I said. "Can't you try now?"

"Absolutely not." Zid dashed for the trees. "I'm sorry, Carlos. May the light be with you."

"Fine, be like that." My nostrils flared. If Zid wanted to give up, I'd have to try this myself. Tio never wrote anything about training a dragon, but somewhere between the Fernweh Express and the peaks of Kesterfall, I'd gained something. Without mystical orbs or the full moon, I could hold my own in the wild, be it in front of a wolf or even inside the leviathan's throat.

This was my final test, pass or die.

I faced Verdoro and begged my heart to be still. *This is possibly the stupidest thing I've ever done. Probably the last thing I'll ever do.*

"Hey, Verdoro." I summoned my most confident, assertive tone. My Diego Rosas voice. I pointed to my eyes with two fingers. "Look here. Come closer."

I could feel Niraya's and James's stares on me. James tugged on Niraya's sleeve. "How much bounty's on this beastie, love?"

Niraya elbowed him and pressed a finger to her lips. "Wait."

Smoke curled from the dragon's nose in black wisps. Verdoro grunted and beat his tail against the ground three times.

I counted to ten before I dared move another muscle. The seconds crawled by. Verdoro wasn't blinking. I wondered if maybe I shouldn't be, either. Was there something in Tio's journal about eye contact? I spread my empty arms apart, like a police fugitive putting my hands up to show I was unarmed. Zid swore dragons could understand us. I hoped with all my heart that included gestures. I held the pose for a minute, and then I put a finger to my lips. "Shhh. I won't hurt you."

*Please don't hurt me, either. Not after all this.*

Tapping my chest with my thumb, I said, "Charlie." I made a heart shape with my fingers and held it above my head. *God, I feel ridiculous.* "Friend."

Verdoro roared, spewed fire, and bent down, infusing panic in my veins. I prepared for pain. What had I done wrong?

"Charlie." Niraya sprung to her feet. "Be careful."

But instead of eating me, Verdoro lowered his head all the way to his ankle, stopping to lick a raw area where his scales were chapped and the flesh had swelled. A single, moonlit tear pricked the dragon's eye as it licked the wound.

A memory flashed in my head, and I was six years old in Tio's dining room. *Even the scary things can be beautiful,* he'd told us.

I took another step, more confident this time, and studied the chafed dragon skin. "Oh man, that's where Falk whipped you, isn't it?" I put my hand above the wound. Against my fingers, his skin was like a pair of rough leather boots left out in the sunlight for a day. Somehow I thought he'd be colder, like a snake, but I shouldn't have been surprised. With all that fire within him, Verdoro had the heat of a Tucson summer in his blood. Like me. I waved the pirates over, and they took feather-light steps toward me and Verdoro. "We're not gonna hurt you, okay? We want to help."

Verdoro made a soft, gentle sound with his throat.

A second memory flashed in my mind. *Down this path, an innocent life requires your help, greatly misunderstood by many. There will be pain with no guarantee of healing. Your predator is certain to catch up to you. You will take much longer to reach your destination.* I thought of baby Oliver in the trap, trying to free himself from the rusted metal cage.

What if this was what Lady Constance meant all along? What if Verdoro was the innocent life and Falk was the predator?

I knew one thing: I never wanted to see another creature in pain. This was the path we were meant to take.

I cracked a smile. "You're not just a flying death lizard after all, are you? I'm gonna help you, buddy. Maybe we can help each other."

With my hand on Verdoro's leg, I stared up at the top of the basin that trapped us down here, the cogs spinning to life in my skull. *Bees make honey to put on your waffles,* Tio once told me.

And dragons . . . dragons fly.

# KARINA

## RUMBLE
## IN THE JUNGLE

--·•——•·--

I overanalyzed every itch as Uncle Diego and I hid
from Falk in a thicket of shrubs I'd never seen before.
They could've been poisonous. Then again, this whole
island seemed poisonous.

My uncle put a finger to his lips. "Stay quiet. We
can't let that man hear us."

"What about Charlie?" I whispered. "And the
others? We have to go back for them."

"I'm going back for them." Uncle Diego pressed
Falk's silver pouch into my palm. "Can you hold onto
this for me?"

I closed my fingers over the drawstring bag. The
responsibility added ten pounds to it. If I lost the

stones and Falk got them, I could change every man and woman's destiny for the worst.

"Put it in your pocket," Uncle Diego whispered, and I obeyed.

"Aren't you gonna make me promise not to move?" I asked.

Uncle Diego ruffled my hair. "Rina, you're so much mightier than you know. You made it all this way without me telling you what to do. I won't start now."

Muddy footsteps squelched nearby, and Falk strutted into view, studying the area with hawk-like intensity. "Come out of the trees, little roses."

When Falk's back was to the shrubs, Uncle Diego spread the bushes apart with all the care and patience of a surgeon.

*Don't go*, I mouthed.

When the twigs snapped, Lord Falk spun around. My palms went cold as he locked eyes with me, teeth showing in an impish grin, and raced toward the bush. "Aha."

"Let's move." Uncle Diego grabbed my wrist.

"Your pack." I threw my uncle's bag on my shoulder, and we ran.

We followed the path, mud squishing beneath our feet. I desperately wished for more places to hide, to veer off the trail and lose the juggernaut behind us, but Verdoro's fire had devoured so much of the jungle that there was little more than a narrow strip of trees leading up to the mountain. I almost collided with Zid when he emerged from a pocket of withered tree stumps, hands flailing and face crimson with fatigue.

Despite his legs being shorter than mine, he nearly kept pace with us.

"Dragon!" Zid flailed his arms. "Verdoro is angry—wild. He'll devour us all."

Zid's toe connected with an overgrown tree root, tripping him. He hit the ground, and a collection of grapes spilled from his pack, rolling across the jungle like marbles.

I wheeled around. "Zid."

In my hesitation, Falk sprung toward me with a flying leap and yanked my ankles out from under me. The muddy ground rushed up to meet my chest. Falk turned me over and pinned me down, his hands clasped over my wrists. In the fiery glow of the jungle, he looked almost demonic when he grinned. "I'll have my prize now."

"Get off her." Uncle Diego bolted for the overlord.

*Use the pendants against him*, my mind urged me. But I didn't know how to use them or what kind of power they possessed. What if I used them incorrectly? What if I hurt someone or ensnared the dragon again? I would be no better than Falk.

Lord Falk took his hands off my wrists, reached for Uncle Diego's leg, and twisted. My uncle went down, but Falk didn't let go. He gave Uncle Diego's leg another twist, and there was a sickening snap followed by an earth-shaking cry that echoed through the jungle.

I lifted my shoulders and saw my uncle writhing on the ground, his right leg twisted into an awkward angle. Tears streaked his eyes.

I pounded my fists against Falk's chest. "You monster."

Falk tilted his head back and laughed. "Oh, I'm not the monster today, girl. Now, let's have that pouch in your pocket."

"No," I said.

"It wasn't a question." Lord Falk patted my sides until his veiny hand passed over the lump in my pocket. "It's a shame you and your family couldn't cooperate. It might behoove you to be on my good side when I have the Wheel of Fortune." He dug his fingers into my pocket and drew out the silver pouch.

Before he could open it, a distant voice cried into the wind, our names echoing in the trees that remained.

Uncle Diego studied the canopy, squinting and projecting his voice with cupped hands. "Charlie, where are you?"

I shielded my eyes with a palm as the wind picked up, shaking the leaves and jiggling the mud around my ankles. Verdoro circled the air like a hawk over its prey. Then he spread his wings open, glared down at me, and descended into the jungle with a hard nosedive.

Charlie called our names again. "Up here."

That's when I understood my brother was on top of the dragon, riding its neck like some Renaissance cowboy. Niraya waved from behind him, and James sat slumped against her back, his hooked hand dangling over the side.

Uncle Diego looked as though Charlie had climbed a skyscraper, hung upside down from the flagpole, and taken a selfie. "Carlos!" He tore his hands from his hair and flailed them over his head. "What are you doing up there, loco?"

Charlie beamed. "What would Tio do? You're the family daredevil."

"Well, I don't approve of this," Uncle Diego said. "Because if you don't fall off or get eaten, your mom will strangle you. And then me. And then I'll strangle you."

Falk sneered. "So you think you can ride my dragon? You people are brave . . . wily. And far too late."

He pulled the drawstring pouch open and tipped it upside down.

A handful of colorless pebbles spilled into his palm.

Falk squeezed the meaningless rocks, his arms trembling as his face reddened. "Who duped me?" He launched the pebbles far into the distance, where they scattered and sank into a puddle of mud. His hands went back to my empty pockets. "Give them to me."

"She doesn't have them," Uncle Diego said. "I do."

I half-expected him to pull them out of my ears, the way he used to do with Oreos and quarters. Classic Uncle D.

As Falk sprang to his feet, my gaze trailed to a stump on Falk's left hand, where his ring finger should have been. I thought about the long boat ride from Florindale to Kesterfall with Charlie and Niraya . . . the tentacle I cut from the leviathan. And I remembered that with one of those stones, Falk could be anything he wanted to be. *Like a kraken.*

More on a whim than anything else, I jumped up and seized a handful of Zid's spilled grapes from the mud then slammed them onto the back of Falk's neck. The sour red juice trickled into his armor, raising hives on his skin. He clapped a hand to the back of his neck and rounded on me, nostrils flaring with rage.

Man I was glad I paid attention to my brother.

At the same time, Verdoro landed with a *whumph* that ruffled the trees again. Something was different about him. He looked at me without fuming, snapping, or thrashing. I planted my feet and steadied my nerves. My brother was insane, but he'd done it. He tamed the dragon.

"Hey, jerk," Charlie said. "Up here."

Falk snapped his whip in the air. "Verdoro, my fire slave. As your master, I command you to consume these heathens."

Verdoro leaned down and sniffed the top of Lord Falk's head. When the dragon's gaze trailed to the whip, he exposed his teeth.

"Don't you snarl at me!" Falk whipped Verdoro's nose.

James chuckled lazily. "I don't think he answers to you anymore, mate."

"He answers to nobody," Charlie said. "He does whatever the heck he wants. But I think he might be open to polite suggestions." With his ankle, he gave Verdoro a slight nudge. The dragon stepped forward, knocking Falk face-first into the mud.

"Keep him on the ground." Niraya slid down and pinned Falk by his shoulders.

"I have a rope in there." Uncle Diego reached for his backpack and pulled a coil from the main pocket. "Tie him."

"To the beastie's leg," James said. "Let's take him to the king and let Florindale decide what to do with him."

Lord Falk lifted his head, a beard of mud framing his lips. "Never. Wait! We can talk. You can live in fortune and glory. You can help me make the greatest discovery in the history of all realms, and I'll see to it that you never suffer. Luck will always be on your side."

Uncle Diego tossed the rope to Niraya. "I'm okay with the luck I have, thanks. Fortune's only ten percent. The other ninety's on you."

"Optimistic words for a helpless man. The winds of fortune doomed you here."

"Be that as it may, some creatures have wings." Niraya patted Verdoro's neck. "Zid, can you get us out of here?"

As Niraya looped the rope around Lord Falk's ankles, Zid flexed his fingers and stretched his arms over his head. "Curse it all if I don't try."

James ran the back of his sleeve against his forehead and bit down on his fist, sweat beading up on his neck. "Another dragon ride with Zid. This is exactly why I left the Order in the first place."

"Another?" I asked.

"Will you cease your blubbering?" Zid ground his knuckles into his hips. "Listen up, all. I'll attempt the flight back to Florindale, but you better hang on. I've flown many a dragon in my life, but this one hasn't got any reins, saddles, straps, or in-flight beverage services. You're going to have to brace yourselves and deal with it."

The word attempt made my heart drop, but it didn't stay down for long. We were going back to Florindale, and that meant we could all go home. "Have you ever done this before, Zid?" I asked. "Flown a dragon without reins?"

"Nope."

Charlie slid down Verdoro's neck like it was a banister. After he helped Uncle Diego to his feet, all his weight on one leg, they assisted me, Niraya, and Zid with the binding. Falk put up a pretty good fight. He was a thrashing mountain, threatening to break free and bury us in his wrath. Crying out like La Llorona, he bucked and used his weight to throw Charlie to the ground. But I kept the brute in check with some of the grapes, which I crushed in my palms and threatened to smear on him if he didn't cooperate.

"Your time is coming," Lord Falk growled. "You don't know what you're doing, chaining me up like this. You know not the meaning of your selfish actions. I require the Wheel of Fortune."

Zid slammed Lord Falk against the dragon's leg and wound the rope around him. "You require a strong kick in the pants, sir."

I chewed on the inside of my cheek as we tied man and beast together. Would this really hold him? What if we landed in Florindale and Falk wasn't with us? What if mid-flight, he escaped, climbed up, and stole the stones from Uncle Diego's pocket?

"You do have the stones, right, Uncle Diego?" I asked.

And in true fashion, he pulled them from behind my ears.

My jaw fell. "Seriously? How do you do that?"

"Can't tell you, *mija*."

"Then there's only one thing left to do." Zid climbed Verdoro's tail and found a comfortable spot on the back of his neck. "Escape this cursed place. Everybody climb up and hang on."

Before Charlie helped me onto the dragon, I stole another glance at the overlord strapped to Verdoro's leg. We bound his arms to his sides, and already his wrists were pink from rubbing against the rope. I wanted to believe we'd strapped him pretty tight, locking him in figure eights, loops, and Niraya's sailor knots. Unless Falk could conjure a blade out of thin air or breathe fire like Verdoro without the stones, I saw no possible way for him to escape.

But my stomach still churned when he winked at me, sending goose bumps rocketing up my arms.

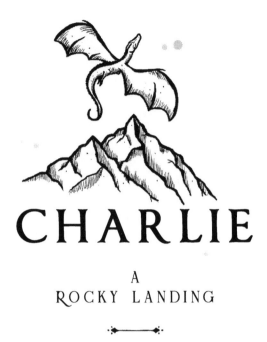

# CHARLIE

A
ROCKY LANDING

·—◆—·

Good thing I liked roller coasters, because Verdoro was the grand poobah of them all.

We crammed together—me, Karina, Tio, James, Niraya, and Zid—bags strapped tight and knees squeezing Verdoro's back for security. Zid put his hands near Verdoro's ears and leaned in as if he were about to share a secret with the dragon. "All right, my beastly beauty. This is your new pal Zid speaking. I'm not your boss. I'm not your master. I am your friend. We need to get to Florindale Square. Can you find it?"

Verdoro grunted, pawed at the ground, and spread his wings. For a second, I thought of the black, holey sails flaring up on the *Red Hood*. There was never any question that Verdoro was huge, but until we got an actual view on top of his back, we underestimated how massive the dragon's wingspan really was. We could've fit a mansion or two on each wing—maybe even a neighborhood.

The wind whipped through my hair as Verdoro ascended, and my stomach stayed on the ground. He hadn't gained much altitude when I'd flown him over the jungle to help my family, but now Zid was in command, and we were in for a long flight high over water. I was grateful Verdoro's wings blocked my view of the ground.

I looked over my shoulder to see my sister squeezing her eyes shut and biting her lip. Tio sat behind her and wrapped his arms around her waist. James was the last in line with a death grip on Niraya's shoulder.

"Zid," I said, "how long will this take?"

"Different dragons, different speeds." Zid shrugged. "Draco could make this trip in a couple turns of the hourglass. A smaller dragon, we might expect to see the sun rise before we make it. I'm not familiar with Verdoro's temperament or speed. With his size, he could very well get us home by dawn, if he chooses. There is also, of course, the problem of the scoundrel tied below."

"He's still there, right?" Karina asked, voicing one of my own concerns.

Verdoro glanced at his leg, growled, and shot a fireball from his mouth.

A girlish scream sounded below.

"Yeah." I grinned. "He's still there."

Zid threw a fist in the air as Verdoro picked up speed. "*Whoooo!* Feel that breeze on your skin, wild ones. Trust your captain. It doesn't get much better than this."

When I gained control of my stomach, I dared a look up at the stars, and they were beautiful.

"Rina, Carlos." Tio leaned forward and patted my shoulder. "Thanks for coming back for me. Let's not tell your mom about this, but this moment right here? This is the time of my life."

"Better than Everest?" I asked.

"Duh." Tio winked at me. "How are you holding up, James?"

"Generally not my idea of a good time." James clutched his stomach. "But I suppose I've had worse company. I'm proud to be amongst you brave souls. You'd have done well in the fight against the Ivory Queen."

When the conversation died down, I relied on the adrenaline to stay awake. When would I ever get to ride a dragon again? Every now and then, my mind would shift to other questions, all of which drained my energy. *What happens when we get home? Where's the rest of the Wheel of Fortune? What happens to Falk when we get back to Florindale?* At one point I found myself nodding off and leaning forward. My forehead hit Zid's back, prompting him to turn around and glare.

"Don't make me roll this dragon over." Every word sounded fuzzy, cutting into the strange nether between sleep and wakefulness.

I rubbed my eyes. "K."

"I just had another thought," Karina said. "And stop me if it's stupid, but we're flying back into Florindale, right?"

Zid tugged his beard with one hand. "Aye. And?"

"And Florindale knows all about Verdoro? You put the wanted posters everywhere?"

Zid pulled more slowly. "Aye . . ."

"So, do you think the people in Florindale know Verdoro doesn't actually want to hurt them?"

In the maddening silence that followed, I felt the wind trying to knock me out of the sky. I heard the ocean churning, swishing and swelling, and I imagined the infinite expanse of secrets waiting to fold me under again.

"*Harumph.*" Zid sighed. "I suppose we'll find out."

"How soon?" Niraya asked.

Zid pointed ahead. "Not long at all."

Verdoro dipped below the clouds and lowered his head for us all to see, revealing a faint glow on the horizon.

"At last," James breathed. "Civilization. Sweet, warm civilization. Bed. Food. Yes."

Tio clutched his stomach. "Really hoping for a cheeseburger."

"Tio, I couldn't agree more," I said, though I would've been okay with anything except jackalope meat. Studying the skyline, I picked out the bell tower's silhouette. The warm glow around it instantly made me feel safe, like a candle in a power outage. I could almost imagine what Florindale would smell like when we landed. Like clean linen and new leather, spiced apple pie, and cedar wood.

"What a beautiful view." Zid gave Verdoro's neck a gentle pat. "You're doing good, beastie. Keep us afloat for just a little longer."

The more I stared at the town, the brighter and larger it grew, swelling from the dull pinprick of a faint star to the steady glow of a torch, and finally, an expanding and burning orange light like a fireball.

Or a burning javelin soaring directly for my head.

My breaths doubled. "They're firing at us."

Karina screamed and leaned into my back. Cries of panic burst from James, Niraya, and Tio as well.

"A thousand curses." Zid dug a boot heel into Verdoro's neck. "To the left, chum!"

Verdoro veered over, tilting us a few degrees and forcing us to squeeze tighter. The dragon roared and cut into the dark night with his fire.

The burning javelin slashed through the sky and narrowly missed Verdoro's head. I could hear the *whoosh* and the sizzle of the wood, feeling the heat licking my skin as the javelin soared past us.

I craned my neck. Florindale appeared with more definition, and a few lavender rays of sunlight crept up behind the bell tower. In its dim glow, I made out a sea of armored people on the shore, loading an enormous pole into a wooden contraption. After they secured the pole, a man with a torch approached the tip and lit up the end.

"We're in for a rocky landing," Zid said. "Florindale means to bring this dragon down."

"With us on top of it?" James's voice shook with panic. "What the devil has the king ordered? We were comrades."

"Oh, stars, we never should have plastered those cursed posters all over town. I don't think the king knows we're riding."

"Then get his attention," Niraya commanded.

"This is your fault, dwarf," James said. "You've doomed us all, and if you weren't commanding this beast, I'd skewer you with my hook."

Zid turned around and jammed a finger in James's direction. "Stop distracting me, sea dog, or you'll get us skewered with a flying fire stick. All your hope of survival is on my—"

"Okay, you've made your point." James kneaded his forehead. "Now will you please face forward?"

"Don't tell me what to do, you barking barnacled blubbering bandit—"

"Zid." I clamped my hands over Zid's ears and guided his head until he faced forward again. "Javelin at twelve o'clock."

Zid dug his heel into Verdoro's side. "Hang tight."

Like a roller coaster, we corkscrewed. As in, Verdoro did a full three-sixty, wing over wing. I hated every second of it. I squeezed my thighs together like I was trying to break an egg with my knees, and the sea became the sky for a terrible second.

Hot air licked my cheek when the javelin passed directly under my head—or uh, over it.

And then I heard a splash, and Niraya yelled, "Diego!"

My heart twisted in knots. "Did my uncle just fall?" Verdoro completed the flip, and we faced right side up again. I was not about to lose my uncle again. I jabbed Zid in the shoulder. "Turn back. Now."

The Florindale army released another pole. Their cries and murmurs began to fill my ears. We were dangerously close. Verdoro bucked, swerved, and steered a harsh right.

"I don't know that he'll continue to hold us," Zid said. "Verdoro's all at once angry, fatigued, and excited—a dangerous combination. One way or another, we're going down."

"My uncle could drown," Karina said.

"Not in my waters." Niraya's tone was iron, and before I could ask what she meant, I heard the sound of a kiss behind me, followed by James's scream.

"Niraya."

"We're losing people!" The horizon turned pink, throwing bright rays toward us. I shut my eyes, squeezed my legs against Verdoro's neck, and waved my arms over my head in a series of X's and V's.

"Hold fire." Karina waved her hands with me. "Don't shoot."

James joined in the commotion. "Let us live, land rats!"

I hoped the glare of the sunrise would catch on James's hook and attract some attention from the ground. Karina must have had the same thought, because she made James reach into her backpack and pull out the compact mirror she raided from the train wreck. "Remember?" she asked me, rotating the compact against the sun. "When Uncle Diego got rescued from the desert with the little foil square on the back of a credit card?"

"Half a credit card."

Another javelin shot into the air.

Verdoro dipped lower, generating small waves in the water's surface below. Droplets of ocean spray beaded on my face and forced my eyes shut.

"Stop!" Zid cupped his hands over his mouth. "He shall not harm you."

I opened my eyes. The army froze, exchanging excited chatter.

Verdoro descended with a final glide that dropped my stomach, though I had to admit the landing was smoother than some airplanes I'd been on. The dragon's feet touched the ground, skidded, and Verdoro took three more steps to stop his momentum, tail dragging on the beach.

Karina looked at me and smiled weakly. "We're here."

Here. On ground. In civilization. I played a five second air guitar solo to release my joy.

One of the soldiers shouted a command. "Somebody help those people off."

A lanky man threw a rope ladder over Verdoro's neck, and a second man caught the other end. "Come on down, friends. Let's get you to safety."

With some difficulty, I descended first, both terrified and relieved to make eye contact with a sneering—and soaking wet—Lord Falk still strapped to Verdoro's leg. One of the soldiers had already made his way over with a dagger and the intent to cut Falk free, but as soon as my feet touched the ground, I rushed to the soldier.

"Don't," I pleaded. "He's dangerous."

Zid and James descended next, catching their breath. James ran straight for the beach, threw his coat behind him, and prepared to dive into the water, but the guards restrained him.

Beads of sweat bubbled on my forehead as Falk drilled me with his gaze, an impish grin on his face. "Do you think these ropes will hold me?"

Verdoro began to buck and snap, shaking a wide-eyed Falk like a can of spray paint.

A nearby soldier raised his sword and made a beeline for Verdoro. "Somebody get the king over here, and tend to the survivors. It's time to do something about the Dark Dragon of—"

"No!" Karina spread her arms in front of Verdoro. She was a tiny shield for a massive beast, but she made the guards pause. "Please, don't hurt him."

"This is a wanted beast, young lady," the soldier said. "He's an enemy of the kingdom. The damage he's done—"

"I swear he's good," I said. "If he had been left alone, he wouldn't have terrorized Florindale. That's not a dragon's true nature."

The soldier lowered his sword and wrinkled his brows. "Aren't you the New World siblings who arrived here a little over a week ago? What do you know of dragons and their nature?"

"More than you, Jack Nimble," Zid said. "Carlos tamed this dragon. Independently. Have you ever done the same? Hmm?"

The soldier, Jack Nimble, considered Zid's words. "Impressive. So, who put the dragon under a trance, then? Do we have a witch problem in Florindale?"

"I would say you have a security problem."

A cool blade pressed against the skin of my neck, and a tight, burly arm wrapped around my torso. Fear slithered down my throat. Somehow, Falk had freed himself, even with hundreds of people watching and armed to the teeth. He deceived every eye. Why had we turned our backs to him? Why had we forgotten the knife he stole from Karina?

"Charlie!" Karina said.

The army looked at Lord Falk like he was a bomb.

"Drop the blades," Falk said.

Jack Nimble was the last to let go of his sword. "Who are you?"

"The architect of your destinies." Falk pressed the dagger a little tighter against my neck, cutting off some of the air. "Thank you, little roses, for escorting me back to Florindale. Now, who will be so kind as to take me to the home of Lady Fortune's wheel? Perhaps the bell tower? Time's a-wastin.'"

A new voice, distinctly female, chimed in the crowd. "Excuse me. Let me through, please. Thank you." A man and woman of about twenty years old pushed through the army, parting the soldiers like the Red Sea. The woman wore a faded-red cloak, and she had shiny black hair and beautiful golden-brown skin, like my family. The man wore khakis and a silk maroon button down, and his inky-dark hair was styled in a spiky crew cut. But my eyes were on the ivory daggers they both held in their fingers.

"Falk, is it?" the man said. "Let him go."

Falk's breath was unpleasantly hot on my neck. "And who exactly are you, little bird?"

The woman scoffed while the man laughed to himself.

"We're the king and queen of Florindale," the woman said. "Little bird."

"And I promise you're not our first dragon," the king added. I had never seen two people who looked less like monarchs. They looked more like people I'd see wandering a college campus back home. "Get out of here, Falk."

I swallowed, my neck rubbing against the blade. *Who are these people?*

"You command *me?*" Falk asked. He took a deep breath, pulling me up into the air a few inches, then pushed forward with his chest, sending a beam of red light shooting out of the dagger he carried. The light rolled along the ground, gathering momentum as it charged for the king.

The king flicked his wrist, sending green waves racing toward Falk's red light. The shape of a tiger head rose from the sand, engulfed Falk's red light, then sunk back into the ground.

Falk drew back, pulling me with him, and he pushed forward with a bigger light from his blade.

The queen gritted her teeth, sending another green light charging along the beach, but it wasn't enough. Lord Falk's red light burned through the queen's, knocking the couple on their backs and sending the ivory daggers skittering along the sand.

"You command nothing," Falk said. "People of Florindale, I advise you to seek a king more capable of defending himself. Might I submit my name for consideration? Falk! Remember the name, remember the day—"

A hollow sound echoed somewhere on the beach, like someone blew a spitball, and a second later Lord Falk dropped the dagger and cried out in pain. He slapped his neck like a mosquito. Only when he pulled his hand away, a tiny little dart punctured his skin.

After I ran from Lord Falk's hold, my sister waved a blow dart shooter at me and grinned. I recognized it as the one she'd stolen from the ogres.

That sneaky, wily sister of mine.

Falk dropped a couple seconds later, his eyes rolling back into his head. Verdoro snorted, a puff of steam shooting over the villain's face.

He was down for the count.

The king stood and called for the army to bring some chains, but I didn't care enough about Falk to watch them chain him up. I cared more about the beach, where two people emerged from the waves.

# KARINA

## THE KING OF FLORINDALE

·◦━◦·

Go figure, if anybody could tread water long enough to swim back to shore, it was Niraya Storm and my uncle Diego Rosas. Even though he was limping and dragging his leg, he reminded me of Aquaman, emerging like a total boss with Niraya on his back. We had no idea how the stones in his pocket worked, but it seemed one of them strengthened his leg just enough to support him and the pirate queen when they needed it most.

I started to wonder if maybe Lady Fortune was watching us from her cloud, and if she was, was she sending us the little drops of luck she had left? Did she help Niraya and my uncle, knowing we were trying to protect her wheel in return?

From what Uncle Diego told us, he'd almost passed out before Niraya jumped in and pulled him to the surface for air. A rogue wave had crashed over them and forced them back underwater.

Shortly before the two had come up, Niraya blacked out. I found it cute that James was the one to bring her back. Sigh . . . true love's kiss. Even though Charlie just called it CPR.

Uncle Diego credits his survival to the nature orb, but really, he and Niraya survived because they were strong. Not invincible, but strong.

As for Niraya's hat washing up behind her with the red feather somehow in perfect condition, that thing was invincible.

The important thing was we were all reunited. Not only that, but Verdoro was free, and the real monster was in chains.

The king and queen of Florindale walked toward us, speaking in hushed tones. "How did Falk get a knife like that?" the queen asked. "You don't think he's a . . . ?"

"Carver?" The king shook his head. "I don't think so. There was something off about that dagger. I'm going to have to study it."

My stomach dropped. Falk almost killed my brother with a knife I'd taken from Niraya's ship. All along, I had never known the dagger had magical properties.

The king marched up to us, a warm smile on his face. "It appears there's a lot to discuss." He studied Uncle Diego's awkward stance, all the weight on one foot. "Your leg. Is it broken?"

Uncle Diego shrugged. "It's strange, Your Majesty. That man snapped it with his bare hands. It was definitely broken when I got on the dragon. But after I fell in the water, something happened. It's a little sore, but I can stand on it just fine."

The king laughed. "Please don't call me that. To you all, I'm just Enzo, cool? Enzo and Rosana." Under his breath, he said to his wife, "Next time I see Liam and Snow, I swear . . . Become the king of Florindale, they said. It'll be fun, they said." He grasped Uncle Diego by the shoulders. "Come on. Let's fix you up."

Zid jammed a thick finger in Enzo's face. "You almost had us killed. Have we not earned your respect after all we've gone through together?"

Enzo put his hands up. "Whoa, buddy. You can't be too mad. I thought that thing had eaten you. I didn't see you sitting on his neck. Should I be surprised, though? Zid the Dragon Whisperer?" He waved Jack Nimble over. "Can you escort my friend Zid and his scaly companion to Grimm's Hollow, please? I'm sure Tahlia would love to have a look at this beautiful creature and get him fed. Are these whip marks? From Falk, I assume?"

Charlie nodded grimly. "What's gonna happen to him? To Falk, I mean?"

Rosana bounced on the balls of her feet and clucked her tongue a few times. "We should maybe continue this inside. Are you all hungry? That's a dumb question. Follow me."

Enzo's home wasn't the lavish, eight-story castle I would've expected from a king, but it worked for him, and I would've lived here in a heartbeat. It had two floors, a garden, and was a perfect fusion of modern design and rustic fairytale life. Many items were made of wood, and the house smelled of cedar, rain, and a hint of sweet citrus. I couldn't resist the urge to get a little nosy and trace the walls, studying the little carvings, figurines, and leather book spines. There was hardly a speck of dust to be found, like the books actually got some good use.

Enzo and Rosana gestured to a couch by the fireplace and disappeared for a minute, returning with a tray of cheese, fruit, crackers, and cold cut meats. My mouth watered like a sprinkler. Enzo took a seat across from us and smoothed his hair. "Please, help yourselves. There's more where this came from. Do you need anything else? Baths? Blankets? Coffee? Don't get shy on me. I've been in your shoes."

Charlie exchanged glances with me and Uncle Diego.

"I think we'll be glad to take you up on all that," my brother said.

"Sure, sure," Enzo said. "You're welcome to stay as long as you want. It's good to be in New World company. I heard all about the train, you know. I'm so sorry for everything you've been through."

I rubbed my face. I'd almost forgotten what safety felt like. "We kept thinking it was a weird accident," I said. "Some impossible stroke of bad luck. And then we found out it was all somebody's game."

Rosana nodded. "I'm a little shocked as well. It's a lot to wrap our brains around, living in Florindale and hearing the legends of Lady Fortune, only to discover they're all true. Falk might be one of the greatest threats this place has ever seen, and things were so calm since we beat the Ivory Queen."

Charlie spoke in a hushed whisper. It still felt dangerous to say Falk's name out loud. "Where is he now?"

"Let me worry about Falk," Enzo said. "They're escorting him to Florindale Prison. He'll have every measure of security until I can figure out what to do with him."

"He's going to keep hunting for those orbs until somebody destroys him," I said, thinking of all he'd already gone through. Of Uncle Diego's signature on his arm. *I will always find you, Diego Rosas*, Falk had vowed. *I will hunt you and your family eternally until I have that wheel.* "Can a prison really hold him?"

Enzo made a sour face. "I don't know what kind of man he is without those orbs, or that knife he got a hold of. He may be weak. He may be strong. He may be biding time until we settle back into peace. I want to be optimistic about what a brick fortress can do to keep him in there, especially when the legends say Lady Fortune's chained to a cloud. Then again, there was a day when Florindale Prison couldn't even hold my parents. Or James. Or Zid."

I scratched my head. "Wait, Zid and James were . . ."

"I'll tell you all about it someday." Enzo flashed a wink as if he'd told a brilliant joke. The levity melted from his face just as quickly, and suddenly he looked a little sad. "But as long as Falk is in Florindale, he's my responsibility. If I have to strengthen the chains, thicken the walls, or double the guards to keep him there, I'll do it all. Don't worry about us, and certainly don't worry about Falk. Go home and live your lives, whatever it takes."

"What about the stones?" Uncle Diego pulled the orbs from his pocket and shook them around in his palm. "Can you keep them safe here?"

Enzo stared at the stones for a minute, their brilliant colors reflecting in his eyes. "I don't know that I'm the man to keep those safe, you know? Seems like the kind of thing that's best left forgotten . . . like it's too much for one person. I honestly wouldn't be comfortable storing those in Florindale when there are so many people after them. This place is full of secret nooks and crannies that I'm still learning about, and honestly Falk probably knows every inch of this place better than I do. I should confess I haven't been here long."

"Then what should we do with them?" I asked. "It's not like they're any better in our hands."

"How 'bout this?" Rosana reached over and plucked two stones from Uncle Diego's palm. "You take half and do whatever feels right. Throw 'em in the ocean, bury them in a safe, toss them in a fire. I won't ask. It makes sense to keep them in the New World, though. It's constantly under construction, growing, swelling, changing, and it's unfamiliar territory for an Old World native like Falk. The other half . . . Well, we'll talk to some friends of ours and figure out what to do with them. But it seems like things are worse if we keep them all together, right?"

I stifled a yawn. The crackling fireplace, the deep, soft tones of King Enzo's voice, and the exhaustion of the past few days were really getting to me. "I guess I agree." I reached forward and cut into one of the cheese wheels, pairing a slice with a wheat cracker. "We'll separate them and never talk about them again."

We stayed there for two days, and for the most part, we really didn't talk about the Wheel of Fortune again. Queen Rosana was largely absent on royal business most of the time, but Enzo was an amazing host. He took Uncle Diego and Charlie to a nurse in Florindale who examined their bones and confirmed neither of them had any breaks. For good measure, she gave us a potion that would make us strong and healthy, and I wondered why people didn't drink it all the time. I loved the mysterious green bottle it came in, and it was kind of delicious, hitting my tongue like frothy root beer.

Even though Charlie's arm was fine, he asked for a cast anyway. Pretty sure he just wanted attention. The nurse said no and sent us back to Florindale Square.

"Man, a cast would've made me look heroic and cool," Charlie grumbled.

"Or incredibly dorky and clumsy," I said.

Charlie sneered. "No! It would've been, like, proof that we've been through some stuff, you know? Almost like a souvenir. Think of the stories."

"The stories . . ." I said. I reached into my backpack and took out the leather journal we'd been carrying around.

Uncle Diego's eyes lit up. "You two had that with you this whole time?"

I nodded. "Your stories kept us alive, Uncle D."

He took the book and leafed through the pages, an expression of wonder on his face. "None of them compare to the ones we're about to write together."

Enzo watched us, his arms crossed, a proud smile on his face. "I guess it's a good time to give you your gifts, then."

Charlie grinned. "Ooo, presents? Really?"

"There was a reward promised, wasn't there?"

"We don't need one," I said. "Plus, we didn't slay the dragon."

"No. You saved him. You saved all of us."

Enzo gave each of us a leather bag with a collection of items from our friends. He'd carved us several wooden figurines, including one of the bell tower and one of Verdoro. Rosana gave me a red silk cloak that reminded me a bit of a superhero. Niraya tossed in a feathered pirate hat that looked just like hers. James left us each a handful of gold medallions, and Zid gave everyone a blank leather book to fill with stories of our own. The first pages had already been filled with messages inked by our friends.

I ran my fingers along the inky grooves, where the first message had been scrawled. *To the fiercest young woman I know. May our ships meet again on new waters. Niraya.*

My gaze drifted to a rough sketch of a hook. *Never 4get. Thx for saving my life, lass. J.*

From Zid: *You and your brother tamed the beast! Remember how I always knew you could do it? How I never doubted you?*

The book was one of the most special items I possessed, and I couldn't wait to fill it with pages about my adventure with my family. I sat there brainstorming as we had lunch in the Hansel and Gretel café, where Niraya and Uncle Diego hit it off. They talked like old friends, swapping stories of the wild, of adventure, and the art of survival.

"I can see where these brilliant wildlings get their resourcefulness," Niraya said. "You're all right, Diego Rosas."

Adding to my amusement, strangers in Florindale Square clamored to sign our books and give us little trinkets, though I suspected most of them just wanted any excuse to get close, soak up my uncle's good looks, and hear us tell the story of our time in the dragon's den.

"Is it true you tamed Verdoro?" they asked Charlie. He loved that question. He smirked and nodded every time.

"You're Diego's niece?" they asked me. "Did you really fight off a clan of werewolves and yetis?"

I shrugged. "Meh. It's all in the details."

After Uncle Diego, Charlie, and I said most of our goodbyes to the people of Florindale, Enzo led us to a quiet area on the edge of The Woodlands where few people wandered. "You're legends now," he said. "Forget Lord Falk and Lady Fortune. People wanna talk to the family who calmed the untamable dragon. Hope you're ready for fame."

"Oh, it won't last," Charlie said. "You know how it is back home. We can't talk about any of this once we cross back into Arizona. We'll be the pariahs of the desert. Mom'll send us to the mental hospital."

"I can't say I envy you," Enzo said. "My parents were the ones who had to explain all the weird stuff to me back in the day. My best friend can fly, and my father . . . Well, come back someday and I'll introduce you. Maybe you can bring your ma to see Verdoro one weekend?"

Uncle Diego cringed. "Please don't. My sister will freak. By the way, speaking of Verdoro, something's bothering me. I know why he took me, but why James? Does he have a stone, too?"

"Nah, I think Verdoro was just mad at him. You got to know James pretty well out there." Enzo laughed. "If a dragon flew over his ship right now, do you really think he'd leave it alone?"

Enzo had a point. James wasn't exactly a *have an Oreo* sort of guy.

"Trance or no trance, a dragon's still a dragon," Enzo said. "Respect the wild—"

"And the wild will respect you," Uncle Diego finished.

Charlie and I exchanged a grin. Did our uncle just become best friends with the king?

"If you get into any trouble back home, keep in touch with me," Enzo said. "I have some good friends back there. If things ever blow up again, we'll find each other."

"We've got your back," the queen added.

Enzo approached a thick pine tree and slid his blade down the center with one smooth stroke. A white light spilled from the wood and opened into a sort of doorway, too bright to see through. "As promised, the New World awaits. Say hi to home for me."

"I have one more question first," I said. "Do you think the Wheel of Fortune really is here in Florindale somewhere?"

Enzo rubbed his chin for a second then shrugged. "I really don't know. Up until today, I didn't believe it existed. There are some strange things under our bell tower that survived all the fires and construction, but I'd have to look into it. It might even be closer to you, somewhere we'd never expect. Hopefully, it will never matter."

I considered Enzo's words. I didn't think I'd ever care about the remaining stones or the wheel either, but now that home was right in front of me, I was going to miss the adventuring with my familia, the feeling that I was protecting something. A guardian of fortune.

"I hope we get to see you all again," I said.

Our goodbye with Niraya and James had been short and snappy. I think somewhere deep down, we all knew we'd meet again.

"Soon."

"And under better circumstances," Enzo said. "Until then, I wish you the best."

We all shared our final hugs then pulled away when a dark, cold shadow passed over us.

"So long, younglings," Zid's gruff voice called from above. We looked up and saw Verdoro spiraling over The Woodlands and shooting playful wisps of fire and smoke from his mouth.

"Goodbye, Zid," I called back. "Thanks for all your help."

*Goodbye, Verdoro. Enjoy your newfound freedom.*

Charlie and Uncle Diego stepped through the bright light and disappeared. I put one foot through, which tingled.

"Will you tell the queen we said goodbye?" I asked.

Enzo smiled. "Goodbye for now, at least. I'll give Rose your best."

As I stepped through the portal back home, I smiled. *Rose.* Like my family name. Something beautiful that knows how to prick if you mess with it.

I liked her.

# CHARLIE

## NOT
## THE CHOSEN ONES

---

I only took three steps before the pine needles and dirt fell away and the linoleum appeared at my toes. The transition was so jarring that I stopped mid-step, looked around me, and—

Someone rammed me from the side. Baggage spilled from a trolley and rolled into my shin.

A red-haired teenager ripped his earbuds out. "Hey, you can't just stop like that! Gotta watch where you're going."

I helped the guy with his luggage. "Sorry, dude. I'll be more careful next time."

"You legit came out of nowhere, bro." Under his breath, he added, "I swear it's a jungle in here."

"You literally have no idea." I packed the last suitcase onto the trolley and let the guy continue.

I let my gaze linger for far too long on everyday objects as I tried to ground myself in reality again. *Windows, luggage, marquee. Departures.* People of course had to stare at the weirdo who suddenly became mesmerized by things everyone else took for granted, like the coffee stand and a little rack of five Euro key chains near me. *I'm at a train station. Great. Where's my family?*

"There you are." Karina pushed her way through a food court and rushed in for a hug. Our uncle walked behind us, testing the strength of his mended leg. "So that was an experience."

Understatement of the year. I rubbed my eyes. "And we lived."

Tio pulled us in for a hug, and it hit me just how happy I was to be reunited with our crazy uncle, to have survived the long road with my sister, and to be a few steps away from the nearest sandwich shop.

"Tio," I said, "you're absolutely crazy."

"Yeah? Well, maybe it's time for a rest. What do you two want to do? By the looks of things, I'd say we're in Geneva. We have some options here." He sat down on a metal bench and propped his foot up on a leather stool.

Karina raised an eyebrow. "Such as?"

"Depending on the day of the week, we can finish the trip to Switzerland and explore like we intended, or we can catch a train to the airport and get you two back to your mom so she can bean me with a spatula. Otherwise, the world's our oyster, whatever that actually means."

I looked at my boots, hesitating to ask my next question. Assuming we could actually return to a normal life, what would that be like? A part of me wasn't quite ready. "Can we go look for the rest of the wheel? And those stones? We're like, the chosen ones."

Tio shook his head. "There's nothing chosen about us, Charlie. Fortune chooses ten percent. We choose ninety. Let's put all this behind us and stop picking up gemstones. Take only pictures. Leave only—"

"But I mean, if somebody's going to find them one day," Rina said, "shouldn't it be us? We're good people. We can help Enzo and Rosana keep them safe."

"If it's meant to be, we'll work with our luck and make it happen. But for now, let's focus on these." Tio patted his pocket. "Can we agree on that? We'll take them somewhere far away and hide them in a place only we know. It's like Enzo said. As long as these two are safe, we don't have to worry about the others, right?"

I thought for a minute.

Maybe. Fortune was weird, though. If Tio found one orb by accident, who was to say we weren't meant to find and protect the others? To free Lady Fortune? To break the Curse of Jericho Harbor? If not us, though, maybe there were good people who would and could. Yes, people can be scarier than dragons sometimes, but most of the time, people are awesome and kind and want to do what's right. People like Zid, James, and Captain Niraya Storm, the fiercest pirate queen in the waters.

"Then can we go climb the Alps and look for wolves?" I asked. "And dragons and treasure?"

"You're kidding, right?" Uncle Diego laughed. "After all that?"

Karina pumped a fist in the air. "I'm with Charlie. I vote for some adventure time."

"How 'bout lunch and a thrilling adventure to a hotel, where we can rest first?" Tio shut his eyes and crossed his arms behind his head. "Then we'll talk."

## THE END

# ACKNOWLEDGMENTS

Just like Rina and Charlie, I was always fascinated by the classic stories: the ones with the dashing, roguish dude battling his way up the dragon's tower to rescue the princess and whatnot. *Roses in the Dragon's Den* is sort of the inverted version that lived in my heart, where two Latinx kids get to be the heroes. One of the most powerful themes that kept coming up was strength in familia, whether you define this strictly by the branches on your family tree or by the pirates and dragon tamers you choose to roll with. Below are people who became part of my *Roses* familia and made this book possible.

Thank you, Hannah, Maira, Silvia, Lucas, Katie, and Janelle for being a phenomenal crew of first readers and proofreaders! I'd bring the six of you with me to Kesterfall any day.

Thank you, Mom, for keeping me safe from La Llorona.

Thank you, Scrappy Dog, for the memories.

Thank you, Karina and Uncle Ed, for showing me two different sides of the unique and immortal bond between uncles and their nieces and nephews.

Thank you, Krystal Dehaba, for your continued guidance, encouragement, editorial superpowers, and soccer coaching skills. Charlie couldn't have outrun Verdoro with you, and I couldn't have, either.

Thank you, Melissa Stevens and Amalia Chitulescu, for breathing visual life into this book! Your work solidifies my belief in magic.

And of course, thank YOU, dear reader, for coming on this journey with me and the Rosas family. By Lady Fortune's hand, there will be many more adventures to come!

# ABOUT THE AUTHOR

When Jacob Devlin was four years old, he would lounge around in Batman pajamas and make semi-autobiographical picture books about an adventurous python named Jake the Snake. Eventually, he traded his favorite blue crayon for a black pen, and he never put it down. When he isn't reading or writing, Jacob is probably geeking out at a comic book convention or blasting Italian pop rock music in his car. He does most of these things in southern Arizona.

# OTHER BOOKS